Hazel and Elijah Find Out

First They F*cked Around

Marty Vee

Newsletter Fun!

I love my newsletter, it's my favorite way to connect with my readers. Stay in the know about exciting news, upcoming releases, fun stuff, and freebies. https://www.subscribepage.com/martyvee

Contents

Content Note

While this book is a romantic comedy Elijah has experienced religious trauma, and has an emotionally manipulative and abusive parent. It also shows on page shunning from a tightknit community.

Dedication

Dedication
To Beth, who like Hazel, would never be reckless.

Part 1

Hazel and Elijah Don't Get Caught

Chapter 1

Hazel

Everyone in Grand Ridge, Michigan knew Elijah March. He'd been a senior when I'd been a sophomore. Having a crush on him had been almost a right of passage for people my age. *Oh, you graduated between 2010 and 2015? What was your Elijah March phase?*

Mine? I'd signed up for all of them.

Baseball Elijah? Yeah, he wasn't our star player, but he was the only reason I showed up to games.

Golden-boy Elijah? Yes, please, he had a smile that could charm anyone. It was never directed at me—a nerdy younger girl with frizzy brown hair—but I was still charmed by it.

Rebellious Elijah? Oh, hell yes. He still had the smile, and played baseball, but with a little extra "Fuck You" on his shoulder. He skipped school to do... whatever kids who skip school do; I was never one of them. And he joined the other rebels to drink in Ol' Mr. Miller's backwoods—or so I heard.

His major rebellion, though, was sleeping around; rumor around school said he was *very* good at it. Again, I wouldn't know because I didn't have sex in high school, good *or* bad.

But I was late to class once because Sarah Hillis was telling Olivia Vazquez salacious details about him. In my, and their, defense the girls hadn't realized I was in a bathroom stall. It would have been too awkward to leave, so I waited until they had gone. It was worth it for the details I inadvertently discovered.

The rebellious stage was right around the time his mom left his dad, and the church-going, God-fearing community had certainly had opinions on the matter. After Elijah graduated, he and his mom moved to Nashville—or Memphis; I wasn't sure—he'd been estranged from his dad ever since.

I only knew the last part because his dad was my mentor; Dr. March, our town's veterinarian.

When he talked to me that morning to say Elijah was visiting and planned to help us later I was curious, but not overly invested. I wasn't the fawning, nerdy girl with an unrequited crush from ten years ago. I was now a nerdy woman a month away from taking over Dr. March's vet clinic.

My vet clinic. Almost.

I was too busy and overwhelmed to pay much attention to handsome—or not handsome—men.

It made Dr. March's next warning unnecessary. "You need to stay away from Elijah. He'd be bad for your reputation."

I blinked, completely caught off guard. "My reputation? I don't think we need to worry about that."

"He will try to take advantage of you."

"Why would you say that?" The corners of my mouth turned down.

Dr. March shook his head. "I know my son."

"No one is going to take advantage of me—"

"Hazel, stay away from him," he said with a razor-sharp edge to his voice. "My son has a history, and it would be unwise to ignore it. If you get involved with him it could affect the sale of the clinic."

"How?" I'd seen the ownership documents; Elijah March wasn't insinuated anywhere on them.

Dr. March's face grew red, and his jaw set. "Do as I ask, please."

By the time evening rolled around, I'd mulled over the conversation. It was still on my mind as I put on a summer dress that ended at my ankles and fit like a T-shirt. The perfect outfit to prep for our annual pet adoption event on the local library's side yard.

The sun was setting when I parked my vehicle next to the historical, large-stone building. There were a few patrons inside, but I was the first from the clinic to arrive. A half hour later, Nora, our business administrator, and Dr. March were directing our other two veterinarians, Brooks and Remi, as they lined up the temporary fencing on the side yard.

Car tires crunched over loose stones on the paved parking lot, catching my attention. The car was black and sleek, but not overly sporty. Through the windshield, I could make out that it was a man driving.

Then he stepped out into the summer evening, and I swear by all things I know to be true, time slowed down. It was like a scene out of an early aughts romantic comedy, with the warm breeze rustling through his chestnut-colored curls and a beautiful smile underneath dark sunglasses.

Completely absorbed in the way his gray T-shirt draped over his shoulders and chest, I lost track of my slack-jawed expression. Until Nora turned to share a wide-eyed look.

This was Elijah March all grown up.

He made polite introductions, not even sparing me a lingering glance—which was fine. Really.

He helped us prepare, diligently working while making conversation. The whole time, he and I orbited—but never entered—each other's space. That didn't stop me from noticing the way the fine muscles in his forearm flexed as he painted the welcome sign, or the bulge of his biceps as he hammered the temporary fence posts into their bases. Or just the general way his thighs filled out his jeans.

My gaze seemed to land on him, no matter what I was supposed to be focused on.

By the time we finished Nora and I had had a silent chat with eyebrow raises, suppressed smirks, and pointed staring—more or less meaning, *Are you seeing how hot he is?*

We really needed to actually talk.

Elijah said goodbye and left. Shortly after Nora and I were in our separate cars, and before I'd even put my car in drive, I dialed her.

"How is your heart doing?" she asked through the speaker.

"Palpitations. Did you see that man?" I answered, my voice pitched high.

She snorted. "Yeah. Got a whole eye full."

"Shoot. What do I gotta do to get more eyes on him?"

"Such an important question, and I don't have an answer. But did you see how weird Doc was with him?"

"He was weird earlier today, too, when he was talking about Elijah coming tonight."

The conversation weaved through different degrees of "he was really polite," and "it was nice of him to help out," and "he is so hot," until I parked in front of the clinic. I had a few things I needed to grab for tomorrow's event.

I pushed my key into the door with my phone pressed to my ear.

"So, is this an official reentry into 'I want to marry Elijah March' town?" Nora asked.

"One hundred percent." My voice carried across the empty lobby and the front office. "What the fuck was evolution thinking when it made him so goddamn fine?"

Her smile was clear through the phone. "Superfluously good looking."

"Like, I get it, I want him to impregnate me. You don't have to keep making such a point of it."

"Yeah, every angle of that man had something new to appreciate."

"Goddamn gorgeous." I pushed through the door to the hallway lined with exam rooms on the right. Taking a left, I entered the office, heading to the files at the back of the room. "I thought I'd outgrown my 'Elijah March Scrambles my Brain Phase,' but I have not."

"I do what?" a deep male voice said from behind me.

I made a sound somewhere between a gasp and a scream, turning around so quickly I pushed a couple files off the shelf. They slapped onto the thin blue carpet. My hand pressed to my chest.

In my ear, Nora sounded worried. "What's going on? Are you okay?"

Elijah sat back in a black office chair. One of his ankles was propped on the thigh of his other leg. The cotton of his shirt draped and stretched across his chest in the most delicious ways. His chin rested on his fist. The fingers of his other hand relaxed over the armrest. His hair was ruffled, the curls flipped in all directions. A hint of a smile flirted with his lips.

His green eyes focused on only me—interested and playful.

My mouth hung open. A warm blush filled my cheeks. I should say *something*, but my thoughts had gone to ground like a scared animal; abandoning me to static between my ears.

"Tell me you're okay. Fuck. I'm coming to you," Nora's voice continued through the speaker. It took me a second to comprehend her words.

"I'm fine. Sorry, I'm okay. You don't have to come here." My calm tone was a total lie.

"Are you sure?"

"Yeah, Elijah March is here."

"No!" Nora drew out the word, loud enough that Elijah raised an eyebrow.

I continued my fake facade. "Yup, I was just startled."

"Ohmygod! No."

"Mm-hm, I'll talk to you later." I ended the call.

"Sorry to startle you," Elijah rumbled.

I was too mortified to appreciate the rich timbre of his voice, which was a shame. "No need to apologize. What are you doing here?"

"Helping my dad with something; he let me in. I'm just waiting."

I decided ignoring that he'd heard me was the best way forward. "Your car at the back of the building?"

"Yeah, that's why you didn't see it."

"Great. Well, I'll leave you be."

I was fully ready to disappear into my office and wish for death, but he said, "You think evolution went too far with me?"

With my back to him, I allowed myself to cringe.

"I'm sorry?" My face was neutral when I turned around.

"That's what you said."

I remember.

"You heard that?"

"Yeah, you might not recall because I scramble your brain?"

"No need to rehash the past."

"Why not?"

"Because I'm flustered." Embarrassed would be more accurate. Humiliated. Where was the hole I could hide in?

"I'm a little flustered, too."

I grimaced. "Oh yeah, you seem it."

"I'm just better at hiding it than you."

"Hm."

He tilted his head, considering me. "We had a biology class together, didn't we?"

"I think so."

Definitely.

"You raised your hand a lot."

"Good of you to remember."

"You were cute."

"Yeah, I'm sure."

"You're still cute."

Was Elijah March flirting with me? How was I supposed to respond to this? It'd been so long since anyone had shown interest in me that I was out of practice. But despite having built him up in my memory, he was just a man. And I was a grown woman.

There was no reasonable reason for me to feel like I was melting.

"Thank you," I said to my ballerina flats. My hands clasped against my thighs. My shoulders shrugged forward, as if I could hide standing right there. My body language made me recall my wallflower days, before I'd gone to college and had come into my confidence. It was enough to convince me to roll my shoulders back, straighten my spine, and lift my chin. "I think you're cute."

Oh my god, I wanted to swallow my tongue. I'd flown too close to the sun. How had I thought I could go from him hearing my gossiping to telling him he was cute without it being weird?

A slow, easy smile spread across his face, and the full force of it was overwhelmingly charming. I'd never been so charmed in my life. I would die a charmed woman.

Elijah met my eye. "I was told you're a good girl."

My jaw dropped, his words filthy and enticing.

The pink tip of his tongue moistened his lips. "Are you a good girl?"

I had to swallow to answer. "Usually." Air rushed from my lungs as the lie settled into my blood, and I corrected, "Fucking *always*."

I had always been such a good girl. So mature for my age. So driven, and focused. And I'd never wanted to be anything else. I liked being good, dependable. In my twenty-six years, I'd never put my foot out of line. But right now Elijah was making me want to be anything but good. To ignore the warning—possible threat—his dad had given, and experience something I'd always wanted but thought I could never have.

The way Elijah's gaze swept over my body made me think I could have everything.

He gripped the arms of the chair. "I was told to keep my distance."

A flair of irritation shot through me—knowing exactly who had overstepped their boundaries. Dr. March and I would be having a conversation about him staying in his lane.

I raised my chin. "I don't remember telling you that."

Elijah's eyebrows shot up, and he nodded. "That's a good point. That's a good fucking point."

He stood in one graceful movement. "Is this too close?"

I rolled my eyes, but the effect was ruined by the giant grin on my face. "No."

He took a step closer, only a few feet away now. Close enough that I could smell faint wisps of something smoky and sweet. "Is this too close?"

"No."

Was this really happening?

He reached for me, slowly. Softly, he asked, "Is this too close?"

His fingertips slipped up my hips to my waist. My chest felt tight. My heart was racing. My mind could only process so much information over the flurry of electricity shocking through my nervous system. There was a darkening of stubble on his jaw. One peak of his Cupid's bow was slightly sharper than the other. In his eyes was the question he'd asked.

"No," I breathed.

A shiver ran down my spine as he slipped his hands around to my back. Instead of moving closer to me, he pulled me into him. My breasts pressed to his chest. I took hold of his arms, just because I could—just because I wanted to. The firm contours of muscles were even better under my touch than I'd imagined.

He tilted his head, his lips parted inches from mine.

"It's not close enough," I answered before he could ask.

Swallowing, he nodded. "Yeah."

One of his palms moved up my back to cup my neck at my pulse. His thumb drew a line along my jaw. "Your heart's beating fast."

"Mm-hm," was all I could actually say.

"Are you sure you're okay? Do you feel safe?"

His question caught me off guard, and I instinctively searched for the answer. He was wrapped around me, firm and strong. Real. So much more than a fantasy.

"I do." I sank into him, noticing the way his heart thrummed against his chest.

"Good."

"Do you feel safe?"

He blinked. His hold on me tightened. The corner of his mouth curved as he lowered his head to brush his lips along my earlobe. I gasped as intense sensations flickered through my body.

I felt more than heard him groan. "Yes."

I'd never done this. He wasn't a stranger, but he nearly was. Everything about this fought against my logical mind, but even my logical self said, *Don't question it.*

Against my thigh, his cock twitched.

Heat pooled in my core—a throbbing need.

My eyelids drifted shut as he skimmed his lips along my jaw; turning me to liquid. Bewitched by the gentle caress of his touch. Anticipation coiled in my stomach, waiting as the pressure grew. The corner of his mouth brushed mine. I turned my head, ready for real contact.

The back door closed with a loud thud. We jumped apart as if we'd been splashed with cold water. The spell was broken. My head whipped in the direction of footsteps coming closer down the hallway.

Elijah ran a hand through his hair, his fingers tangling in the curls. One corner of his mouth turned up in an apologetic and bashful smile. "Fuck, sorry. You're..."

I leaned forward to hear his quiet words.

"You're really fucking beautiful."

Nothing was working like it should—my jaw was slack, my hands hung at my sides, and if not for the shelf behind me, I probably would have fallen to the floor.

At a normal volume, he said, "It was nice to talk to you." Then, without any more explanation, he left the office. "Hey, Dad."

"Hazel in there?" Dr. March asked.

"Yeah."

I bent to pick up the files that had fallen when I'd come in, and placed them back on the shelf where they belonged. Dr. March stepped into the room, and I hoped my voice was as level as Elijah's had been. "I swung by to grab some adoption applications."

"Well, good thing you remembered." He looked from me to Elijah, who was standing in the doorway, but I wasn't sure what he was looking for. Whatever it was, I hoped he didn't find it.

"Of course." My expression felt natural enough, possibly a bit forced. "Anyway, I won't hold you two up. It was nice to catch up with you, Elijah."

"You, too."

I tossed a wave over my shoulder, and found Elijah watching me leave. Even from the other side of the lobby, I could feel the intensity of his stare. A regret of what had almost passed between us. A promise for more.

The past few minutes didn't feel real. It was already a hazy memory of bright emotions and awareness.

But I knew without a doubt that I wanted it to happen again.

Chapter 2
Elijah

Fucking around with Hazel was a terrible decision.

My dad supported her taking over the family business—even though she wasn't family. Not only because I had never wanted to be a veterinarian—which might have been the first time I'd truly disappointed him in a long line of disappointments. But also because he thought she upheld the evangelical and puritanical image he valued so much. An idea he was obviously wrong about.

She was multi-faceted. A woman who blushed one second and sank into my arms the next. Who arched her body into mine. Who gasped at the slightest brush of my lips on her skin.

He'd told me to keep my distance, and he did not like to be disobeyed. I knew better than anyone that his high morals were just a facade; a tool to manipulate.

The roiling ball of anger that had resided in my stomach since reconnecting with him grew leaden and hot and uncomfortable.

What the fuck was I doing here? What had compelled me to think I should make amends with this man? A man I resembled in appearance only.

Taking a couple weeks of vacation on Lake Michigan's coast had seemed like a good idea a few months ago. Mom had encouraged me to reconnect with people from my childhood, despite her personal apprehensions.

"Honey, it's a small town, but there are a lot of people other than your dad in it," she'd reasoned. "You could reconnect with Ransom. How long has it been since you've spoken to him? And I hear that Ben kid you used to hang around opened up a bar in town. There's a new generation taking over and building things. People and places change, maybe it's different from when we used to live there. If you talk to your dad and it doesn't feel right, then there are other ways to spend your time."

Five days in, and I had already gotten into an argument with Dad, gotten too drunk at Benji's Place with Ransom and his cousin Sterling, and nearly kissed Hazel. Who knew what would have happened if Dad had come in through the front door instead of the back?

Twelve hours later, I knew it had been a terrible choice. I didn't need to complicate my relationship with Dad even more. I would leave town in just over a week. But every time I let my mind wander, it went to her closed brown eyes and her lips parted. Waiting.

The floral smell of her hair, faint in my nose. Her breasts pressed to my chest. Need thundering through my body with an intensity I hadn't experienced since I was a young man.

It was eight a.m. in Michigan's Bible Belt and I struggled to conceal a semi down the pant leg of my jeans in front of a library. And Hazel hadn't even shown up yet.

She had an effect on me I couldn't understand.

The pet adoption event would begin in less than an hour on the green grass of the side yard. The front of the large stone building was taken up by concrete stairs and a ramp. I gripped one end of the Grand Ridge Animal Clinic banner's string. It would display between the dramatic columns on either side of the front door.

When my dad called out, "Hello," I looked over my shoulder so fast I thought I might have pulled something. But Hazel wasn't approaching him.

His white hair glinted in the sunlight as he waved to a middle-aged woman in a gray polo with the humane society logo on her left breast.

"Hey there!" She waved back.

"Patricia, always good to see you," he greeted.

She beamed up at him, her black eyeliner making her blue eyes luminescent in an almost unnerving way. "Dr. March, are you really gonna retire next month? Who will do this next year if you don't?"

He rested his hands on his hips and gave an apologetic nod. "It's time. But you remember Hazel?"

"From last year?"

"And the year before. She'll be taking over. You'll like her. She's good people."

Patricia's lips pursed to the side of her face. "I'm sure she is. Can you introduce me again?"

"Of course. Speaking of..."

I followed his gaze down the street. Strolling up the sidewalk in a lavender-colored sundress—this woman's array of dresses was going to be the death of me—was Hazel. A row of brown buttons ran from her chest to just above her knees. She held an iced coffee in one hand and a cardboard carrier with three more cups in the other. She had dark sunglasses on, and her shoulder-length mahogany-colored hair swung from a ponytail high on her head.

"Hello! I brought coffee!"

She was my type—pretty and brainy—but that didn't explain why I was so drawn to her. My eyes only wanted to rest on her—to take in the soft, full curves of her body. I should have more control—for her sake, if nothing else. But my intuition told me this wouldn't just go away.

I tried to focus on tying the string of the banner through the loop, but my fingers had grown too large and uncoordinated.

She gripped my arms, her thumbs trailing up my biceps. "It's not close enough."

A shiver ran down my spine, and the string slipped from my hand. The whole banner fell to the ground like a thunderstorm, echoing off the stones.

"Ya all right, son?" Dad called from a few feet away.

"I'm good."

"Want help?"

"No, I'm all right. Thanks, though."

"He looks so much like you," Patricia remarked. "Couldn't deny him if you tried, huh?"

God knew he'd tried. Maybe that wasn't fair. Maybe that was just how it had felt as a teen with newly divorced parents, in a town of people who'd shut their doors to my mom.

If she could find forgiveness for them, and my dad, I should at least try.

But it didn't feel like he'd changed. Did he deserve my forgiveness?

"I don't see it," Hazel said.

I glanced over to the group to find her considering me with her head tilted.

A little smile tugged at one corner of her lips. "You're obviously related, but I don't think you look too much alike."

Dad laughed. "That's because you've only known me as an old man."

"Well, here's your old-man coffee—black, no frills." She pointed to a cup in the holder, then indicated to a second one and said to Patricia, "Millie down at Country Grounds said this was your preferred order—a caramel white chocolate mocha."

"Oh my goodness! Look at you; that's so sweet. You're Carol Matthew's daughter, aren't you?"

Hazel nodded. "I am."

Patricia made a *tsking* sound with her teeth. "Well, no wonder you're so thoughtful."

"Isn't she a sweetheart?" Dad agreed.

Hazel took four strides toward me, holding out the last cup in the tray. "I didn't know what your order was, so I just got two of mine—it's an iced vanilla latte with an extra shot of espresso."

I let the string of the banner go again, this time laying it down on the cement. "Sounds delicious. It really is nice of you to think of me."

"Can't really stop," she said just under her breath.

My stomach dropped. It took all my self-control to keep my composure. My polite smile was practically plastered onto my face. I lifted the lid to my mouth and tilted some of the sweet liquid in.

In a normal volume, she asked, "What is your usual order?"

Swallowing, I answered, "Usually just a plain latte with an extra shot. But I wouldn't change this. It's perfect."

"I'm glad you like it. I'm enjoying mine, too." She turned to face Patricia and my dad—who squinted at me in warning. "So, we got pretty well set up yesterday, looks like Elijah has the banner under control, and volunteers will be here in about thirty minutes. Patricia, would you like me to ride with you to get the pets?"

"A woman with a plan. You were right, Doc, I'm gonna like her just fine."

The two women chatted as they walked to the humane society van.

Setting my drink on the cement, I picked up the banner again.

Dad moved to join me. "Son, let me help you with that."

"I really do have it," I argued.

He took the string from between my fingers anyway. I sighed and stepped back.

"Now, I know Hazel is a pretty girl—"

"Woman."

"—and as my son, she might not understand your character the way that I do—"

"Have you ever considered that maybe I don't have a bad character—that that's just the way you choose to see me?"

He blinked, clearly annoyed at my interruption.

"No? Okay."

His fingers began working a few simple but tight knots into the string, securing it to the pole. "But I have made myself clear. I will not have your negative influence on that young woman. It would force me to make changes to her and my agreement. So, even if she shows interest in you, I need you to do what's right."

I blinked at the back of his head of thick white hair, trimmed and neat. It took me a moment to realize my mouth was hanging open as I tried to put my thoughts in order.

Ice ran through my veins. I shook my head, sure I was misunderstanding him. "Your agreement? Are you saying you won't sell her the clinic?"

He turned, facing me. His eyes were blue, but otherwise shaped like mine. A few deep creases were etched into the skin at the corners. He looked exhausted. Weary.

And disappointed. Always so fucking disappointed.

"Do I have your word?" he asked.

I crossed my arms over my chest, then ran a hand across my lips, wondering just how far to push my point. "I will show her respect. That includes not running away from her if she comes near me. This conversation feels very uncomfortable. It feels like we're discussing what behavior would be...*becoming* of her, as if she wouldn't be the best person to decide what that is."

"We both know you better than she does."

"I was a reckless teen—"

"Still no accountability for your actions."

"Of course I hold myself accountable. But I'm not to blame for everything."

Dad's face twisted in disgust—a rage brewing just beneath the surface, a twin flame to the anger growing in me.

In a hoarse whisper, he demanded, "*How* did you come from me?"

"I ask myself that every day!" I shot back.

We stood with matching set jaws. Wielding our glares like daggers. Birds carried on easier conversations in the trees overhead. Cars drove by full of people who didn't know how foolish I'd been harboring hope for a relationship with this man. And for what? Because he made up half of my DNA?

All the years that had passed since I'd been trapped under his control. The smiles I'd forced—to appear as the good son, because failing meant harsh consequences. There were plenty of ways to hurt someone without ever raising a hand. When Mom finally left him during my junior year of school, I'd exercised my new freedom. Doing exactly what he'd taught me to do—hurt him without raising a hand.

A sick pattern I didn't want to be a part of anymore. I didn't want Hazel to be a part of it either.

The accusation and warning in Dad's eyes made me resent whatever he was going to say next.

"Don't make her pay for your sins."

Chapter 3
Hazel

I didn't know Elijah well, but it was obvious there was something wrong. There'd been a tightness to him since I'd brought him coffee. His hands were balled into fists inside his pockets, and his shoulders were bunched and corded. His warm smile looked brittle and tight—so close to breaking.

Clearly, something had happened between him and his dad, because Dr. March wouldn't even look at his son. No one else seemed put off by their tension. I doubted anyone even noticed.

With a bundle of folding chairs under each arm, Elijah disappeared around the library and down the slope of the yard to the basement side door. Dr. March was saying goodbye to the last of the volunteers. The pets were already on their way back to the shelter; a few adoption forms had been filled out.

All-in-all, it looked like the day was a success.

I grabbed the mugs full of pens and strode up the large cement stairs between the pillars of the grand main entrance. The familiar musky scent of books greeted me.

I set the cups on the checkout desk next to Mrs. Simon's computer. "Here are your pens."

She had been head librarian here for as long as I could remember, as much a staple of the town as the library itself. She stood behind the front desk, with a brightly colored silk scarf wrapped over her hair contrasted with her dark skin. "How was the turnout?"

"Really good. Thank you for getting the Euchre Club involved. I haven't seen exact numbers, but it was definitely more than last year."

"Oh, those ol' busy bodies are always looking for somethin' to talk about. I'm sure they blabbed about Elijah March, and everyone came to see the young man return." She set the cups on a shelf under the counter. "He's grown up just fine, hasn't he?"

"Sure."

She raised a thin dark eyebrow with a skeptical smirk.

A blush crept up my cheeks. "I'd say so."

Her lips pursed. "Yup."

"Mrs. Simon," I said, a little shocked.

"I see what I see."

I wondered if what she saw was a handsome man, or how I lusted after him. The first would be obvious; the second would be humiliating.

"I'm gonna double check that everything is taken care of downstairs. You have a good day." I pushed off the counter.

"You, too."

Descending into the basement, I trailed my fingers along the large wooden railing with its ornately-carved knoll post at the landing. The finish was beginning to flake, and I wondered if the Board had commissioned its repair yet.

I hadn't expected to find Elijah in the storage room—but I had hoped. At the sight of his slouched shoulders, my flurry of excitement drifted away. I wanted to ask if he was okay, not just because I had definitely formed an ill-advised crush, but because I hated to see people or animals suffering.

"Hey." I tried to keep my voice low, but the cinder block walls amplified every sound.

"Jesus." He startled and pressed a hand to his chest.

"Sorry, I was actually trying not to scare you."

"I thought you were the ghost that haunts this place."

"You believe in that?"

"I don't know." He swept an arm out in a vague gesture, encompassing the space. "It's a creepy old place, and there's been sightings."

I scoffed. "Yeah, from people like Shane Briar, and I don't think he could even point to the library on a map."

That brittle edge was there in the corners of Elijah's smile. Like old glass that had grown thin in places, warped and unclear. "Probably not."

"It's kinda—it's obviously none of my business, but are you okay?"

"Sure, why do you ask?" He stood straighter, his shoulders pulled back.

"You seem sad."

"I'm all right."

"Okay."

But I knew he knew I didn't believe him. I also wouldn't push him any further.

I jerked my head toward the open door behind me. "Wanna see one of my favorite places?"

He nodded with a wistful look in his eyes that made my chest hurt. "Yeah."

He stared at the hand I extended between us. For a few seconds, he seemed to go back and forth on whether he should loop his fingers with mine. I was about to drop my arm to my side again when he slipped his fingertips along my palm. His touch was warm as his hand fit into place.

I hoped my expression hid all the ways that small touch thrilled me.

The human body had somewhere around seven trillion nerve endings. And every single one of mine was alight.

My stomach flipped, and my heart began to race. A shiver ran down my spine. My scalp tingled. My toes curled. And deep within my core, a quiet ache grew louder.

Time stretched and wrapped around us, drawing us closer together. In reality, it was likely only a few seconds, and it was probably just me leaning toward his warmth and strength.

His green eyes dropped to my mouth, and I wondered—hoped—in my dazed state if he'd kiss me.

I registered him forming words, but I couldn't hear him.

"I'm sorry?" I asked.

He swallowed, and his Adam's apple bobbed. "Lead the way."

I most likely failed to hide anything. On the plus side, based on his thickened voice, he wasn't unaffected.

The basement held the denser nonfiction stacks and local historical materials. Holding hands from the storage room to my spot was most likely safe. We shouldn't be caught. I still cast a quick glance out the door before pulling Elijah along behind me. We hurried. Once we got to the back corner, it'd be unlikely anyone would discover us.

He chuckled, and I glanced over my shoulder to see if his smile had healed. There was humor and something even warmer—something I was too scared to name—alight on his features. I giggled as we zoomed past stack after stack of dusty tombs. He almost passed the opening in the wall as I ducked into it.

It was hard to see the entrance. It was barely wide enough to walk through without twisting sideways. The exterior wall was cinder block like the rest of the foundation, but the other side was lath and horse hair. It was all painted in a yellowed pale pink—every inch of it covered in faded handwritten quotes. All about love. Some were sad and some were happy. Some were romantic and some were... for lack of a better word, horny. Each in swooping, beautiful cursive from a time before computers, when penmanship was taught in schools. At the ceiling and floor, the wood trim was etched with initials and hearts, some of them with jagged broken scratches going down the middle. A reminder that not all loves last.

"Where are we?" Elijah asked; his voice echoed in the small dimly lit space.

I shushed him, my finger pressed against my lips.

He shrugged his shoulders near his ears and bit his lip.

Pointing to the permanently closed small iron door leading to the outside, I kept my voice barely above a whisper, because all other sound would amplify. "It's where they used to throw the wood or coal for the old furnace."

"How did you find this place?"

"I was a nosy kid who spent a lot of time at the library."

"How doesn't everybody know about this?" He turned his head this way and that to read line after line.

"Well, I like keeping secrets, so I never told anyone. But most people don't come to the basement, and the section out there is, like, the history of watching grass grow or something. I think Mrs. Simon keeps it a secret on purpose."

"It's probably lead-based paint and they'd have to cover it."

"Yeah, just don't eat any paint chips while we're down here, okay?"

"I'll do my best."

We settled into a comfortable silence, him reading with a crease between his eyebrows. I searched out some of my favorites quotes. There were Emily Bronte words that had inspired me to read *Wuthering Heights*; "Whatever our souls are made of, his and mine are the same." It was such a lovely idea—to be woven from the same cloth. I was less impressed with the book itself.

"We should talk about yesterday," Elijah said.

My eyes settled on a line from Jane Austen's *Emma* about love not being in her nature.

"Why does it sound like you're going to let me down easy?" I asked.

He was silent long enough that I looked and found him staring at me with an apology in his eyes. "I'm sorry. My dad... It's complicated."

I was grateful for the darkness that hid the blush rising up my cheeks. His choice had more to do with his relationship with his dad than me, but it still hurt.

It didn't make me feel any less rejected.

"Okay." I was relieved my voice wasn't strained.

The silence was less comfortable this time. I wondered how long I should wait before I ducked out. I couldn't right now; it'd look like I was running. Which I wasn't. Mostly. Maybe a little.

Were either of us even reading anymore, or was he pretending just like me?

Then I felt him pause at my side, and I followed the direction of his gaze. *"Have loved and lost."*

I breathed in through my nose. This quote had followed me for a long time—four words haunting me. There was pain in those swooping letters, enough that for years, I'd mulled them over. Wondering why they made me feel loss, when I'd never felt loss before. It had taken a heartbreak in my freshman year of college to understand. It had taken experience to discover the knowledge. Instead of their edges growing dull, the letters had sharpened—driving the cut deeper.

Elijah lifted his fingers to brush over the words. "This one..."

"I have a theory." I hadn't forgotten my embarrassment, but I could never pass up an opportunity to be a brainiac.

"I'm listening."

"So, it's clearly from, 'It's better to have loved and lost, then never to have loved at all.'"

"Yeah."

"Which is already a sad quote, but it's hopeful. This person... wasn't able to see the hope."

He made a thoughtful sound.

"It's more than that, though, isn't it?" A new understanding lit me up, something not fully formed. "Maybe this person didn't experience loss. Maybe they realized in its lack, they didn't experience love at all. I think it hurts because..."

I turned, finding his attention had shifted from the words on the wall to me. In the dark, surrounded by poetry full of victory and angst, I saw him without bravado or poise. He was honest and unfiltered. Vulnerable.

"I don't know why it hurts." I was trapped in the green depths of his eyes. They pulled at me, urged me. Making me admit what I really knew. "It's sad, because it's lost before it's yours."

The press of his chest put me firmly against the wall, right before his mouth claimed mine.

Chapter 4
Elijah

Hazel's body gave to the pressure of mine. Her breasts pressed to my chest as her surprised gasp was captured by my kiss. Her arms wrapped around my neck, pulling me in tighter. Her scent of cut grass and some kind of sweet flower had filled the small space. I'd been called to it like a cartoon bear called to the smell of freshly baked pie on a window sill. Something I was bound to devour if left unattended. And now that her taste was on my tongue, I was less the harmless, dopey bear, and more the actual wild animal.

I had enough awareness to swallow down my moan, but just barely.

My hands dug into the flesh of her hips. My fingers drove into the top of her ass. It was lush under the cotton of her dress. She ground her pelvis on the leg I had between hers. Her core was hot on my thigh through the denim of my jeans. The shiver that went through her whittled at the self-control I thought I'd already abandoned. When her touch drifted down my sides, I trapped her wrists and pressed them to the hard cinder block over her head. The other gripped her leg. My fingertips slipped under her skirt.

I tilted my head, and licked the sensitive skin over her pulse. It drummed a frantic rhythm against my tongue.

"I don't get to touch you?" she barely breathed.

I drew her earlobe between my teeth. "Not here."

Her breathing shuddered, and she rocked her hips.

I should stop. Pull back. Breathe. And I would. Just as soon as I tasted the tops of her swollen breasts. Just as soon as I sucked on her parted lips, again. Just as soon as I...

I should stop, but I didn't see an end in sight—not one that didn't end with me speared deeply inside of her—her legs wrapped around my waist. Both of us coming in near silence.

But then a voice cut through the sounds of our breathing. One that had the effect of dumping a bucket of ice over my head. It sounded like it was right outside the cove we were in. Actually, it came from the storage closet on the other side of the basement, the sound bouncing off the walls.

"Just making sure we're locked up," Dad said, talking to someone out on the library lawn.

Regret flooded into me, but not for kissing Hazel. Not at the possibility of getting caught with her, but at the reflexive way I'd pulled my mouth from her skin.

"Good stuff, good stuff, glad to hear it," my dad went on. "You take good care of that little pup."

Her heavy-lidded, big brown eyes were dark with desire.

"Have you seen Hazel anywhere? I wanted to go over some things—" Dad's voice cut off with the closing of the door.

A groan rumbled from Hazel's throat, and she pouted. I wanted to drag her full bottom lip between my teeth. Instead, I eased my hips back, away from the warm, welcoming pressure of her body. Convincing myself to release her wrists was even harder. I liked the way she looked, her arms held over her head. The hem of her skirt rumpled high on her thighs. Soft pink lace peeking out of the gap between two dark-brown buttons.

"I should go," she said.

I nodded and removed my hands from her. I missed her nearness. I already missed the feel of her skin, warm and soft. I missed the way her teeth had scraped my neck.

With my back pressed against the cold cinder block opposite her, I took in her tousled ponytail. Her mouth looked like she'd been ravished. A red bruise stood out on the pale skin of her breast. She looked perfect.

It made my cock ache. I wanted to take her back into my arms. I wanted more of what I couldn't have.

Whatever her pull on me, I was lost to it. She'd been under my skin from the second I saw her, like she was layered into my DNA.

We were reckless—I was reckless. It would be her who paid for that. Whatever motivations my dad had didn't matter; it would be Hazel caught between me and the man who wanted to hurt me. There was only one way to protect the life she'd built, because I was going to destroy it otherwise.

My shoulders hunched as resignation settled atop them. "I'm gonna leave in the morning."

Soft lines etched into her forehead. "I thought you were here for another week or so."

I shoved my fists into my pockets and rocked back on my heels, shaking my head. "It's best I leave."

Understanding crossed her features. She smoothed her ponytail before tugging her dress back into place. "I'll see you tonight."

"It's a bad idea."

"You're staying in a Rustic Resort cabin, right?"

"Yeah."

"Which one?"

"Three."

"I'll see you tonight." Then she was gone.

My cheeks puffed out as I exhaled, my eyes landing on a quote on the wall; *"Pleasure's a sin, and sometimes sin's a pleasure."*

Waiting was not an easy task. I liked to *do*. It was the pause between action that made my knee bounce, and my hands twitch. But all there was left was waiting. I'd washed the last of my dishes and set them in the cupboards. My clothes were folded and in my suitcase. I'd taken out the trash, ready to leave first thing in the morning.

A part of me wished Hazel had changed her mind, and I'd wait all night. In the morning I'd be groggy and unfulfilled, but her profession wouldn't be jeopardized. The other part of me couldn't wait for her to show up. The part of me that couldn't forget the feel of her body trapped between mine and the wall—the soft give of her thigh in my hand. That part of me was the loudest, the most desperate.

The moon was large and vanilla colored in the navy-blue sky. Its light casted shadows across the sandy grass, the branches of trees patterned like filigree webs. It was quiet except for the gentle lap of Lake Michigan against the beach.

I was sitting in the metal rocking chair on the back deck, finishing my second beer, as white headlights illuminated the trees. Gravel crunched under the car's wheels as it drove up the cabin's driveway. Unease settled alongside my anxiety and anticipation. I should have realized she'd drive. She didn't realize how vital it was that she didn't get caught with me.

And this was why my better self had hoped she wouldn't come. She didn't even know the risk she was taking. I would tell her, but I wouldn't send her away. Even though, I should.

If she left, it would be because she chose to. Not because of gallantry on my part.

Swallowing one more drink, I set the longneck on the little table next to me.

I squinted at the headlights, raising my hand in a wave before shoving both hands into my pockets.

The engine quieted, and she opened the driver's door. My night vision was still hazy from the sudden brightness, making her impossible to see.

"Hey," she called softly, the smile on her face carried in that single syllable.

"Hey. Are you sure you wanna be here?" I asked.

"Do you not want me here?"

My eyes were beginning to adjust enough that I saw the self-conscious way she crossed her arms over her chest.

My heart sank. I didn't want to make her feel bad or self-conscious. Jerking my head toward the front door, I took a step closer. "How badly I want you here is the problem."

She shifted her weight from one foot to another.

I shrugged toward the cabin door. "Wanna come in?"

"Yeah."

The cabin was small. All of the lights had an amber hue to them, as if we were stepping into an old photograph. Knotty pine lined the walls and made up the floors—maybe it wasn't an old photograph, but the inside of a tree. Floral curtains covered the little windows. The only pieces of furniture were the table the television sat on, a futon in the couch position, and a two-person kitchen table with chairs. A window air conditioner had been permanently installed in a hole in the wall, its whoosh of cold air drowning out the sounds of the lake and the rustle of leaves in the wind.

Turning, I gave Hazel a small smile, holding the door open for her to walk through. She was still wearing the lavender dress from earlier today with the line of dark buttons down her front. Her hair was loose around her shoulders now. She looked like a librarian or a school teacher—in a very hot way.

"Would you like something to drink?" I offered.

"Sure." She glanced in the direction of the open door to her left that led into the cabin's only bedroom.

"I have water or beer."

"A beer would be great."

I didn't even have to move to open the fridge and pull out two long-necks. Using the bottle opener screwed into the wall, I snapped the tops off them both. Hazel's lips around the rim of the glass made the blood in my body surge south. But I needed to be honest with her.

"I'm concerned for you to be seen here. If coming back here has reminded me of anything, it's that nothing remains quiet in this town."

"Are you embarrassed to be seen with me?"

"No." The word came out harsh, but it was from irritation with myself. The more I spoke, the worse I was making everything. Calmly, I went on, "No. I'm concerned about *you* being seen with *me*. Best case scenario, they talk about you like it's any of their business. They make opinions about you."

She shook her head with an annoyed twist of her lips. "Why do you think anyone cares? I guess you're a big deal to everyone around here, but I'm just not. No one talks about me."

"Jesus, I wish that was my experience."

"I don't know; it can suck to be invisible." My eyebrows pinched together, but she rolled her eyes and spoke before I could. "Let's forget that I said that. It's just... I'm always so dependable—predictable. I just... I don't know." She shrugged one shoulder. "I don't want it tonight."

"If my dad finds out, Hazel..."

"He's not gonna do anything."

"He's threatening to take the clinic from you."

"He'd never do that. I've brought in new veterinarians, and we're doing more community work. One more month and he's retired. He's so ready. And... he wouldn't do that to me."

I rocked back on my heels. She was so close to being out from underneath his thumb.

"Have you signed paperwork already? Is there some sort of deadline in the contract and all of that?"

"Yes, but we still have to sign a release when the business changes into my name."

"What if I came back in a month?"

She crossed her arms over her chest and leaned to one hip. "I don't know who you think has the power in my sex life, but it's me. If you don't want to have sex with me, you can just say it. You don't have to be so weird about it."

"He hates me—"

"He doesn't hate—"

"He *hates* me." My words hung between us.

She didn't believe me, and maybe she wanted to argue further, but she didn't. It was always hard for people with loving parents to know their situation wasn't always the case for everyone else. Sometimes the person who was supposed to love you the most just made you feel bad.

"He will hurt you to hurt me." Having to convince her of the truth only made it cut deeper. "I won't tell you to leave. I won't even ask you to. If I can have a night with you, I'll take it."

Raising her longneck to her mouth, she considered me. Under her scrutiny, I realized I'd raked my fingers through my hair. I probably looked half-crazed, spouting about my father issues. I wouldn't blame her if she decided to leave. I'd practically begged her to.

When she set her beer on the counter, I took a step away from the front door, offering her an easier exit.

Instead of making an excuse and shuffling past me, she held my stare. Lifting her hands from her sides, she eased a button through its loop. The V of her neckline dropped lower, and pale-pink lace showed just above the second button. Unhurriedly, she opened that button. Then the next.

I drank in every fresh inch of exposed skin. The roundness of her stomach under her belly button. The matching pink-lace triangle over her dark pubic hair. By the time she was done, I was hard and throbbing. I forced myself not to move, to let her see me want her. Needing her. Let her see the power she had over me.

Her dress hung open like a robe. She grabbed the open collar and let it drop from her shoulders. Close to her bra was a small red circle where I'd sucked too hard earlier today. I'd try to be more gentle with her tonight—but, then again, I liked the mark I made on her. I wanted to make more.

The wet tip of her tongue slipped over her bottom lip.

"Touch me." There was a gentle plea in those two words that squeezed my chest.

The wood floor creaked as I stepped closer. She tilted her chin upward to hold my gaze. In the deep brown depths of her eyes was an echo of her words, silently begging me to explore her curves and valleys. Her eyelids fluttered closed at the barest brush of my fingertips.

She was so fucking beautiful with her thick dark eyelashes and the rosy flush on her cheeks and the way she sucked on her lower lip. My cock twitched inside my jeans.

I trailed my touch up the line where her thighs pressed together, then over her mound. Her stomach flexed and she drew in a sharp breath.

"Is that how you're going to respond to me all night?" Just above her bra, I twisted my wrist and pressed my palm to her sternum. Her heart thudded beneath my splayed fingers. "Is every little touch going to make you gasp like that? I'll be honest with you"—I cupped her throat and urged her chin up to look at me—"that's gonna fuckin' ruin me."

Chapter 5

Hazel

Elijah must have felt me shiver. It had taken so much for me to unbutton my dress while he watched. His stare devouring and intense; his desire pulled tight like a rubberband about to snap. It had taken all of my bravery to drop my dress off my shoulders and tell him to touch me.

And he'd said I would ruin him.

I might have found it laughable if I hadn't been engulfed in flames. They licked through my veins, eating up all the oxygen in my body. Leaving me gasping as he brushed his lips on mine.

His fingers twitched at my throat. Groaning, he pulled me closer with his free hand on my back. "You are, aren't you? With your shy eyes and your fucking body." He reached down and squeezed my ass cheek to the point where it pinched. "You're gonna ruin me."

"Please," I whined.

"Please, what?"

I didn't know, but then I was saying, "Kiss me, fuck me—"

The rest of whatever I was going to say was swallowed by his mouth on mine. His back flexed under my fists as I clung to him. The denim of his jeans brushed against my legs.

I wasn't in my head at all. I was the sensation of his teeth scraping my lip, and his thumb tracing the lace of my bra. My nipple pinched, wanting his touch lower—his lips, his tongue.

My thong pulled tight against my sensitive clit as he ran a hooked finger up and down the back string. "You've got too many clothes on."

"You're the one fully dressed."

"I'm not worried about me," he said, but the hard length of his erection against my hip made a liar out of him.

There was no room to argue further. His tongue against mine demanded all my attention. He wrapped his arms around my ribs and pulled me in tighter. I found the hem of his shirt and slid my palms up his sides. The skin of his back was hot and smooth. I pressed my thumbs into the flexing muscles underneath. He arched, groaning.

It made me thirsty for more.

My bra drew tight as he plucked the clasps apart at the back. He stepped, away pulling the straps off my shoulders.

My nipples were hard—my tits full and heavy. I loved the way he looked at me. Cupping me, he lifted my breast to his mouth. Through his lashes, he watched my face as he circled his tongue around my beaded tip. When he pulled the hardened peak between his lips, my head fell back and my eyes closed.

I was so wet, and aching.

He moved to the other nipple.

My hand went between my thighs, rubbing my clit through my panties.

"You need it that bad, baby?" Straightening, he replaced his mouth with his thumbs.

"Yes," I whimpered, my hips bucking.

Gently, he shifted me back a step. Something firm hit the back of my calves. I would have fallen, but my one arm around his shoulders kept me up.

"Take off your panties, and sit down."

I did as he directed, slipping my legs free from the scrap of lace. I didn't even look where I was sitting, just landing on a cushioned surface; my tits bounced with the impact. His cock strained against the fabric of his pants. Incensed, I pressed a firm hand on his balls as I placed a series of kisses up his length to the imprint of his tip.

His fingers tunneled through his hair, watching me.

Staring up at him, I said, "I want you in my mouth."

"Not until I fuck you."

"Then fuck me."

"Not until you come on my face. Put this behind your back," he commanded, handing me a pillow.

Poised at the edge of the futon, I spread my legs further as he knelt between them.

"Are you comfortable?" he asked, his breath puffing along my damp upper thighs.

I nodded, my mouth hanging open.

He placed three kisses up my leg, so close that the scruff on his chin scraped against my sensitive lips.

"Yes," I answered, but it was more of a plea.

"Are you sure?" His lips brushed my mound, and he hooked my thighs over his shoulders. "I'm not rushing through this." He continued peppering my thighs and lips with kisses and scrapes of his teeth.

The anticipation pulled my need tight, stringing my muscles taught, and I gripped the cushion at my sides.

He took hold of the tops of my legs, easing them even wider. "I asked you a question."

"Yes, yes, please." I wasn't even sure what I was agreeing to anymore, but if it would give me release, he could do anything.

"Look at me."

My chest rose and fell on uneven breaths as I met his gaze.

"Put your hands in my hair."

The wavy strands were silky and thick between my fingers.

"Now ride my face like you're doing me a fucking favor."

A sound I didn't know a human could make ripped from my throat as he *finally* buried his face in me. He urged my hips up and down, grinding my clit along his nose. It took me barely a second to lose all semblance of restraint. My fingers twisted in his hair. Pulling him tighter and pushing his tongue deeper. His grip on my thighs did the same, tugging me.

I came undone fast. I couldn't comprehend time. I was electricity firing through my system and nothing else. I might have forgotten my own damn name—but didn't have a mind to check.

I crashed in waves, curling over and staring down his still clothed back. Shivers raked through my limbs, but I was aware enough to untangle my fingers from his hair as I fell back again.

My eyes were half closed when Elijah stood, pulling his shirt over his head. Strong, lean arms reached up, elongating the lines of his obliques. A trail of dark hair traveled down his abs and disappeared inside the jeans he unfastened. I was a mesh of arousal and satiation. My brain wanted more, but my body didn't know if it could take it. I felt like I was sinking into the sofa with each aftershock of my orgasm.

Elijah wiped his shirt on his face, then pushed his pants and boxers down. He was so hard and thick and gorgeous. And the tides of my will began to shift.

My thighs had red marks that would likely bruise from his strong hands. One of those hands now cupped my jaw, and he ran a thumb along my lip. "Let's get you ready again, baby."

Chapter 6

Elijah

Hazel laid face down on the white sheets of the bed. I'd gotten a burst of masculine pride when she'd wobbled, as if her legs didn't work correctly, during the short walk to the bedroom.

"Mmm, laying down was a dangerous move." Her words were lazy and muffled by the blankets.

Her bare ass was round and plump, and I couldn't resist filling my hand with one cheek. Her sigh made my balls tighten and my cock twitch. I was so hard for her. I wanted to sink inside her so badly. I needed her to squeeze me just before she came apart—again.

Kneeling with her legs between mine, I drifted my touch to her other cheek, then twisted my wrist to sink my finger between her wet folds. She arched, pushing into my touch. Her responsiveness almost robbed me of all the self-control I'd had in the living room; it was even worse here.

Leaning on my elbow, I kissed her just behind her earlobe. "You don't think I can convince you to stay awake?"

My erection throbbed between my stomach and her plush ass.

"I believe in you." She sighed, relaxing even further into the bed.

I kissed across her shoulders and down her spine. The need to fill her growing more intense as she groaned and tightened around the finger gently fucking her. My erection was nearly painful—my desire a persistent, pulsing beat. But I loved the little sounds of relaxed pleasure she made. A rumble deep in the back of her throat. A breath held and then released. The quiet rustle of the comforter shifting under the rocking of her hips. The brush of my lips, finding new places to touch. Revisiting the places she seemed to like best.

I wanted more of this. To trap this moment in amber. To suspend all of reality and keep drawing out her pleasure. I wouldn't last long once I was inside her. Precum already dripped down my shaft.

Her breath was beginning to catch, and her hips moved more urgently. The hushed sounds she'd been making becoming louder.

"Elijah," she breathed.

"Fuck," I whispered in her ear, "I like my name on your lips."

"I don't want to come again without you inside me."

"That's even better."

Her giggle shot through me, leaving me dizzy.

I grabbed a condom, my fingers glistening in the dim light. She peaked over her shoulder and licked her lips as I rolled the latex over my shaft.

I leaned down and kissed her. "You want it just like this? On your stomach?"

"Is that okay?"

Chuckling, I nodded. "Everything about this is okay."

This time, I knelt between her legs. With my hand at the base of her spine, I pushed inside her. Her walls squeezed me.

I growled between clenched teeth, urging my movements to be slow and deep even as my instinct was to take her fast and hard.

At the roll of her hips, I had to close my eyes and breathe before I lost it right then.

The even pace I kept gradually grew less controlled as I gave over to something primal and wild. An insistent need to claim her. To make her cry out. To make her whimper my name.

"Harder, please." Hazel's lower lip puckered and lust clouded her beautiful brown eyes. She was so gorgeous, with her cheek pressed into the sheets and her hair splayed out. But it was the *please* that really did me in.

"Only because you were so fucking polite about it." I smiled, taking hold of her hips in both hands.

A grin spread across her face until I plunged into her—pulling her to me as I rocked deeper. Our skin clashing together in a loud smack. She cried out, and I stopped before doing it again.

I ran a soothing hand along her side. "Can you take that, baby?"

"Yes, more, Elijah, please. I want that."

Something broke free inside my chest. The break felt uneven, leaving splinters. Making me aware of the power she had over me. Whatever drew us together was more than desire, and far more intimidating.

I tried to bury it below the lust, but I could still feel it. A jagged splinter lodged somewhere near my sternum.

I pounded into her, over and over as she begged for more. As I growled out her name over and over. Saying things I couldn't recall as soon as they left my mouth. Praising her for how well she took my cock. Telling her how beautiful she was with her mouth open and her eyes squeezed shut.

My thrusts grew impatient and punishing in their speed. Her ass rippled with each clap of our hips. Her mouth hung open in a silent scream—the waves of her orgasm squeezing and milking me. I lowered my stomach to her back; my movements were still unrelenting as I neared the edge.

I urged her to turn her head and take my kiss like she was taking my cock. Demanding and needy. Her pulse was frantic against my palm. She sucked on my tongue until I couldn't take it anymore. I dragged my teeth down her neck, and I bit down on her shoulder, spending into the condom.

Early morning sunlight dawned through the gap in the bedroom curtain, casting Hazel in a warm glow. I probably should have let her sleep more. She had to work later today.

But I couldn't stop touching her. Even after hours, I still needed her.

Eventually, we'd moved to the shower to wash away our salty sweat. I meant to let her sleep after that, but she curled into my side and kissed me so sweetly.

"You know," she whispered, "you still haven't fucked my mouth."

Hours later, we both needed to shower again.

Hazel sighed, and nestled deeper into her pillow.

I should just let her sleep, but I wanted to see her face. I wanted the memory of how peaceful she looked. With the softest touch, I brushed the silky chestnut strands of her hair behind her shoulder.

Her eyelashes rested on her cheek, and her lips were slightly pursed. She looked content. Something grew in my chest, bright and tempting.

I should rollover, stop taking in her gentle curves or the lush pink of her skin. I should try to protect myself from the feelings taking root in my chest. I should try to get some sleep, too.

But I never was good at doing what I should do.

Chapter 7
Hazel

"**Y**ou've been distracted today." Dr. March appeared at my shoulder as if conjured out of thin air. It was probably more accurate to say I'd been staring off into space, remembering all the ways Elijah had filled me, and touched me, and made me feel more than I had known possible.

"Just tired," I said. By the time I had gotten home this morning, I'd had just enough time to shower, change into my scrubs, and get to work. I'd read the chart for my first patient while French braiding my wet hair.

"Didn't sleep well?"

Nora Vasquez's typing paused for a moment as she glanced at a sticky note next to her mouse. I wanted to talk to her about everything, but we hadn't had a moment of privacy all day.

And it was kinda killing me. I wasn't going to spill all the... *details*, but I was feeling... *feelings*.

My body was sore, but relaxed. I'd never had a night of sex like that. I'd dated all of my partners before Elijah—dependable men who'd gotten me off like it was a task on their to-do list. Last night had not been about agendas. It had been hot. And sweet. So sweet, it had left my heart as tender as the rest of me.

I looked down at the chart I was filling out. "Yeah, not much sleep."

"Well, I hope you sleep well tonight."

"Thank you."

"Doc," Nora said, swiveling in her office chair to face us. Her curly black hair had begun escaping her braid a few hours ago, and now there was a frizzy halo around her oval face. She rocked side to side, fidgeting as usual. "I heard that Elijah cut his vacation short. Is everything okay? Was there an emergency or something?"

Dr. March straightened. His shoulders lifted a degree. "Not that I know of, but my son can be flighty."

She pursed her lips. "Huh, okay."

"He didn't seem flighty to me," I argued. I didn't like the tone Dr. March had used; it dripped poison.

He jerked his head to look at me, and I rocked back on my heels. His normally friendly blue eyes sharpened to a point. "How well did you get to know him?"

It was unnerving—like glimpsing between cracks and realizing there was something completely different underneath. Possibly even more un-nerving, Nora had gone still.

"My dad hates me." Elijah had said, and I was seeing what he'd meant.

"Not as well as I would have liked, honestly, but he seemed to feel that you wouldn't want him to get to know me." The whole time, everything had been framed as if I needed protecting, but maybe that hadn't been the case. Had it just been an excuse to control Elijah? Had it actually been about Dr. March protecting himself?

"He was right. Consider yourself lucky, Hazel."

"What's wrong with Elijah?"

"What's right with him would be a shorter list," Dr. March hissed.

Nora and I shared a look. I was glad she was there to see this as well. Otherwise, I might not believe it actually happened. What else had I seen but reasoned away, because this was kindly Ol' Dr. March, my mentor? The man who had picked me to care for the pets and livestock of our community.

I hadn't listened to his vague threat about how getting involved with Elijah could affect the sale of the clinic. Elijah had been concerned about me being seen with him last night. As light dawned on the truth of the situation, I was getting concerned, too.

I don't think I would have made a different choice, though.

Just a couple weeks to go, and as long as no one had seen me, the sale would go through and the danger would be behind me.

"That's too bad." Nora leaned back in her chair and crossed her legs; her foot bounced. "It'd make me really sad if my parents talked about me or my sister that way."

"Well, you're a good kid." The pleasant mask fit back onto Dr. March's face, but it didn't seem to fit right anymore. "It's been a long weekend and I'm gonna say goodnight, ladies."

Nora made a *"hmm"* sound of acknowledgment.

The most polite thing I could bring myself to say was, "It has been a long weekend."

Nora turned and began typing again. I went back to jotting notes in my chart. When the employee entrance opened and closed, I looked up to find her looking over her shoulder at me.

"Is he gone?" she mouthed.

I held up a finger and walked to the hallway where there was a view of the door. Back in the office, I nodded.

"Okay, that was fucking weird." The corners of Nora's lips pointed down in disgust.

"What was that?" I asked, not expecting her to have an answer.

She sighed. Her foot began to bounce again.

"What?" This time I did expect an answer.

"Mom made a comment once, and I... I guess I never really had any evidence to believe it."

I remained silent, waiting.

"You know Mom and Dr. March's ex-wife used to work together?"

"No."

"Yeah, Insurance United." She rubbed her fingertips and her thumbs together. "Anyway, she said there were a couple of times that Doc seemed really... like, I guess, possessive or controlling of Mrs. March. She said he seemed to kinda make her small."

"Like, verbally abusive?"

"I guess so. I just couldn't see it until, like, now."

My eyebrows drew together. The whole picture was becoming clear. I'd been around fourteen when Mrs. March had moved her and Elijah out of their house. The separation had rocked the community in the early 2000s. No one could understand why she would leave such a nice and generous man—a doting father. Then Elijah's rebellious streak began, and everyone saw that as proof that Dr. March had been the best influence. But in this new light, I wondered how much of that had been true.

How much of it had been fabricated?

I hadn't planned to go to Benji's Place that night. The atmosphere was different on a Monday evening than on a Friday or Saturday. There were a few tables filled, one with a couple and their kids eating burgers and french fries. Benji's was not a dive, but it did have a reputation for getting rowdy—much like the owner himself.

I spotted broad shoulders and auburn hair at the bar. Ransom Strauss sipped amber liquid from a short glass and glared into the middle distance. Taking the stool next to him, I forced my shoulders to relax. We both had grown up in this town, had graduated from the same school.

Yet I could count on one hand the number of times I'd spoken to him directly. With his blue eyes narrowed and his stubbled jaw set, I understood why.

He was an intimidating man.

He'd be handsome if he weren't so terrifying.

I would have preferred to speak to the always easy-going Sterling, Ransom's cousin. But then, I'd prefer to speak to almost anyone else.

He doesn't bite—unlike a number of animals I worked with today.

At least I could rely on him not to tell another soul what I'd come here to do.

He lifted a ruddy eyebrow in my direction, but said nothing.

"Hi." I tried to smile, but I knew it looked forced.

"Hi?" The creases of his scowl deepened. It was unclear if it was the word that was foreign to him, or if it was my presence.

I stared too long, waiting for him to say anything else.

Rolling my eyes at myself, I squared my shoulders. I sat up straight, and got to the point. "Do you have Elijah March's number?"

Part 2

<u>Hazel and Elijah Find the Fuck Out</u>

Chapter 1
Hazel

I had the feeling I should be upset. Dennis seemed to think I would be. With his apology sketched in every line of his handsomely boyish face at the tail end of his, *It's Not You Breakup Speech*.

"I think you're great, and if things were different..." Atop the table between us, he rubbed the calloused pad of his thumb across the back of my hand.

Blinking, I glanced through the window into the dining area. Bettie's Pour House was one of the more popular places to eat in town—which had more to do with the lack of options than the quality of the food—and it was beginning to fill up. Dennis and I were the only people seated on the patio. The temperature had dropped overnight, and apparently, no one else wanted to weather the cold.

So, while everyone inside was likely just eating their meal and spending time with their friends and family, I felt like I was in a fishbowl—being watched.

The white receipt from our meal flapped in the breeze.

I glanced down at Dennis' beagle, Banjo, who tilted his head at me. He didn't seem to understand any more than I did.

My hands slipped easily from between Dennis' fingers and I folded them in my lap. I leaned forward with my mouth slightly open, trying to decide exactly how to say what needed to be said.

He waited. His face was trapped somewhere between hope and apprehension.

"Are we," I began, then started again, "I think, maybe, we're on two different pages."

"How so?"

"I thought we were casual."

Wrinkles folded into his forehead.

I drummed a nervous beat on my thighs. "That we weren't dating exclusively. That we could have dated other people the whole time."

His dark eyebrows shot up, and his blue eyes widened. "Oh, really?"

"Yeah."

The feet of his metal chair scraped against the concrete as he leaned back. "Huh, I've never done that before."

"I'm sorry." My cheeks warmed, a blush rising up my neck. "I haven't been dating anyone else, but I just...I thought we weren't serious."

He picked up his beer, then set it back down.

Gesturing between us, I said, "But we're good, this is good. You thought you had to breakup with me, and now you don't."

"Okay."

A sliver of relief seeped through the less comfortable feelings I was dealing with. "I just thought, we're both busy, and this is convenient"—I held my hands out—"not that you're a *convenience*, or a hardship for that matter, it's just like..."

I'm making a mess of this.

My hands continued in their random movements. "I thought we weren't... I just didn't think that we were like a *thing*."

"We see each other a couple of times a week."

Pointing at his dog attached to the leash draped over his thigh, I said, "I'm Banjo's vet."

The beagle was a special pup, and between his diabetes and the random things he ate constantly, I saw him almost weekly. Dennis also brought wounded wild animals from Sleepy Pines State Park to my vet clinic for treatment and rehabilitation. Our paths crossed regularly. It was mutually beneficial that we were of similar age, single, and I found him attractive. But a serious relationship with him hadn't crossed my mind, and especially not when I was still in the first year of owning the clinic. My available free time was almost impossible to come by. And I definitely didn't have the emotional bandwidth to date anyone seriously, not with the demand to pay off my business loans and numerous daily choices taxing my brain.

Dennis was a nice man, but I wasn't interested in him for anything long-term.

"Yeah." Dennis nodded, his mouth still hanging open slightly. He looked shocked, but not angry, and I decided that was a good thing.

I hadn't planned on having this conversation, but as he started explaining that he'd gotten a remote research opportunity to evaluate the migration patterns of salmon for the next six months, it became clear where the conversation was going. I'd been internally processing the email I'd read from the Grand Ridge Greater Area Humane Society, and brainstorming ways to correct the bind I was in. But now my mental energy was going in a completely different direction.

"We can still be friends." I leaned over the table, lowering my voice. "We can keep sleeping together until you leave."

"Uh...I don't know." His shoulders hunched as he scratched his pant leg. "Now it feels like I like you more than you like me."

The role reversal was startling. I sat back in my chair, blinking. "Dennis, you were *just* breaking up with me."

"I know."

"So clearly, you don't like me *that* much."

"I kinda do… I didn't *want* to break up with you."

"I am so confused right now."

"Yeah."

"If you didn't want to break up with me, then why were you?"

He sighed, puffing his cheeks out. "It seemed like the right thing to do. I'm gonna be gone for six months with a heavy workload."

"Don't you think *asking* me what I wanted would have been the right thing?"

"That's a good point. I guess I should have. What would you like?"

There was the root of my issue with Dennis. He was kind, handsome, and the second best lay I'd ever had, but he was not a deep thinker. There wasn't anything wrong with him, and if I wasn't pining for someone who wasn't even around—and whose number had gone unused in my phone for over a year, I might be more interested in the possibilities of Dennis.

I brushed the loose strands of my French braid from my face and stared at the pinks and golds reflecting on the surface of Grand Ridge Lake across the street. Behind me, two car doors opened and closed. I'd set myself up to be asked a question that I didn't have an answer to. The longer the silence stretched, the more uncomfortable it grew.

"Dennis," I began, but Banjo growled and barked, surprising me quiet. I had just enough time to glance down and see him dart through the fenced area.

Dennis snatched at the leash dragging on the cement, but missed it by less than an inch. His chair clashed to the ground as he jumped the fence to chase after his dog. I took a beat to roll my eyes before chasing after them.

If he won't take obedience classes, could he at least hang on to Banjo's leash better?

"Mom," a man's voice warned from a few feet behind me.

Banjo barked.

The man moved to place himself between a woman with reddish brown hair until the beagle charged past her, and directly for the man.

I exited through the gate. The woman pressed her hand to her mouth, Dennis raced after an incensed Banjo.

Realizing the dog's path was headed right for him, the man turned on his heel. He was strong, and lean, and took hold of the top of the eight-foot retaining wall and pulled his entire body up it. The sweatshirt he wore concealed the flex of lithe muscles, but his jeans were more transparent about what was inside—his thighs strained against the denim and fabric clung to his ass. It only took seconds for him to place his tennis shoe on the grass and leverage the rest of his weight to stand safely above us.

Banjo barked and clawed at the wall.

The man's chest heaved as he took a few deep breaths, his hands resting on his hips. And I was transported to the middle of the night in a cabin on Lake Michigan's shore. His naked body above mine, his chestnut curls plastered to his sweat-slicked forehead. His whispered words as he sank inside me again, *"I can't get enough of you."*

The memory was so vivid, I could practically smell him on my skin.

My heart drummed in my ears, drowning out the chaotic noises around me, a persistent beat. *Elijah*.

My unattainable high school crush, and the estranged son of my former mentor, and the most beautiful man on earth. The one I had an incredible one-night stand with the summer before. The one whose phone number I'd had for the past fifteen months. The one I hadn't called or texted because of my deep-seated anxiety about just how *him* he was, while I was just nerdy ol' me.

"Eli," the woman called, "are you okay?"

Holding out a grass- and dirt-covered palm, he answered, "I'm fine, Mom."

Dennis had Banjo's leash and commanded the dog to sit. "I'm so sorry. He gets protective around men."

The beagle had stopped barking, but still wasn't sitting.

"You need to get that dog more training," Elijah's mom insisted.

"Yes, ma'am."

"I'm fine," Elijah said again.

Her hands went to her hips, her shoulders set. "You just escaped up a retaining wall."

"Dogs can be weird."

"You could have gotten hurt." She turned her green eyes on Dennis. "If your dog bites someone—"

"He knows, Mom. It was a mistake. Nobody is hurt and everything is fine."

She pressed her lips together as if it was the only way to keep words from continuing to tumble out.

"I really am so sorry. Is there anything I can do?" Dennis asked.

"No, man, I'm good. You and your girlfriend"—there was the slightest hesitation as Elijah's eyes finally landed on me, and all the air pressed out of my body—"go enjoy your night."

I didn't know if I should say "Hi" or scream "He's not my boyfriend." But nothing came out of my mouth, I didn't even wave. I was too busy noticing all the changes to Elijah's appearance since I'd last seen him. There was a couple days' old dark beard on his once cleanly shaven jaw, and his hair was trimmed above his ears. I was too busy being shocked to see him at all. I was too busy just seeing him. The way he stood, perfectly balanced, with his feet shoulder-width apart. His hands fisted in his pockets in a way I hadn't known would be so familiar. Thinking about him, wondering about him, had become such a frequent activity that it was more like a song that was stuck in my head.

I didn't know what it meant now that he was here.

I didn't know if it meant things could be different between us. If he'd want things to be different between us. I knew that I did.

The semblance of a greeting formed at the back of my mind, but then he was looking away as a muscle flexed in his jaw.

"If you change your mind, I'm Dennis Rickman, I'm a DNR officer. You can just call the office and tell them you need to talk to me."

"Sure thing." Elijah's gaze landed somewhere near his feet.

Dennis turned and tugged the leash. "Hazel, do you mind if I take you home?"

"Yeah, sure." I started walking next to him, his hand settled on the small of my back. Glancing over my shoulder, I found Elijah watching. But I couldn't make out his expression through the distance growing between us.

Chapter 2
Elijah

I watched for too long as Hazel left with Captain Forest Ranger and his hell hound. His hand rested on the small of her back like it was a familiar spot. And why wouldn't it be? It'd been over a year since I'd been back in my hometown. She was single when I left, and there was no reason to think she'd stay that way. Over a year of wondering what she was up to. Over a year of her having my number. Over a year of her not using it.

Now I knew why.

It was probably a good thing I'd canceled the previous trips I'd half-heartedly planned to visit. It was probably good that I had stopped myself from contacting her through social media or calling the clinic's number. Every time I considered it, I'd reason that she knew how to get a hold of me but wasn't, and I should probably respect that.

She looked good. The sweater dress she wore ended halfway down her legging-covered thighs—and did nothing to hide her generous curves. The silky strands of her hair were pulled back from her face in a loose braid. Her skin was lit in the warm light of the setting sun.

I expected to run into her, but not like this—and certainly not with me fleeing a rabid dog. When I imagined it, I was on my game. I even let myself picture her being happy to see me. I'd tell her how I couldn't get her out of my head, and then we'd go out to dinner. I'd kiss her good night outside of her front door and see if I could take her to breakfast the next morning.

But all of those plans and hopes were embarrassing now.

I'd been in romantic limbo since spending just one night with Hazel, and I'd been there alone.

A fact that took my embarrassment all the way up to humiliating.

"Eli, do you need help down?"

Bending my neck, I found my mom standing at the bottom of the retaining wall—which was well over her head. "Sure, Mom. How?"

She held her arms out with a goofy grin on her face. "I'll catch you."

Some of the tension left my shoulders as I laughed. "I've got this."

I dropped down to join her on the sidewalk.

Expecting me to follow, Mom started walking toward the restaurant's front door. "Did you know her?"

"Who?" I played dumb, even though it was useless.

She lifted an eyebrow and gave me a look that expressed she was not fooled. "The young lady with Deputy Dipshit."

"He seemed like a nice enough guy."

"I don't care. He let his dog get away from him, and that little shit wanted to tear your face off."

I took hold of the handle and open the door for Mom to walk through first. The interior of the building was like stepping into a childhood memory. It all appeared the same with the dark green vinyl booths lining the walls, the rectangular tables filling the center of the space, and the bar with stools screwed into the floor just beyond them. Large lamps hung with thin '70s-era chains swooping from the ceiling and even the black-and-white checkered floor was the same. Old photos displayed on the walls, showing the town's past, stoic people standing still next to Model T's and the library surrounded by trees, instead of the parking lot and Westside general store.

We stood next to a "Please, wait to be seated" sign.

"It feels so strange to be here," Mom whispered.

I nodded. "You okay?"

When she and I had moved to Nashville just after I graduated from high school, it gave us a chance to start over, something we both had needed. Divorcing my dad—the well-loved veterinarian—had unsettled the community, and he'd used that destabilization to paint my mom in terrible shades. And those terrible shades that were easier to spread because of scandalous rumors about me.

Rumors that were only partially untrue.

"I'm okay," she said. "You?"

I shrugged. "I'm good."

"So, did you know her?" Mom asked.

"Know who?" I didn't know why I was avoiding talking to my mom about Hazel. Maybe because I'd kept this secret for so long. Maybe because I felt like a fool for pining over her for all this time.

"You know—"

"Table or booth?" a teenager asked, his tan skin speckled with pimples.

"Booth, please." Mom gave him a polite smile.

He grabbed two comically large menus and gestured for us to follow him. We slid into a booth and gave him our drink orders.

When we were alone again, Mom held up a warning finger. "Now, don't play dumb with me again. Do you know her?"

I forced my smile to be easy, as if it was just a stupid joke. "Yeah, that's Hazel Matthews. She was a couple of years younger than me in school, and she took over Dad's clinic."

"That's Hazel?"

"Yup."

"I think I remember her. She was such a mature kid."

I tried to remain nonchalant.

The teenager returned with our drinks, then left so we could look over the menu.

"She's pretty," Mom said, scanning her open menu.

I nodded. "Yeah, she's really pretty."

"Did you meet her when you came up last year?"

"Yup."

"You didn't mention her."

"I was preoccupied with Dad being a dick," I mostly lied.

Yes, my dad had been an asshat, and I'd cut my trip short because of it. His main asshattery consisted of lording control over me by threatening Hazel's takeover of the veterinary clinic if she and I spent time together. In the end, she stayed in my rickety cabin rental for one night—a night I couldn't stop thinking about. Craving.

Mom patted my fisted hands on the table between us. "I'm sorry, sweetheart. You don't deserve that."

"It wasn't all bad." I closed the menu and set it on the edge of the table. "I reconnected with Ransom, and we're gonna get together while you and I visit. I mean, I'm the one who convinced you to take this trip, so I must not be too traumatized."

A trip I was hoping to get to know Hazel better, but I'd find something else to do with my time.

"I guess not," she said.

"How do you feel about running into Dad? The town is so small, and it's kinda inevitable."

"Uneasy. There are a couple of people here I'm nervous to run into."

She held my questioning gaze for a moment, knowing I didn't actually have to speak for her to understand.

Lifting one shoulder and letting it fall again, she explained, "I wouldn't have come back if I didn't feel like it was the right choice. I don't know. Maybe it's because I retired or getting older, but I just wanna put the nonsense behind me."

I opened my mouth to reply when a woman with short white hair approached our table, staring down at a pad of paper in her hand. "Are we ready to order?"

"Ginny?" Mom said apprehensively.

The waitress glanced up, her eyebrows pulled together before her eyes widened and her jaw dropped open. "Susan? Susan March?"

"I thought that was you! Ginny, how are you?" Mom stood, pulling the slightly smaller woman into a hug.

"Well, I'm just great! How are you?" Ginny didn't wait for a reply before she continued, "You look *gorgeous*!"

"You, too!"

She flicked a dismissive hand. "Oh, I don't know. Every time I look in the mirror, I ask myself, 'Who is that old lady?'"

Mom leaned on one leg and rested her hands on her hips. "I completely understand that. In my mind, I'm trapped at thirty-five, and that was *so* long ago!" She flipped a hand in my general direction. "My goodness, my son will be twenty-nine this year."

"Oh my! You are Elijah March, aren't you?"

"I am." I twisted in the booth to speak directly to Ginny.

"Look at how handsome you are." To Mom she gushed, "He is so *handsome*."

Laughing, Mom nodded. "He is."

"He looks just like his dad!"

"He does."

"But then you were always such a cute kid. I remember, you had the most mischievous little smile. You probably don't remember me."

"I think I do." Looking at Mom, I asked, "We went to the same church, right?"

Mom laughed harder and gripped Ginny's elbow. "Yes, he loved you because you swore under your breath at church."

Throwing her head back, Ginny cackled at the ceiling, drawing the attention of other diners, who went right back to their meals. "Oh shit, that does sound like me."

"Oh goodness, Ginny, it's so good to see you."

"You, too. How long will you be in town? We'd love to have you over for dinner—a bunch of us ladies get together and play Euchre."

"That'd be lovely. We're around for a couple of months, actually. We're planning on spending the whole fall up here. I'm retired, and he works remotely now, so why not?"

"Really? What do you do?"

"I co-own a business in network securities. We protect businesses from ransomware."

"I did not understand any of that."

I was used to that response, but her matter-of-fact tone made me chuckle.

I was ready to explain, but Ginny lifted her pad and pen, then shoved them both into her apron pocket again. "You know who you just missed? Do you know Hazel who took over the vet clinic? She was just on the patio with her young man."

My stomach dropped. Hearing someone else acknowledge that they were together only added to my simmering disappointment.

Mom's smile pinched, and I knew she was thinking about the dog again. "I haven't met her, but Elijah did last year."

"She's doing a great job. That young lady works so hard."

"I'm glad to hear it."

Ginny pulled the items out of her apron again. "What can I get you two?"

After taking our order, she promised to be right back with everything.

"She is a hoot." Mom slid back into her seat.

"She seems fun." I draped my arm over the back of the booth.

"If she actually invites us over, will you come with me?"

"Of course, Mom."

"She was always so nice to me, even when... well, when it all got bad." She left unsaid how the community had ostracized her, blaming her for tearing apart our home. They couldn't understand how she would leave such a kind, godly man, and they refused to believe the truth of who he was.

"I know," I said simply.

I shifted the conversation to Mom's plans for the following day. Our talk was easy enough that I could devote only half of my attention to it, while the other half wondered what it meant that Hazel and I didn't even say hello. Was there really only one night between us? Had it just been sex for her? Something to get out of her system? Had I fabricated our connection?

Or had she heard something about me that made her change her mind? Had she realized just how bad associating with me could be for her reputation in this little town that thrived on credibility?

That cut into a wound that was always tender. I'd winced at the slightest pressure on it—a pain that had always been there, a whisper that I was bad news.

"You okay?" Mom's concerned voice cut through my line of thought.

"Huh? Yeah, I'm good. You good?"

"I am. I'm glad to be here with you."

"Me, too."

Chapter 3
Hazel

"The vet clinic is fine financially, though?" Remi asked. His arms were crossed over his broad chest. The creases in his forehead set his usually friendly expression into something much more intimidating. He was still wearing his white lab coat from working his shift. I didn't blame him for asking with the slightest tinge of resentment in his voice. Less than two years ago, I convinced him to leave his job in Arizona to treat animals here.

"Yes, the clinic is fine. It's not thriving, and there are some repairs to the building that I need to figure out, but it's going to be okay. I just can't afford to make the yearly donation to the humane society." I swallowed and lowered to lean against the front desk behind me. "And I know they rely on it."

Brooks, our large animal veterinarian, ran a hand over his unruly beard, the tip of his tongue pressed on the inside of his cheek. He looked a bit out of place in his worn jeans and T-shirt. On the infrequent days he worked in the office, he usually chose to wear scrubs and a white coat as well, but he'd come in on his day off for this meeting. Without his usual uniform, he looked even more disheveled—like a small bear taught to play-act as a human. He'd probably be more comfortable in a bear's natural habitat, anyway.

Nora, our business manager, met my eye. This problem wasn't a surprise to her. She and I had been trying to find a solution for a week, and honestly, it was a nice distraction from the other issue we usually fought over. The one where she demanded a reason why I hadn't texted Elijah, and I continued to not have a great answer.

She did not accept my insecurities—or anyone else's—easily.

But I had grown up not catching the attention of people around me, and now that I was a business owner in this community, the attention was microscopic. People discussed and tore apart my choices, and it was messing with my confidence.

The first time that Elijah had actually *seen* me had felt surreal. He'd been sitting in the chair Nora was sitting in now. I'd been completely astounded when he'd started flirting and we nearly kissed. It was possibly even more shocking that I'd been able to set my nerves aside and flirt back. The whole affair felt more like a lust-infused fantasy than a night that actually happened in my life.

I had avoided telling her that he was in town. She would be intolerable if she knew.

"I don't want to leave them in a lurch," I said helplessly.

In the original negotiations for the transfer of the clinic from my former mentor—Doc March, who was Elijah's dad—to me, this donation was factored into expenses. But the week of the sale that consideration was removed, and the sale price adjusted up.

I shook my head, remembering, not for the first time, that I owed Elijah a thank you. He'd shown me his dad's true nature. The one where Doc gave the illusion of being kind and generous, but was, in fact, always looking for a way to manipulate the people around him. I'd seen it firsthand as Dr. March went back on the deal.

He insisted that in order for me to take over at the agreed upon price, he'd need to maintain significant control and receive a monthly paycheck—something we had never discussed. He did it with the most fatherly smile and promised to only use the privilege if I asked for help.

But because Elijah lifted the veil from my eyes a month before, I saw the truth of the offer, and I said no.

The deal went poorly from there.

Dr. March even used public opinion to sway me. I endured many members of our community trying to persuade me to "look out for the ol' boy."

There was a drop in clients after that—a hurdle we were still jumping over.

The financial hit affected me, but the loss of my mentor when I needed him the most was harder. Part of the reason I'd become a vet was because of Doc's encouragement. I'd started working at the clinic when I was fifteen, cleaning rooms. It was only a few hours a week, but I'd fallen in love with the idea of working with animals. I'd become very good at that part of the job, but actually running the business...

It was painful how much I didn't know what I was doing.

Remi sighed, his large chest rising and falling. It looked dramatic on him, even though it was a completely normal action. He was the biggest man I'd ever seen in person—as if he was normal-sized but scaled up by fifty percent. "I can ask Owen what sort of fundraisers his work does, but it'll take money to throw one."

"That's right, he works for that dog shelter, doesn't he?" I mumbled against my knuckles.

Remi, Owen, and I had met in veterinarian school. He and Owen were friends, but Owen had been quiet and shy, so I'd never gotten to know him well.

At the opportunity to hire people to work for me, Remi was the first person I'd thought of. But then he'd actually moved across the country. There were people relying on me to make this business successful.

"Yeah, I'll ask him."

"Thank you."

It was something, but we needed to draw in a lot of money.

The actual residents of the town were tight-knit enough that if I didn't know someone directly, we were only one acquaintance away from knowing each other. The clinic only afforded three veterinarians because our livestock and horse population outweighed our human population. The entire community was struggling more than usual. Tourism was our strongest industry since we were surrounded by a couple of state and county parks, and only a few miles from Lake Michigan and its beaches. And as much as our town feuded with the more affluent, neighboring town of Darling, their cute boutiques and ski lodge also brought people to Grand Ridge.

It wasn't uncommon for households to make the majority of their income between spring and fall, but making those funds stretch through winter was growing less feasible. My business' cash flow reflected the strain, as folks were forced to make hard decisions about the care of their pets and livestock, or to buy groceries.

Yet another problem that I didn't have a solution for. How could I better the state of the vet clinic, and ensure the animals around us were well taken care of?

But that wasn't the issue at hand; the humane society was expecting a sizable donation in just under two months. And that was money I did not have or know how to get.

"You don't have any ideas?" Brooks asked.

Nora and I shared a look.

She swiveled her chair in Brooks' direction. "You won't like mine."

A sound very near a growl rumbled in the back of his throat. He and Nora had been good friends since we were in school—long enough that a conversation passed between them without any actual words.

Remi tilted his head in silent question, but I only shrugged.

Brooks narrowed his gray eyes. "How sexual in nature is it?"

Smacking a hand on his chest, Remi laughed as I threw my head back, laughing at the ceiling.

"*Barely*," Nora insisted.

"Hell." Brooks shook his head.

"We should do a bachelor auction!"

Remi's eyes widened. "What?"

Even though she and I had this argument more times than I could count, I said, "It will be divisive at best."

"It will draw attention."

Brooks ran a hand over his beard and muttered, "It's attention grabbing, for sure."

I continued with my point, my hands making little boxes in the air. "Half the town will be completely bawdy—"

"Oh no, not *bawdy*." She rolled her eyes.

I went on as if she hadn't interrupted. "—and inappropriate. While the other half will go to church and condemn us for being sinners and take their animals to Holy Immaculate Pet Care in Darling."

"Goddamn, Bible Belt."

Holding his hands out, Remi made a calming gesture. "Bible Belt and the community aside, this sounds hellish."

Brooks nodded, his bushy eyebrows raised toward his baseball cap.

Remi looked between me and Nora. "Imagine standing on a stage, with strangers—"

"—Or everyone you've ever known—" Brooks contributed.

"—shouting bids at you—"

"—or saying nothing at all—"

"—for a date with you. What would they expect from us?"

Nora wasn't deterred. "I don't know, a man buys me one goddamn dinner or two, and he expects me to put out."

"Good luck finding bachelors willing to do this. I won't do it," Remi stated.

"It's for the *dogs*. You won't do it for the *dogs*?"

"I will not have sex for dogs."

We shared a collective blink, shocked into silence for a few seconds before falling into a laughing fit that had me wiping the moisture from under my eyes. "Should I get a sexual harassment training video? I think we might have a toxic workplace."

"I will consider it harassment if you make me watch that video." The patch of skin on Brooks' cheekbones was bright red, which I knew was from the laughing and not from embarrassment.

"So, what do we do?" She held her arms out as if welcoming new ideas. "We're not gonna make the kind of money we need selling cookies. I know Ben would let us hold it at Benji's Place—he probably wouldn't even charge us for it. We could sell tickets at the door that provides a drink or two and a buffet. We could have dancing before the main event, so everyone is having fun."

"How did you get from selling cookies to..." Remi's lip twisted as if he'd tasted something gross. "I don't even want to say it out loud."

I stared at the colorful rows of files organized vertically behind him and wondered how I hadn't found a better solution. The unfortunate reality was this was the lowest cost event I could think of. Nora was right about the venue, and it already had a speaker system to hook up one of our phones to play a playlist—no need to hire entertainment.

She was punching away on her phone screen—probably looking up the best songs for auctioning a date.

There was no way we could do it, and it was very annoying that nothing else worked as well.

I was so lost in my irritated thoughts that I didn't notice the phone she was typing on was mine. "What are you doing?"

She didn't even look up, she just continued with her task. "Texting the menfolk to see what kind of interest we can get in participating."

"You're not much of a listener, are you, Nora?" Remi remarked.

"Well, if you're right and no one will participate, then we can move on completely."

I tried to keep my voice nonchalant, but even I could hear I wasn't successful. "Nora, what menfolk are you texting?"

She kept typing. "Just the guys who aren't in my phone."

"Have you gotten to the E's?"

Her thumbs froze, and she slowly looked up from the screen. "Oh no, Hazel…"

"You didn't."

"Didn't what?" Remi asked.

"Whose name starts with an E that's so bad?" Under his baseball cap, Brooks' eyebrows drew together.

My stomach was somewhere around my knees. "What did you say?"

She pursed her lips and shook her head. With jerky movements, she extended the phone for me to read.

I might be sick. Blood rushed from my face, and my vision went dark on the edges.

On the screen was a message from me to Elijah March. It was the first communications we had between our numbers. After all these months of trying to figure out the right way to start a conversation with him—of typing and deleting possibility after possibility, of questioning if I should just leave him alone to live his life—there on the screen, was a single message.

Would you be interested in auctioning your body?

Chapter 4
Hazel

I looked down at my phone. Again.

It had been two days since Nora messaged Elijah. That goddamn text. It was ruining my brain. When I woke up, behind my closed eyes were those stupid words. When I drove to work, the only traffic light in town blinked a chorus of, *He hasn't texted back.* I'd eat my lunch and reason that he probably doesn't have my number, anyway. I probably wouldn't reply to someone I knew asking if I'd auction off my body, let alone a strange number. He'd never have to find out it was me. If, for any reason, he actually *asked* for my number, I'd lie through my teeth and get a new one.

But regardless, I couldn't stop checking my phone. Mostly because now, I didn't have a way to reach him. Now I just had to hope to run into him.

I shook my head, disgusted with myself. It's not like I was using his number, anyway.

The familiar sinking feeling pressed into my chest. I should have texted him a long time ago. Building up the courage to ask Ransom Strauss for Elijah's contact was stressful, and it shouldn't have been hard to actually send out a little, *Hi, this is Hazel.*

I flipped my phone screen-side down on my desk. The clinic was emp-ty, and I just needed to get these last few tasks done. Remi had offered to stay and clean the examination rooms, but I'd turned him down. It wasn't in his job description, and I didn't want to take advantage of his friendship. I'd packed away the cleaning supplies a little over an hour ago and responded to a post on the town's social media community page from Deb Creger, our town hall clerk. She'd shared a photo of her ancient Yorkie with the caption, *Sweet Hazel took such great care of Mrs. Merryweather today! Thank you, Sweet Hazel!*

I considered for a moment adding a post of my own, but then I glanced at the stack of paperwork that needed accomplishing before I could go home to obsess over the text to Elijah, instead of obsessing here.

It was long workdays on top of long workdays that kept me from being able to justify getting a pet. I hated not having a dog or a cat. It felt unnatural to love animals like I did and not have one of my own to dote on.

Every other man Nora had asked had messaged back. Almost all of them variations of *What the fuck?*

When I explained further, the response was more varied. I was surprised to discover how many men were willing to consider the auction if it was clear what they'd be doing after the purchase.

To which Nora groaned. "It's a *date*. What do you like to do for a date? Take them to that. Tell that man-boy it's a *date*."

"That's too broad; it needs to be more specific," Brooks had replied as he scrawled a quick note on a chart.

"What do you mean?"

He closed the file and slid it into place on the cabinet. "How would the women know the kind of date they're purchasing?"

"It would be included in your description. Here's Jack Brooks. He's thirty years old, enjoys hiking and mountain biking, and for the lucky winner, he'll prepare a lakeside picnic, or whatever."

A crease formed between his eyebrows. "How do you know so much about this?"

"Romance novels." She shrugged.

He shot a questioning gaze my way. "Are they all bachelor auctions?"

I snorted. "Guess you'll have to read to find out."

He rolled his eyes and exited to the hallway lined with exam rooms.

Nora's face was overtaken by her smile. "I've been getting some good responses, though."

Her face lit up even more at my sigh.

"You have too, haven't you?" she squealed. "That's why you're disappointed."

"It's not there yet."

"What do you mean?"

"It's too broad." I used Brooks' phrasing.

She considered me. "So, if we told them what the date would be...?"

A feeling a lot like seasickness swished in my stomach. "No. I don't know... There has to be something else."

"It's sexual in nature, and that's why you don't like it, right?"

"Yeah, it feels exploitative. If this was a bachelorette auction, even *you* would feel uncomfortable with it."

She threw her hands up, and they slapped on her thighs when they came down. "Because of the patriarchal power dynamic. We can't compare our experiences as women with the experiences of men, because they are *different*."

"Yeah, but that doesn't mean it's not exploitative."

"I'm gonna figure this out."

No one could deter Nora once she got a plan in her head. I usually loved it—her tenacity was invaluable most of the time—but in this exact situation, I wished she would shift her focus.

In my office, I rubbed my shoulders and rolled my head from side to side, trying to work the tension that was always there. There was more to do, but I wasn't going to finish it tonight. I made a few notes on a sticky note to remind me of what needed priority tomorrow, then stuck it on my desk next to my keyboard. Standing, I stretched my arms over my head, and my spine popped a few times.

"I need to set timers to remind me to move around," I mumbled to my empty office, flicking off the lights. After putting my phone in my pocket and zipping up my jacket, I pulled my office door closed, exiting into the hallway, but it bounced off the doorjamb instead of latching. It'd been doing that. The only way to close it was to grab the handle in both hands and pull with all my weight. My step faltered as I added it to the mental list of things I needed to fix.

I strode to the exit. The only illumination was through the windows from the floodlights on the building's exterior, but I was so familiar with the space that I could have made this walk without any light at all. They strobed slightly. I chewed on my lower lip, wondering if I should hire an electrician, but then wondering where that money would come from. And then I'd need to find an exterior siding person. And then an HVAC technician. The list went on and on.

Maybe I could find someone willing to trade their services with mine.

The list was growing long. It wrapped around me and squeezed. Suffocating.

I wasn't lying to Remi; we were fine financially in the sense that I was clearing expenses with just enough to live on, but absolutely nothing else. If I didn't have my personal cost of living—pesky things like mortgage, car insurance, and food—then I could put more into the building's needs.

Maybe I could move into the basement of the building. I shuddered at the thought, considering all the dusty boxes packed down there, some of them probably older than me.

"Nope," I whispered to the empty clinic. "There's got to be a better way."

The night sky was dark blue with bright stars as the storm door slammed shut behind me, and I absentmindedly tugged on the handle to be sure it was locked up. A cold gust of wind carrying the smell of dry leaves and wet soil caught my hair and blew it across my face. I gathered the strands over one shoulder.

That's when I saw the man leaning against the hood of his car, directly under one of the lampposts.

Gasping, I stopped halfway down the paved walk to the parking lot. My keys were in my hand. I was about to whip around and run back into the building when he raised his hand in a tentative wave.

"I texted, but I'm guessing you didn't see it." His voice carried across the distance between us, gentle and deep.

I took a couple of deep breaths as the instinct to flee deflated from my muscles. All the tension gushed out of me.

"Yeah, I didn't see that." Pulling my phone from my pocket, I read Elijah's message, ***I'm outside the clinic***, just under the only other correspondence between our phones. I almost laughed. How had he sent it in the only thirty-second window I hadn't been fixated on whether he'd text?

"I know it's late, if your..." He stood and pulled the opening of his jacket more tightly closed. "We can schedule another time to talk."

I chewed my lower lip at the formality of his words. They sounded nothing like the lover I'd experienced, with his sweet whispers and dirty groaned appreciation. I swallowed, but the pressure on my sternum didn't lighten.

With a few strides, I stood under the same halo of light as he did. The rest of the world was swallowed in darkness, and all I could see was him. His chestnut-colored curls peeked out of a black stocking cap. As I neared, he leaned away.

I didn't want to see the ways he pulled back from me, so I stared at the parking lot's cracked asphalt. "No, we can talk now." Apparently, formality was catching because I said, "What can I help you with?"

"First, my dad doesn't have any more leverage on you, does he?"

"No, he tried, but no," I answered. "Thank you for the warning, by the way. You really helped me out."

"You're welcome. I'm sorry he put you through whatever he did."

I looked up to find him watching me with careful eyes.

He sighed and shrugged deeper into his jacket. "Can you explain that text message?"

I puffed out a breath. "How did you know it was me?"

"Obviously the area code was from here, so I asked Ransom and Sterling if they knew whose number it was."

I was grateful for the cold already turning my cheeks pink, because I was definitely blushing. "Sterling, huh?"

"Yup."

"Solid detective work."

"Thank you." His mouth tugged up on one side, scrambling the few brain cells I had strung together. "So, Hazel, why is some other guy's nice girlfriend asking me to auction off my body?"

"I'm not a nice girlfriend."

He squinted, casting sharp swooping shadows from his eyelashes across his cheekbones. "Are you trying to set me up as your side piece?"

"No!" My eyes grew so wide, they nearly fell out of my head. I didn't know what was more shocking, the idea of him being my *side piece*, or the fact that he thought I could finesse something like that. "I don't have a boyfriend."

He straightened, his broad shoulders squaring in his dark denim coat. "Then what's up with the ranger guy I saw you with?"

"Dennis and I had a casual thing, but it just ended, actually."

Elijah took a tentative step closer to me. "People around town don't seem to think it was casual."

I chewed my bottom lip. "Well, most of the people around here have a very traditional sense of what spending time with someone means."

He exhaled, and his breath glinted silver in the white light for the briefest moment. His green eyes locked onto mine. The force of them sent electricity along every inch of my skin. A smile grew on his lips, and I remembered the feel of those lips on mine, my neck, my chest. All of me. My heart skipped and raced against my ribcage.

He leaned close enough for his shadow to drape across my chest and the lower half of my face. I shifted closer, as if there was a string tied between us, and he was drawing me to him inch by inch.

I knew that it was just as cold as it had been when I stepped out of the building, but the energy around us had shifted. If I wasn't a woman of science, I would have sworn that the air was warmer. Maybe the sun had even come out, defying all the laws of physics.

His lowered voice whispered through me, suggestive and playful. "So, what do you wanna do with my body?"

Chapter 5
Elijah

"**S**o, what do you wanna do with my body?" I fucking loved the way Hazel looked at me. She had the richest, roundest, brown eyes lined in long eyelashes. There was the slightest hint of something wild and unfed concealed in her buttoned-up exterior. Feeding that untamed piece of her had become a point of fixation. But now that I got the opportunity to really take her in, I could see the darkened skin under her eyes and how her cheekbones were more prominent than they had been last year.

I liked hearing she was single... a lot. But I wanted her to see me as more than just a man in her bed. Of course, the suggestive question I'd just asked didn't really lend to that impression.

"How long do you got?" She tilted her head, and her buttoned-up personification slipped. I wanted to peel it away like the bulky coat wrapped around her, but there were a few things I needed to understand first.

"I've got a while. Let's get you outta the cold and get you some food. What's open right now?"

She blinked, her eyebrows lifting. "That is not what I was expecting for you to offer."

"Come on, what do you want?" I nudged her tennis shoe with the toe of mine.

She dropped her gaze to the zipper of my pants, then back to mine.

"To eat, Hazel."

She lifted an eyebrow.

I chuckled, my mouth pulling to one side. For a second, I considered pressing her against the side of my car and kissing her, long and deep. Nothing more than that, not while we were lit up with a spotlight overhead. Just enough to remind her that what simmered between us would ignite with the slightest friction. Just enough to make her dizzy and breathless. Just enough to settle this persistent need tearing through my veins.

It was torment to close even more space between us, but I couldn't stop myself. She had wrapped me up in so many knots, and I wanted to tie a few of my own. She stood completely still as I bent low enough to nearly brush my lips on her ear. "Benji's should still be doing food."

Her surprised breathy laugh puffed through the scruff on my jaw.

She seemed caught between irritation and entertainment, but I jerked my thumb over my shoulder. "You want me to drive?"

"Fine."

I held her door open and waited for her to scoot onto her seat. She watched me round the hood of the car with an arrogant grin on my face. The smile didn't leave as I turned over the engine.

"Feelin' pretty impressed with yourself, aren't you?" she asked.

For a moment, I considered saying something flirty, something that wouldn't let her see the truth of my good mood. It took bravery to be vulnerable when I said, "I came here tonight thinking you were seeing someone else—now I know you're not. It's good news for me."

I turned the car onto the empty road, my hands sweating on the steering wheel.

She lit up the entire car with a grin so beguiling it made me feel like I was driving under the influence. Just like that, my honesty was worth it.

"It is?" she asked.

"Yeah. I don't know what that text was about, or why you haven't texted me sooner, but I get to take you out to dinner, and I like that."

"You do?"

I pulled into an angled spot on the street just outside of Benji's Place. Putting the car into park, I turned the key and shifted to look at her. "Yeah."

"I like it, too." Her incredible smile hadn't faltered, but it had turned a bit shy.

I considered giving in to the desire to kiss her—to see if she tasted like the giddy light in her eyes. Could I pull that excitement in and give her some of mine? I'd pined for this woman for month after month, berating myself for not asking if it was okay if I reached out to her when the sale of the clinic was done. The way my dad had lorded the sale over her to control me, I didn't want to threaten her stability. I found her social media platforms, typed out messages, and then deleted them. Without so much as sending a friend request.

I assumed if she wasn't calling or texting, when she'd gone out of her way to get my number from Ransom, there had to be a reason.

But now she was in my car, looking at me like I'd just told her something she'd hoped to hear.

Fuck, I wanted to kiss her.

Displaying incredible self-control, I stepped out of the car.

I was determined to make a point that I wasn't just a guy she'd fuck around with every few months. If she didn't want a relationship, I couldn't give her anything else. I liked her too much, and it would hurt to not be liked back.

It was a weekday, so there weren't many other patrons, but we still got glances from the few that were there. A table of women who appeared close to our ages shared excited whispers about us. I thought maybe I recognized one of them, but I wasn't sure. Judging by their reactions and age, we probably all went to school together. Which meant they knew my...*reputation* from high school.

A reputation that was earned. It was fueled by a flirty nature, being a horny teenager, and a need to claim control of my life in some way.

And of course, getting caught with someone I shouldn't have been fooling around with...

Hazel must have been aware of my history, like everyone else in town. As a grown man, my monogamous relationships were few and far between. I only entered them if I really cared for the person and saw potential for a future.

And that was exactly what I wanted with her, a future.

Hopefully, my past wouldn't get in the way of that.

It had been a long time since that sweaty summer day. The earthy smell of the shed's interior. The blinding sunlight slicing through the dark. A booming angry voice making Hannah's body turn rigid in my arms. Her sudden fear as sharp and potent as mine was in me.

I took Hazel's hand and led us by the gossiping table, walking by them as if they weren't there. Her fingers were cold and strong. They fit nicely in mine.

She let go of my hand and slid into a navy booth, sitting with her back to the other women.

"Sorry about that," I mumbled, lowering to the booth across from her.

Her eyebrows drew together. "Why are you sorry?"

"I didn't realize us being seen together would cause a scene."

"Elijah, you haven't lived here in like over ten years, and they're still using you as gossip fodder. That's... embarrassing for them. Also, I think it was more about what they thought of me being with you."

"Why would you think that?"

"Just the expression on Lily's face." She shrugged. "I've never been one of the cool kids."

I opened my mouth to tell her they were wrong when a familiar voice boomed, "Eli, I was wondering when you were gonna darken my door again. Why do you always keep me waiting?"

Ben Hart strode around a table between us and the bar, two paper menus in one hand. The lines around his blue eyes and smirk were deeper than they had been when we were in school, but he was just as welcoming as ever.

I gave Emily, the bartender, a wave that she returned.

Standing, I hugged him, both of us pounding on each other's backs. "Anticipation makes the heart grow fonder."

In one motion, he shook my shoulder and handed Hazel a menu before sliding into the booth next to her. "This jackass. Hazel, how are you?"

"I'm doing well, thanks." She leaned against the wall to speak directly to him.

"No, please, have a seat. Make yourself at home," I grumbled, not appreciating the way his arm was slung across the backrest, or that I couldn't talk to her about the things I needed to.

He shot me a shit-eating grin. "I will, thank you." To her, he said, "I haven't seen you in a couple of weekends. You doin' okay? The first year of this place nearly killed me."

Back in my seat, I watched her closely.

Her shoulders lifted toward her ears. And while she kept her features comfortable and easy, there was tension in her body. "I'm good. I've needed quite a bit of sleep on the weekends."

"Weeks can get long."

"They can."

"If there's anything I can help with, just let me know. I should've asked for more help that first year. I didn't have to do everything alone."

She sucked her lips between her teeth and squinted between me and Ben.

"What's up?" I asked.

A groan rumbled in the back of her throat. When she spoke, it was quieter than before. "Did you get a weird text from Nora?"

Ben pinched the bridge of his nose. "About selling my body? I did. I decided not to step into what I hoped was a philosophical conversation."

All my thoughts screeched to a halt, and instead, only one question roared in my mind, *Why did Nora send a text to Ben that was just like the one Hazel sent me?*

Hazel's cheeks grew bright red before she hid behind her hands. "I don't even want to say this out loud." Her hands lowered to her throat. "She wants to hold a bachelor auction."

"A bachelor auction?" he asked.

"Where people buy dates?" I asked.

She nodded. "I don't like the idea, but I don't know what else to do. We're in a bit of a tight spot..."

"What's going on?"

We all leaned in to hear better as she explained about the donation the humane society was expecting, and how she didn't have the funds for it. Her anxiety was woven into every one of her words.

My hand clenched in a fist under the table. "Dad didn't tell you about this?"

"He did, but we had to redraft the pricing at the end of the deal. One of the things that was no longer in consideration was this donation." She held my gaze, conveying that there was more to the story, but that we'd have to talk about it later.

This was right out of his playbook. If Hazel didn't make the donation, then everyone would talk about how she wasn't running the clinic well. My dad would come out of the ordeal appearing like the better man for offering help that she turned down. It didn't matter to him that she would look flaky and foolish.

I didn't know how, but I would not let that happen to her. Even if I was disappointed that it had been Nora who'd texted me, not Hazel.

"Do you need some of the money to come from the bar?" Ben offered.

"That'd be amazing. But, um…" She bit her lip and tilted her head down. "If we do the auction, can we hold it here?"

We all leaned back in our seats, considering each other. In the short time I'd spent in town, I'd seen that there was a shift happening. A more accepting and less staunchly evangelical sector of the community was beginning to grow. But there was still a large portion of the population that would be beyond offended by an event that could be seen as salacious.

After a few moments of silence, Ben shifted. "Why… this?"

"Nora thinks it could bring in a decent crowd, and we'd have a relatively low investment. You know, we could ask Sterling to make some graphics and do some posts on social media. The auction itself would be the entertainment. But…"

"Obviously, this could backfire." He ran a hand through his dark blond hair.

"Yeah."

"My dad would not like this," I pointed out. "He'd definitely push people to boycott."

She swallowed. "Yeah."

Ben gave her an encouraging smile. "Well, I'm happy to host an event. We just need it to be square with most everybody in town. This auction would raise too many hackles."

"I think so too, but you know how Nora gets."

One side of his mouth lifted, and he nodded. "She's determined."

"What sucks is how many men have said they're willing to do this."

"Really?" I knew the town had changed, but that seemed further than I would have expected. I couldn't see older generations willing to help with the auction.

"I know. They're willing to sell their time, but they don't know what to do once their time has been bought."

"They could sell their trade," I suggested.

"Meaning?" Ben's eyebrows drew together as understanding dawned in Hazel's eyes.

"You'd sell a weekend of free drinks or something, Sterling could sell marketing work, Ransom would sell masonry, I'd sell computer repair. Your vets could sell off a certain number of appointments or something."

"Like a silent auction?" she asked.

"No, because Nora's right; it's gotta be a little risqué, a little naughty. Get people talking about it, get 'em showing up. The men would still stand on stage, and people would still shout out bids, but it's wholesome enough to not cause an uproar."

"That might work." Hazel covered her mouth to hide a yawn. The energy had been leaking from her little by little in the past few minutes.

"Hey, man," I said to Ben, "can you get her some food so I can get her back to her car?"

"Sure thing. Let's get you home, Hazel. I'll reach out to Nora, and we'll start figuring shit out." He took our order to-go.

"We can eat here," she said, but her voice was showing signs of exhaustion.

"It's okay, I'll bring you lunch tomorrow, and maybe we can talk then. I sprung this on you."

"It's a busy day tomorrow... I wasn't planning on taking a lunch."

"Then I'll just bring you food, so at least you eat something."

"I always have food in the work fridge. It's the only way I eat during the day."

"Okay." I tried to keep my shoulders from hunching. It seemed that whatever I thought had passed between us last year was one-sided. She didn't want me the way I wanted her.

We talked about the clinic and my business. I felt worse and worse for bringing her out as she massaged her temples and struggled to stay alert. When the food arrived, I paid, and we got back into my car. She argued that I didn't have to follow her home when we got back to her vehicle.

"Are you uncomfortable with me knowing where you live?" I asked.

"No, you just don't have to. I'll be okay." She pulled her keys from her coat pocket.

"I'd really like to make sure you get there safely."

She nodded, covering her mouth on another yawn. We leaned across the center console for a hug. I was torn between the way she fit her head on my shoulder and how she felt in my arms, and the ache of knowing that she wasn't noticing those things as well.

Holding up her to-go box, she reached for the door handle. "Thank you for dinner. I'm sorry I'm not much fun to be around right now."

"I'm the one who should apologize. I've kept you from getting the rest you need."

Her blink was a bit too long. "No, it was my choice. I could have gone home. It was nice to see you."

Nice. I cringed inwardly at the word.

"It was," I half-heartedly agreed.

"I wish I could think straight right now. It feels like my brain is underwater, like, sluggish."

"It's okay, you know how to get a hold of me."

"Yeah?"

"Yeah."

She slipped out of my passenger seat and into her car.

I drove behind her into a little neighborhood near the elementary school until she pulled into the driveway of a cute house. There was a porch swing lit by the front door and pots of fall-colored flowers. I parked at the curb, waiting for her to get inside. She waved before closing the door behind her.

There was already so much stacked against us. How likely would it be that we would connect enough in a few short weeks that we'd be able to carry a long distance relationship? Ending before we began would be better in the long run.

"It's okay," I said to my empty car. "Not everything works out."

But it didn't feel okay. It felt fucking terrible.

Chapter 6
Elijah

"You look nice, Mom. Where're you off to?" I looked down at my sweats and wrinkled T-shirt.

"The Briars invited me over for dinner. I thought I told you about it? I'm gonna use your car, remember? You gonna go out tonigh—" She turned away from the mirror, putting the cap back on her lipstick. Narrowing her eyes, she took in my disheveled appearance. "Son, what's going on? The past couple of days you've been... not yourself."

Stuffing my hands into my pockets, I leaned against the bathroom doorjamb. Our cottage was better than the one I'd stayed in last year, even if the decor was heavy on biblical cross-stitch and doilies. It also had a distinct Pine-Sol scent.

I shrugged. "That hangover a couple of nights ago was rough, just getting my energy back."

It was mostly true. I had walked to the beach and got very drunk after ensuring Hazel got home. Falling asleep on the blanket I'd laid out on the sand hadn't been advised—waking up with a headache, a sore neck, and cold. Really cold. Late September nights did not hold their heat along Lake Michigan.

"Okay." Mom zipped her makeup case. "You should go out tonight. Find your friends."

"I think I'll just stay in." I backed up, giving her room to exit into the hallway. "You've been busy lately. Having a good time?"

"Honestly, it's surprising how healing being here has been. Ginny even apologized for not coming to my defense all those years ago."

"That's great, Mom."

"I'm really glad we came back."

"Me, too." If only for her to find this closure.

"All right, I'm heading out."

"Have fun."

"I will." She put on her pink beaded sandals and opened the door. "Don't wait up."

She closed the door, leaving me surrounded by sky-blue-painted walls and white Jesus.

My phone buzzed on the coffee table. Striding into the living room, I found a text from Sterling, **Heading to Benji's, you wanna come?**

I considered it for a moment, then typed out **I'm gonna pass tonight.**

Lame.

I snorted, shaking my head. **Have fun, Princess.**

He sent a GIF of Cinderella transforming from pink rags into a blue shimmering dress.

Outside of the sliding glass door, colorful leaves drifted to the grass on a gentle breeze. It looked like a great night. They'd probably be seated on the patio with outdoor fireplaces fighting back the chill.

I considered meeting up with my friends. Mom had my car, but I could take my bike or ask Sterling to pick me up.

Then I remembered that I'd have to change out of my sweats and into jeans, and decided it wasn't worth the trouble. A Friday night alone at the cabin would be relaxing. There was a grill in the shed, so I could cook a steak and veggies that Mom had bought from the farmers market.

The rejection from Hazel had taken more out of me than I wanted to admit.

She said she wasn't dating the ranger guy, and I believed her, but it was obvious there was something between them—everyone in town mentioned his name with hers. I'd seen him coming out of the clinic earlier this week. Clearly, she was more willing to make time for him, and all I could do was accept that.

Maybe they were just meant to be, and it had nothing to do with me. But I couldn't help wondering if it was my tarnished past that kept her from wanting more than a good time from me.

Regardless of the changes happening in the community, one's reputation carried a lot of swing still.

My shoulders dropped with my sigh.

One more night.

I'd let myself feel bad about it for one more night.

Again, my phone buzzed. Sebastian's contact image filled the screen. I answered his video call.

"Hey, man," I greeted.

"Holy shit, Eli, you okay?" His hazel eyes were wide under thick dark eyebrows.

"Yeah, why?"

"You look rough. Did you lose your razor on a wilderness hike or something?"

I chuckled. "Why would I have my razor on a hike?"

"I don't know what you do out there. I don't like to go to dirt-road places." Red brick filled the background of his video, and the sounds of Greektown were static in my microphone.

"There's a lot more beards here, and not in a styled, polished way, but in a 'I don't feel like shaving' sort of way."

"I would not call your look polished. Are you at your grandma's?"

"No, this is the rental Mom and I are sharing."

He shook his head. "You gotta get outta there. You're becoming too uncool for me to do business with."

I laughed, rolling my eyes. "Did you call just to be an asshole?"

"Kinda. I miss you." Sebastian's openness was one of the first things I connected to when I met him. He never took anything too seriously, and he was clear about his feelings. Which meant he rubbed people the wrong way sometimes, but for me, it was a relief. My dad was disingenuous, and Seb's honesty was something I could trust.

"Come up, I'm sure Mom would be happy to see you."

"Nah, one of us has to stay down here and run the business."

"You could hang for a weekend; it's not that far away."

He cringed, his lips pulling to one side. "Dirt roads."

Snorting, I nodded. "All right, fine."

"You gonna... I don't know, go feed the wildlife or somethin'?"

"Why would I feed the wildlife?"

"I don't know what those countryfolk do for fun."

"We don't feed wildlife."

"We..." He narrowed his eyes at the camera. "I don't like this *we*."

"Don't worry. You're still my number one."

"Damn straight."

"You getting drinks with your brother?"

Sebastian's brother, Angelo, was always looking for a fun time, even more than Seb.

He nodded. "Yeah, I showed up twenty minutes late, and he's still not here. What are you doing?"

"Gonna take it easy tonight. Stay in, grill a steak, watch TV."

"What? Hit up your friends. Don't get old on me."

"I was invited to hang out, but I feel like chillin'."

His eyebrows drew together in a sympathetic look. "So, your veterinarian chick still didn't call or anything?"

I didn't like the way my stomach sank as he pointed it out. He was right, but I didn't like it. "Why would you assume that?"

"Because if she had, that mess on your face would be shaved and your hair wouldn't be in such a sad state. You'd be lookin' sharp and out the door."

"Come on, I'm not that bad."

"It's been many a drunken night of, 'Goddamn it, I can't get her out of my head.'" Sebastian's imitation of me was not flattering. I sounded like a dope.

I couldn't help but smile. "All right, I'm not sticking around for this kind of abuse."

"You should go out, have fun."

"Got it, Seb."

We said our goodbyes and hung up.

Silence echoed through the empty cabin—bouncing off the walls like an unwelcome house guest, leaving too much room for my own thoughts.

Striding into the kitchen, I pulled the steak out of the fridge to prepare for grilling. I'd use food and drink to distract myself. Take a little time to focus on a good meal, and not the jackass I've been, moping over a woman who didn't have any interest in me.

Music, that was what I needed. I leaned my hip against the counter and took my phone out of my pocket. I clicked the app and was about to search for an Outkast playlist when I realized there was an unread text message. I must have not felt my phone buzz.

Are you coming out to Benji's tonight? Hazel had sent it just a few minutes before.

I gazed down at the steak on the counter. It felt like she'd made it clear that she wasn't as into me as I was into her. I'd tried to see her for lunch the other day, and she put up roadblock after roadblock. Then, with each day passing without contact, it grew more obvious that there wasn't anything real between us. I'd fabricated the whole thing, and it was nothing more than a sad, one-sided infatuation.

If she was asking me out now, it was probably the equivalent of a booty call. Which I told myself I couldn't do. But now that the option was in front of me, it seemed possible that I could.

Typing fast, I sent, **Yeah, I was thinking of meeting Sterling there. You planning on going out?**

If you're gonna be there.

A stupid, ill-advised grin spread across my face. **I'll be there in a bit. See you.**

I put the meat back into the fridge, before jogging down the hallway to my room.

Mimicking Seb's mocking voice, I said, "Goddamn it, I can't get her outta my head."

I was a dope.

Chapter 7
Hazel

I sat on the back patio of Benji's Place, which afforded a great view of the parking lot. But now that the sun had set, I couldn't make one car out from another. They were just headlights coming and taillights going—and even if any of them were Elijah's car, I couldn't tell.

Fridays were usually busy days at the clinic, but today had been a bit light. I was trying not to freak out about it, especially since news about our auction was starting to spread. The community page was divided, just like I knew it would be, but with an added bonus of people like Lindsey Goodman posting, "Hazel Matthews is doing this? I didn't know she had it in her."

I didn't. But I was desperate and doing it anyway.

Even though the workload wasn't really mine; Nora, Sterling, and Ben were coordinating all of it. For a moment, I considered Ben's offer from the other night to help if I needed it. He'd be able to show me how to be a boss, to run a business. I wouldn't ask, though. He'd only offered because I was suddenly cool enough by association to Elijah.

Ben was a nice man, but we did not exist in the same social circles.

He had always been a ringleader of the cool kids—Sterling Strauss, Shane Briar, Elijah—Ben had never shown interest in knowing me before. It wasn't a failing of his. We all had our groups we fit into naturally, mine leaned toward bookish people like Brooks, and our point person,

Nora. But then, she could flit between groups. Her assertiveness meant that she went where she wanted, when she wanted.

Remi sat in the chair to my right with his fingers laced across his barrel chest and his legs extended in front of him, ankles crossed. Brooks was on his other side, staring at a point on the tabletop. Anyone who didn't know him might think he wasn't paying attention as Nora spoke, but I knew—and more importantly, Nora knew—that he was. I'd lost track of the conversation a while ago and was sipping my Moscow mule—probably a little too quickly—and watching people in the bar through the window. Searching for chestnut-colored curls, or a flash of green eyes.

"Who are you lookin' for?" Remi asked, craning his neck to see into the building.

Shrugging, I tried to act normal. "No one, just looking around."

He narrowed his dark blue eyes at me. "You shouldn't lie; you're not good at it."

"Shut up." I chuckled.

"All right, so it's someone of interest," he said.

"Why do you say that?"

"Because if it wasn't, you'd just tell me. But I can figure this out."

"There's no need to do that."

"Well, I could wait and find out when they get here, or I can speculate. I have nothing but time and drink on my hands, so I might as well take a guess."

I rolled my eyes. "Elijah March said he's coming out tonight."

Remi's eyebrows shot up and the corners of his lips turned down. "Good for you."

"I don't know. Maybe." I chewed on the inside of my lip, considering him. "Honestly, you'd be a good person to talk to about this."

"Talk about what?" Nora's brown eyes fixed on me.

I flicked my hand dismissively. "You already know."

It was all the explanation she needed, and she sat back in her metal chair. "Oh, *that*."

Brooks paused with his beer halfway to his lips, considering the rest of us before taking a drink.

"I told you," she said.

I shook my head. She and Brooks were tight friends, so I wasn't surprised.

She lifted one shoulder. "I can't complain to you about you."

He set his drink on the tabletop. "I don't even know what we're talking about."

Gesturing toward him, she argued, "See, he's a steel trap."

I trusted her. If it was something I'd shared in confidence, she wouldn't tell anyone—not even Brooks. But she *did* need to complain to someone about the man I was being stupid about—I was making a mess of this.

"It's fine." I rolled my eyes. Then to Remi, I said, "Elijah and I had a thing last year."

After Remi's divorce a few years ago, he'd had a lot of *things*, and it didn't surprise me when he nodded. "Okay."

"Then he left, and we didn't talk—"

"Even though you had his number," Nora interrupted.

I glared at her. "Yes, I had his number, and I didn't use it."

"Okay," Remi said, again.

"But now that he's back, I was really happy to see him. And the other night, he showed up at the clinic late and took me to get dinner. And he thought I was seeing Dennis—which, apparently, everyone thought."

Brooks shrugged. "I did."

"No, it was casual, and I'm okay that we're not hanging out anymore."

"Thank god." Nora groaned. "If I had to hear about the introduction of nonnative salmon into the Great Lakes one more time..."

"So, what's the problem with Elijah?" Remi asked, ignoring her complaints.

"Nothing, *I'm* the problem." I pointed at my chest.

"Truth." Nora nodded.

I sighed. "I was really tired the other night, and he noticed and made sure I got home safely. Also, he kept on trying to see me for lunch the next day, and I kept pointing out, like, all of the dumbest reasons he couldn't."

"Mm-hmm," she hummed, lifting her drink to her mouth.

"You're really not helping," I pointed out.

Remi disregarded the side conversation between me and Nora, and asked, "What is it you want help with?"

"I don't know," I whined, melting into my chair—an arm draped dramatically over the armrest. "He's my first crush. I have vivid memories of going to baseball games—that I did not care about—just to see him in his varsity uniform. He's so hot, and I like him... I *like* him. But I don't know how to talk to him because he's *so* hot, and I'm so *bad* at this."

"It sounds like he *likes* you, too."

Nora raised her hands, palms up, somehow conveying *I told you so* in the gesture.

She was really getting on my nerves.

Brooks shot her a *Cool it* look, but I didn't have much faith in it helping.

"I don't know if that helps or makes it worse," I said.

"Why would it make it worse?" Remi asked.

"I don't know... Because my stomach is in knots, and I'm sweating in weird places, and I don't know what to do with my hands." I had to pause as we all shared a laugh at my expense. When we recovered, I added, "It's weird because last summer, I didn't have any of this anxiety. Probably because I didn't have time to think about it; I just did it."

"Okay, so what would make it less stressful?"

I pressed my lips together, shaking my head.

One side of his mouth quirked up and wrinkles pressed into his forehead. "You like him, but does that mean you want a relationship, or do you want a couple of fun nights with him?"

"How could we have a relationship? He doesn't even live here. I'm so busy—I shouldn't be out tonight. I should be home sleeping, or catching up on charts, or any number of things."

"You could let us help more," Remi said as Nora demanded, "Will you let us help you?"

I went on as if they hadn't said anything—it felt wrong to ask them to do more than they already were. It was my business, and I should have more responsibilities.

"But I really want to see him." I was sure my helplessness showed all over my face and the droop of my shoulders. "He's great. He's thoughtful, and nice—"

"And unbelievably hot," Nora offered.

I exhaled in a whoosh and smiled. "Unbelievably hot."

My eyebrows shot up in surprise when Brooks said, "People don't stay single forever. If you don't say something... Well, regret fucking sucks."

His observation seemed personal, but I couldn't see how. Then again, he'd never shared that part of himself with me. He stared out at the parking lot in his usually impassive way. White headlights flashed across the contours of his face, but it didn't reveal any more insight about the thoughts underneath.

Nora's expression was void of all emotion and unreadable, proving that she understood exactly what he was talking about, but she'd never let on.

Next to me, Remi's large chest rose and fell. "Regret *does* fucking suck."

I didn't have to look to see how those words wore on him; I understood exactly what he was thinking about. There was a shadow that etched into his eyes the day his ex-wife, Alicia, left. Years later, it was still there—an open wound.

My phone buzzed, and I looked down to find a text from Elijah. *I'm here. Where are you at?*

The organs in my gut flipped.

Patio, I sent back.

Lifting the Moscow mule's copper cup, I toasted before throwing back the remaining contents. "To no regrets."

Brooks began a slow clap, and Remi threw his head back and laughed. Nora whooped, and I tried to convince my insides to appear as self-assured as my outsides.

Chapter 8
Hazel

Elijah March could control time. It was the only explanation for the way seconds slowed as he opened the door from the bar.

My friends were still clapping and hollering, but my attention was fully focused on the movement of his body. The distribution of his weight over his stylish brown boots. The shape of his knuckles holding the door handle as he scanned the tables. His eyebrows were drawn together until he found me, and a dizzying smile spread across his face.

The string of globe lights cast warm hues across his sharp cheekbones, and the freshly trimmed beard covering his jaw. The waves of his hair were tousled; a brunette curl hung over one eyebrow, giving him a rakish quality. My fingertips practically itched to brush it back.

A jean jacket hung open over a forest green flannel shirt he'd tucked into dark blue jeans. It all fit just right—tight enough where I could see the shape of his shoulders and thighs, but only hints of his pecs and biceps. Masculine. Effortless. Mouth-watering.

He closed the gap between us in fluid strides, and my heart thundered with each one. I was so fixated on him that I didn't notice Sterling Strauss, the closest thing the town had to a publicist, trailing behind until they were at the table on the other side of Remi.

That was when I realized I was smiling as well. It was too big, but it matched my emotions—too excited, too nervous, too infatuated.

"Hi." Elijah grinned down at me.

"Hi." I sighed.

"Can we join you?"

I opened my mouth to answer, but Remi stood. "Sure thing, take my seat."

"Brooks, you gonna give me your seat?" Sterling asked, his usual flirtatious smirk and brilliantly blue gaze focused on Nora.

"No, he will not," she answered.

He grabbed an empty chair from a nearby empty table. "Nora, why are you always turning me down?"

She shrugged. "I just like to be special that way."

But that was the last I heard of their conversation, because Elijah had lowered into the seat next to me. He scraped it closer, making room for two new chairs. He was near enough that I could smell his oaky cologne.

"Hi," I said again. Warmth spread up my neck and cheeks. How did I usually start conversations? I suddenly couldn't remember.

He rubbed the back of his neck. "Hi. How was the rest of your week?"

"Good. Busy. You?"

"Good. Chill." With jerky movements, he tugged the sleeves of his jacket down, even though they didn't need it. "I hear the auction is coming together."

"It is. Thank you for volunteering your time, and on your vacation, too. That's so nice of you."

"I'm happy to. I like animals." He pulled his sleeves down again, before exhaling and leaning back in his chair.

I tried to do the same, but as quiet settled between us, my nerves made me shift and fidget with my hair.

"I'm surprised how quickly you scheduled the auction. It's only five weeks away. Has planning it that quickly been a problem?"

Part of me was disappointed with our professional conversation. The other part of me was happy he was making conversation at all, because

I wasn't supplying anything. "Honestly, Nora, Sterling, and Ben have totally taken that over—which I appreciate. So, I really don't know."

The uncomfortable silence came back. It was probably only a few seconds, but it felt like an eternity. I needed to speak—it was arguably my turn.

"I..." I didn't know what I would say next. *I didn't mean to blow you off* felt too blunt. *I missed you* was hive inducing. *I don't know what I'm doing* was way too embarrassing. Finally, I forced out, "I'm glad you're here."

The corner of his mouth twitched as amusement warmed his green eyes. "I am, too."

"I didn't mean to blow you off."

Well, that happened.

"No?"

I shook my head. "I'd like to see you."

His Adam's apple bobbed as he swallowed. "I want to see you, too, but I think we might want different things."

"Why's that?"

He considered me for a moment before leaning on his elbow, putting our faces within inches of each other. "Why didn't you text me?"

I blinked, trying to register his whispered words, but they were so gentle and tender with the slightest rasp to his baritone, brushing like fingertips down my spine.

"Or call me," he went on. "You got my number from Ransom months ago. I was hoping you'd reach out."

Of course, Elijah knew. Why wouldn't Ransom tell him?

My shoulders tensed toward my ears.

After a few more moments of my mind sputtering, I answered, "I don't have a good reason. I just kept typing out messages, then deleting them. I couldn't send them."

A brush of his finger hooking my pinkie made some of the tension leave my body.

Quietly, he asked, "Why couldn't you send them?"

Focusing on our hands slowly intertwining, I found the bravery to say, "You're way cooler than me."

"Not true."

"I don't know what I'm doing here, and it makes me nervous."

"You make me nervous, too."

I snorted. "*Really*?"

His smile did things to my heart, made it behave erratically.

"I could jump out of my skin at any second." His thumb rubbed along my knuckles.

"Because of *me*?"

"I want to get to know you."

Butterflies took flight in my stomach, fluttering wild and frantic. "You could have called me. I'm easy to find, and you knew I had your number."

"It felt... creepy to call the office—you didn't give me permission to do that. I almost messaged your Instagram profile a couple of times... I don't know, I probably should've. I just figured there was a reason you weren't calling me."

My ribs squeezed my lungs. I had to force myself to suck in air. He had been waiting to hear from me. I'd wasted time being too intimidated to text a few words, when really, he was the sweetest man.

He shifted in his seat to face me squarely. His eyes locked onto mine, capturing me entirely. "I can't stop thinking about you, and I don't want to."

I tried to fight back the smile spreading across my face, but it was stronger than me. These fresh, light emotions blooming were such a sharp contrast from the disappointment that was still sinking in my gut.

"I want to hold your hand," he squeezed our palms together, "all the time. I want to take you out or bring you lunch. I want to see what there is between us, because there is something here."

Despite how good those words were to hear, there was still the issue of distance. "What happens when you go back to Detroit?"

"A couple hours' drive is not insurmountable. I'm here for four more weeks. Let's give this a try. See how we fit together?"

Biting my lower lip, but grinning like a fool, I nodded. "I want that, too."

Holding my gaze, Elijah lifted our joined hands and brushed his lips across my knuckles. My breath caught and a rush of my blood whooshed in my ears. That small touch of his mouth to my skin was enough to invoke sensations and memories from our one night together—enough for me to consider asking him to take me home.

He pressed a kiss to the inside of my wrist before he whispered in my ear, "Not yet."

"Why?" I sounded as desperate as I felt, and also completely unconcerned that he could read my mind.

"Did you forget that I want to get to know you?"

"*Now?*"

Laughing, he rested his forehead against mine. "Yes, now."

"Fine," I said with a giddy grin on my face.

I leaned against Elijah's side. His body was comforting and warm in the booth next to me—the chill that lingered in my bones slowly leeching away. We'd moved inside almost an hour ago, when the outdoor furnaces couldn't keep the cold far enough back.

His arm was wrapped around my shoulders. His thumb drew circles on my upper arm, following the knit pattern of my dress. The combination of yet another long week, Moscow mules, and the persistent beat of his heart against my ear caused my eyes to drift shut. But I didn't want to go home. I didn't want to hug him goodbye. I didn't want to say good night.

Not yet.

I wanted to keep soaking up his presence.

"What's your favorite color?" I asked, trying to stay awake.

"Midnight blue. What's yours?"

"Green."

Like your eyes I left unsaid, but just barely. I was halfway through my third Moscow mule and my inhibitions were showing it.

"It suits you." He brushed my hair back from my face and craned his neck to look at me. "Do you wanna go home? You seem exhausted."

I shook my head. "I'm not ready."

He pulled me closer. "Okay."

"Get Low" was pounding from the speakers. Nora, Brooks, Remi, and Sterling were dancing with half the town's population of twenty- to thirty-year-olds. They laughed as Sterling twerked.

I laughed too until Elijah asked, "Would you like to dance?"

I recoiled. "Oh god, no!"

"Don't like dancing?" His schooled expression hid most everything, except the amusement in his eyes.

"No."

"Not even alone in your house?"

"No. I don't like dancing alone. I don't like dancing in front of people. I don't know if there's anything more embarrassing than dancing."

"Aw, baby, don't be embarrassed."

My brain went fully offline, remembering the last time he'd called me that. He'd pushed me to the point where my need was too much, and my hands sought out relief. But then he asked, *'You need it that bad, baby?'* and he sent me over the edge on his tongue.

It took a while, but eventually, I regained the ability to speak. "If you'd like to dance, I'm good. I'm perfectly happy to sit here drinking water and watching you."

In response, he'd tucked me against his side.

I spotted Emily, the bartender, and Millie, the owner of the local coffee shop, share surprised looks at the sight of me and Elijah together.

No one could be as shocked as I was.

A few songs later, I was comfortably nestled against him, my mind adrift and drowsy. The tension eased from my shoulders with each breath.

"Are you falling asleep?" Elijah's voice rumbled low in my ear.

With a sharp intake through my nose, I sat up straight, trying to appear awake. "Hmm?"

"How are you getting home? Is your car here?"

I shook my head.

"I have my bike, or I'd offer to drive you."

"You ride a motorcycle?" I generally found motorcycles to be reckless death machines, but the idea of him on one surfaced a sexual awakening from *Grease 2* I hadn't realized was still relevant.

He scoffed, "My bicycle."

Laughing, I covered my mouth. "Where's your car?"

"I don't want to say; I'm already being supremely uncool."

"Where is it?"

He grimaced at the black iron beams of the ceiling. "My mom has it."

I hid my face in his shoulder as the humor took over. The sounds I was making couldn't even be called laughter anymore; it was more like cackling.

"You rode your bike here," I yelled into the soft fabric of his flannel. It wasn't funny... I knew it wasn't funny. A bicycle was a completely reasonable form of transportation, but still, I couldn't stop laughing.

His finger hooked under my chin, urging it up. Three wrinkles were drawn from the corners of his eyes, and parentheses were etched at both sides of his smile. A tender heat grew in my chest, wrapping around my heart and easing into my stomach, pleasant and soft. Unlike the all-consuming smolder he'd made me feel in the past, this was something new. Gentle. Sustainable.

"The woman I like asked me to be here, so I'm here," he stated.

"You're here because of me?"

"I am in this *town* because of you."

The distance between our mouths was closing in imperceptible increments.

"No way," I whispered.

"Yes."

"No." I shook my head, brushing his lips for the barest second.

"Yes." He nodded, nudging my nose with his. His fingers weaved into the hair at the base of my skull.

And then we were kissing.

And I was falling—tumbling, reeling. Head over heels into a pool I hadn't even realized I was dipping my toe in.

His lips were smooth and soft, and his hold on me was firm. My fingertips trailed down his neck to grip the collar of his shirt, the back of my knuckles against his clavicle. I felt the vibrations of his groaned moan more than heard it as he pulled me against him and deepened the kiss. Tilting his head, he ran his tongue along the inside of my lips. And

I was fully immersed in the smell of his skin—that scent I couldn't place, but reminded me of campfires, and staying up too late, and hot nights under the stars. I couldn't get enough of his taste, the lingering hoppy notes from the beer he drank under the inexplicably sweet taste of his mouth.

I'd heard of this, but I'd never experienced it. Someone who just appealed to every single one of my senses. Maybe it was a pheromone or a gift from god that made him so delicious to me, but I didn't care. I wanted more. I wanted to feel him closer, tighter. I wanted to smell every inch of his skin. I wanted to run my hands down his stomach. I wanted to bite into the flesh of his deltoid as I wrapped myself around him.

Someone bumped our table, and we startled, both of us gasping for air. Somehow, I'd ended up on his lap, and our sweet little kiss had grown into something barely appropriate, even for this dimly lit bar.

His erection strained against the pant leg of his jeans. The skirt of my dress would have been up to my waist if he hadn't held on to it in both fists, keeping it in place at the top of my thighs.

Hiding my blushing face in his neck, I lowered to the booth next to him. "Oh my god."

"Yeah." He shielded his face with his hand, and only I could see his baffled smile. His chest bounced against my cheek.

"Oh good, you came up for air," Nora said, scooting into the booth across from us.

I ignored her, but Elijah snorted.

"Are you getting a ride from me or him?" Her face twisted in distaste. "I hate the way I asked that."

I rolled my eyes. "Classy."

Elijah shook his head. "You'll have to take her home. I'll pick you up for a date tomorrow."

I wanted to ask him to spend the night at my place, but decided I was probably being too thirsty.

"We have the shopping trip tomorrow," Nora pointed out.

"We'll be done by the evening, right?" Elijah asked.

"What shopping trip?" I asked.

She gestured to the sea of dancing bodies to her left. "I'm making the bachelors get clothes that fit their bodies. Most of these men dress like little boys playing dress up in their dad's clothes."

I considered Brooks and his loose-fitting jeans and T-shirt. "Good point. But Elijah dresses great."

"I'm making him, Remi, and Sterling come to do most of the styling. I don't have the energy to be patient with a medium-sized man insisting on wearing an extra-large."

The mental image of Elijah trying on clothes and me getting to sit back and ogle him was enough for me to give up my plans for a productive Saturday. "Can I go, too?"

"Of course," he said as Nora warned, "Only if you're not a distraction."

"Great, I'm coming tomorrow."

"Maybe we can get dinner down there, or I could cook for you when we're back in town."

I nodded, my brain lagging due to his nearness, scent, and touch.

Holding my hand, he walked me and Nora out to her car. She told him the logistical details about the following day, but I wasn't paying attention. All that really mattered was when he held my waist and promised to text me the following morning to make plans.

He combed his fingers through my hair, then cupped my jaw. Leaning forward, he kissed me. It was just a kiss goodbye, but it was slow and full of promise. And I could not wait for our upcoming date.

After closing my car door, Elijah waved. Turning with his hands stuffed into his pockets, he shrugged against the blustery autumn wind. I watched him in the side mirror until he disappeared into the bar.

Nora pulled onto the dark, quiet street. "You two are so cute, it almost makes me want someone to crush on."

I gasped theatrically. "Not reel 'em in and throw 'em out Nora!"

"I said *almost*."

"He said he likes me."

The corners of her mouth twitched. "I'm really happy for you, babe."

I wiggled in my seat, too elated to hold still. "Thanks."

Chapter 9

Elijah

Our shopping assignment was: Halloween rules.

Costume a roofer, but make it sexy.

School teacher, but sexy.

Grocer, but sexy.

And Nora had been wise to enlist help dressing these men. Some of them acted like putting on a button-up shirt was terminal.

I tended to be accepting of other people's limitations, but even I wanted to roll my eyes when Shane Briar complained, again, about having to try on a third pair of jeans. Or when Brooks grabbed an extra-large shirt when he was a lean large, at best.

"It fits tight in the shoulders," he complained.

"Good," I retorted.

"It's restricting my movement."

"What, you gonna do jumping jacks on stage?"

He cupped the bill of his baseball cap. The shirt did strain around his arms and shoulders, but that was the idea. It was no snugger than the shirts I wore regularly.

The three-sided mirror repeated our images from different angles. Behind us, the other end of the hallway opened into the store.

"Do you have the belt on?" I asked.

He nodded.

"Cool, tuck the shirt in." I looked in the other direction, catching an animated conversation between Sterling and Bill Mueller, a local plumber, about the merits of a quality undershirt. The older man nodded, his bald head gleaming under the florescent lights.

To my left, I vaguely registered the rattle of Brooks undoing his belt. Hazel walked into the frame the doorway created. She looked down at a shelf, her hands working quickly through the garments as she talked to someone I couldn't see to her right. Her smile was warm, and when she laughed, I couldn't help but grin in response. It sparked a vague memory of sharing a high school class with her. She'd been this cute, nerdy girl in the front row. I wouldn't go near her, because I was trouble and she was good. I didn't know if she actually wore glasses back then, or if I'd projected them onto her face in my mind—a manifestation of just how clever she was with her hand always in the air, always with the answer to the questions.

We had driven to the mall separately. She'd called earlier that morning, saying she had some work that needed to get done for the clinic. I was expected to get here at the beginning of the shopping trip, and neither of us wanted to risk Nora's wrath. Instead, Hazel hitched a ride with Millie, the owner of Country Grounds, Grand Ridge's coffee shop. Hazel and I hadn't been able to spend much time together all day, and she planned to hitch a ride back with Millie as well. At least this way we could eat lunch together before she left. And, of course, we had a date tonight, where I'd cook for her at her house.

Seeing her again, knowing that we both wanted to give this romance a shot, had me full of energy. I was certain we would be a good fit; I could see a future with her. A life that looked nothing like what I had pictured before. I always saw myself living in cities, building my business with Sebastian, and the women I dated fit into that image. They were career driven—just like Hazel—but they didn't aspire to a small-town life with a yard. If they wanted kids, they wanted to raise them in the city.

I didn't think that was what Hazel wanted. She was building a business she was proud of, and I understood firsthand how important that was.

She didn't have the type of job that could go remote like mine.

If we became everything I thought we could, it would mean moving back to Grand Ridge—a town I had mixed feelings about. But I had the feeling the more I got to know Hazel, the less that would feel like a sacrifice.

Looking up, she caught me staring, and I didn't look away.

She pinched her lips together and shook her head.

I smiled, the tip of my tongue running along the ridges of my upper teeth.

Her breasts rose with an inhale.

The need to touch her, to be near her, grew almost overwhelming. I couldn't wait to get her alone. I didn't know how I would keep my hands off her long enough to not only prepare food, but let her eat it, too. Not with the way her jeans hugged her hips, and the V-neck of her thin sweater gave me glimpses of the black lace of her bra.

Not when just the memory of her gasps and moans made my cock twitch.

Something must have changed in my expression because pink warmed her cheeks and she absentmindedly grazed her fingertips on the pale skin of her neck.

I was going to run my teeth right there. I was going to—

"This what you want?" Brooks' voice broke my train of thought so abruptly, I had to blink, forcing my brain into the present and out of a much more desirable future.

"What?" I croaked. I flicked my eyes toward him, then back to Hazel. She was covering her mouth and laughing down toward her feet.

When I met his eye in the mirror, Brooks appeared equal parts amused and annoyed. He held his arms out, indicating his shirt fully buttoned-up and tucked into his slacks. The gold buckle of the brown belt was bright against the navy blue pants, and the shirt was the same blue as his eyes.

"You look sharp, man," I said.

He gripped the bill of his hat in both hands, the ends of his hair curling out under the rim.

I jerked my chin up. "You know Nora's gonna make you get a haircut."

He nodded. "I'll schedule it today." He shrugged uncomfortably. "I still think it's too tight."

Hazel wasn't outside of the dressing room hallway; instead there was a woman I hadn't seen before. She had bright blond hair and whispered something to her friend, who stood with her back to us. The other woman casually looked over her shoulder before doing a double take. It was easy to see the line of the women's gazes taking in an eyeful of Brooks.

Quietly, I said, "Look in the mirror above your right shoulder."

He did and caught the women checking him out. When they realized they'd been caught, they giggled and one of them gave a shy wave. The smallest tug upward of his mouth was the only indication Brooks gave that he saw them.

As they walked away, he conceded, "Maybe it's not too tight."

Almost an hour later, I held Hazel's hand as we entered a chain restaurant. The walls were lined in booths, and there was random classic film paraphernalia on the walls. It was the tail end of the lunch rush, and most of the restaurant was empty. We'd waited for everyone else to commit to a different place, then slipped away like thieves. Finally, having her to myself was well worth it.

The hostess gave us a welcoming smile that didn't reach her eyes—an expression just as uniformed as her name badge. "How many?"

"Two, please," I answered.

She grabbed menus and led us into the seating area. Gesturing to a four-top table, she asked, "Will this work?"

"Yes, thank you."

She left while Hazel and I slid into our seats across from one another.

With a quick glance over her shoulder, she said, "I love how polite you are."

I shrugged, not knowing exactly how to respond.

"Your dad's polite." She picked up her menu.

"So is my mom. You'd like her."

Without looking up from the laminated pages, Hazel asked, "Are you close with her?"

"Yeah, it was kinda just her and me—like we were the only ones who knew what it was like when I was growing up. We've always stayed close."

Hazel laid her menu down. Giving me her full attention, she tilted her head. "Was it that bad?"

I knew she understood what kind of man my dad was better than most people. But that didn't make it any less uncomfortable to actually explain the nuanced way he controlled me and my mom. I clasped my hands together, swiping the knuckles of my thumbs across my lips. "Uh, looking back, there was a lot of gaslighting. When I got older, Mom and I were able to piece our reality together. You know, there was a way he twisted the truth, and then there was actual reality. And in public, I was just kinda this set piece. I had to anticipate what he wanted and do that. If I got it wrong, he'd get this look, and I'd just know it'd be mental warfare for weeks." I sighed, forcing some of the tension from my body. "I didn't know that wasn't normal; I thought everyone's life was like that. Then I got older and, I started pushing back, and... Mom got us out of there. And... that was good."

"That is good. I'm glad she did that."

"Me, too." I slid my menu in front of me. "What about you? What was your childhood like?"

"Um... I was an awkward little know-it-all who spent most of her time with books. So... pretty awesome, actually."

My mind conjured the memory of the little room in the library where she'd taken me the summer before. I pictured her in her mid-teens—the only age I remembered her from when we were growing up—carrying books clasped to her chest, reading quotes about love and longing.

A smile spread across my lips. "That is awesome."

Logically, I knew we lived hours apart, and opening myself up to the infatuation I'd harbored for her wasn't wise. The likelihood of us becoming something sustainable was low. But I enjoyed being with her too much to completely ignore the thrill of these feelings growing in my chest.

I lowered my hand to the tabletop, palm up. She laid her fingers on mine, and we curled them. Her short nails pressed into my flesh but didn't dig. Her eyes were brown pools, lined in sweeping dark eyelashes. I was being pulled into their depths, adrift and happy to be there.

Until the front door of the restaurant swung open, and a wave of voices poured into the dining area. Familiar male faces filed in.

Hazel's jaw dropped, not even having to turn around to know exactly who just walked into the building. "No, they are not here."

My laugh was more of a cough. "They are."

"But they were supposed to go—"

"I know. They'll sit somewhere else... it's a big building."

Then I saw a shitty sneer pull at the corner of Shane's mouth, and our stupid high school rivalry came back to me in full force. We couldn't stop getting in each other's way back then—going after the same girls, trying out for the same position on the baseball team. It had been annoying, and he'd been an asshole. I had the suspicion his basic personality type hadn't changed since then.

"I doubt it," she said.

I squeezed her hand reassuringly, even though I felt less sure. "We'll tell them we're here together."

She rolled her eyes. "I love that you think they have boundaries. The only boundary these people recognize is city limits."

As if on cue, Shane Briar called out, "Sweet, Hazel and Eli already got a seat."

"Leave them alone," Nora's voice called from the back of the crowd, but I couldn't spot her.

Shane led the way past the apathetic hostess.

I half stood, and gestured between me and Hazel. "Hey guys, we're kinda—"

"Come on, help me push these tables together." He pulled chairs out from the neighboring empty four-top. My hands fisted under the table, my biceps flexed. The sensation of my body preparing to fight happened so quickly, it completely caught me off guard. But then Shane had always been able to get a rise out of me. His annoying-ass face had a direct line to my worst character flaws.

I forced my hands flat on top of my thighs.

"Are you all really *this* oblivious?" Nora asked with her arms open, but the men were set to their task.

"Let's *not* push them together," I said, my irritation sharpening my unheard words.

"It's fine." Hazel shrugged.

"What's fine?" Sterling stood next to Nora before his crystal blue eyes met mine. He must have seen my exasperation and understood the situation. "Oh shit, yeah, guys, come on. We'll sit somewhere else."

"Why?" Bill Mueller lifted his bushy eyebrows as he reached for the chair between me and Hazel.

"Yeah, why?" Shane feigned innocence.

"It's fine," Hazel said again.

My shoulders fell in resignation. "Bill, I'm gonna sit there."

"Here?"

I nodded.

He shook his head, confused. "Okay."

Lowering into my new spot, I shifted to face her fully. I tried to tune out my ornery emotions as easily as I turned my back to Shane. Under the table, my knee brushed hers. I was determined to look on the bright side. I hooked my ankle around hers and said, "I guess this could be worse."

An adorable smirk played at the corner of her mouth. "I guess it could."

Then Dennis took the empty seat next to her.

Chapter 10

Hazel

Elijah's body language tightened—a flex of his thigh against the inside of mine, a straightening of his back, a broadening of his shoulders. I wanted to set him at ease, but I didn't really know how to do that with Dennis less than a foot from my left.

"Hey, I don't think we've actually met." He extended a hand toward Elijah.

Their grip looked firm, but not aggressive, as they shook.

"Not really, I'm Elijah."

"Dennis. Again, I'm really sorry about my dog. Sometimes he gets away from me…"

I resisted an eye roll. Banjo needed obedience classes, but like everything else, Dennis wasn't concerned about it.

"Please don't worry about it," Elijah said.

"Hi, Hazel." Dennis gave me a sweet, boyish—almost sheepish—smile. I couldn't tell if he was as oblivious as the rest of our group, or if he knew there was something going on between Elijah and me. Or it could just be Dennis' innocent face.

It kinda stung that everyone assumed Elijah and I weren't together. As if they all believed my fears—that he was too far out of my league to even consider the two of us a possibility.

But then, Shane knew Elijah and I were becoming an item—he had made it a point to warn me a few hours ago. "Be careful, Hazel. You know Elijah's reputation... He gets off on ruining good girls like you."

I'd been instantly infuriated, but I hadn't been able to express it. I'd wanted to tell him that I was a grown woman—not a girl—who didn't need his protection, and couldn't be ruined. That he'd never talked to me before today, and we should go back to that. But what I'd actually said was, "I'm fine."

Shaking off my irritation at myself and Shane, I asked, "Hey, Dennis, how's your day going?"

"Good. I really liked that shirt you picked out for me."

"You should go back and get it in a couple other colors. It looked nice on you."

I wanted to shift my focus back to Elijah, but it felt rude and dismissive to ignore Dennis.

Elijah picked up his menu and began scanning it.

"I'll do that." Dennis leaned back in his chair. "You getting your usual?"

"I think so."

"You have a usual?" Elijah looked up through his brow, his green eyes piercing. How did just one look from him quicken my heart rate?

"Kinda. This is where we eat when Dennis drives me down to get supplies. We fill his truck every couple of months."

Some of the light in Elijah's gaze dimmed. Possibly. Maybe nothing changed at all. Maybe I was just seeing things because I was uncomfortable. There was nothing between me and Dennis, but we did have history. But then, Elijah had a *history* with quite a few people in town; it was years ago, but it still existed. I was probably being quaint to think he'd be insecure about my past.

I wanted to go back to talking to him like we had before everyone interrupted, especially after he'd just opened up about his relationship with his parents. I really appreciated him sharing that with me, and I wanted to keep getting to know him better. And we would have, if the menfolk hadn't blasted through the door and blown that plan up.

I was sitting in the middle of an incredibly uncomfortable sandwich. *We'll have our date tonight, it'll be okay.*

"I should have driven my truck today; we could have loaded it up before I leave for my research program," Dennis said.

"Yeah, I didn't think about it." I hadn't thought about it because I'd been too excited to see Elijah try on clothes—which hadn't happened. That was more than a little disappointing.

Dennis could be impossibly nice. He didn't owe me anything, yet he valued doing this task that helped me. Sweat was prickling underneath my hair from the combination of guilt and awkwardness sludging through my body.

"I'll rent something. We'll get it taken care of," Elijah offered.

Some of the tension in my shoulders released. The grateful smile I directed toward him was cut down by Dennis saying, "Thanks, man."

He scratched at something on the table's surface. "I hate feeling like I'm leaving people in the lurch."

A muscle flexed in Elijah's jaw.

"Hey, Denny," Nora said from the other side of the table. "Tell me," she paused, "*again* about the research you'll be doing."

He sat up straighter before he began his lengthy and very thorough explanation, and I watched pain seep into her dark brown eyes. I mouthed, "Thank you," and she nodded. I'd stock the work fridge with her favorite creamer, or something. She was the best friend I could ask for. I mentally apologized for anytime I'd called her irritating—while also noting that she *could* be irritating on occasion. Not in that moment, though.

Nora. Was. The. Best.

I needed out of this situation.

Leaning toward Elijah, I whispered, "You know I could really go for a pretzel right now."

"Not that hungry?" he asked.

"Not really... I'm planning on a big dinner tonight."

His smile was enough to break me into a thousand delighted pieces. "Are you?"

"Yeah, this really cute guy offered to cook for me."

His eyes dropped to my mouth. "Lucky guy. Let's get you a pretzel."

We stood, and Dennis looked up to me. "You leaving?"

"Uh..." I nodded at the confused, and slightly sad, expression on his face. How had I ended up here? Me? Of all people. Was I breaking his heart? Was that what this was? It did not fit well. It bound too tightly around my ribs.

I'm not responsible for his feelings, I coached myself. *I'm not doing anything wrong by being with Elijah.*

Everything with Elijah felt right. But hurting Dennis felt very wrong. The two truths walked parallel with each other. Their contradictions did not make either of them less accurate.

"Den, what is the environmental impact of this research?" Remi asked from the other side of Dennis. Remi must have snuck in with everyone, and I hadn't even noticed.

Dennis launched back into the subject, and I made a mental note to do something nice for Remi, too.

I tried to leave the discomfort behind as Elijah and I exited into the mall, the sounds of shoppers bouncing off the tiled floors and high ceilings. It was easier to do in theory than in execution.

We ordered our pretzels and waited while the teenagers behind the counter prepared them.

I searched my mind for something to talk about, but all I could think to do was apologize. As I hadn't done anything wrong, I didn't want to do that.

"You helped Dennis find some clothes?" Elijah finally asked.

"I did. He's offered up carpentry work for the auction, so I found a nice fitting flannel and khakis. It's funny, most of these men are going to be wearing flannel."

"It's a good look."

"Yeah, you were rocking the hell out of it last night," I said to my feet, my cheeks burning.

"Thank you." He grinned.

"I'm actually kinda disappointed. I thought I'd see you try stuff on..." I trailed off as my tongue grew too large for my mouth, wondering if it was a weird thing to say. I really wanted to get back into our flirty rhythm, and this suddenly felt like the wrong route. "Of course, you don't *need* to. I mean, you look great in what you're wearing right now—not that that's surprising. You always look great."

He looked down at his fashionably loose-fitting T-shirt and jeans as I continued to ramble about subjects that no longer seemed relevant.

My words cut off completely when he took a step closer. The heat of his skin pushed back the chill of the mall air. His low rumble lit sparks in my brain. "If you want me to try something on, all you have to do is ask. I'll give it to you."

Behind my shoulder, one of the attendants announced our order was ready. Elijah thanked them, then handed me my pretzel stick and cheese.

Taking a bite of his cinnamon sugar-covered twist, he jerked his head toward the row of shops. "What store do you want to go to?"

"Oh, you don't have to... It's fine. I didn't mean to make a thing of it—" The protest died on my lips when his hand slid around my back.

His thumb dipped into the waistband of my jeans and his fingertips pressed against the curve of my ass. "What store, Hazel?"

I stared at a granule of sugar clinging to his lower lip, wondering if I could lick it off. "I guess wherever you normally shop."

"You don't want to dress me up like a sexy carpenter?"

I giggled. "No, you're sexy just as you are."

That was how I found myself standing outside the dressing room of a store that was much more expensive than I usually shopped at. On the other side of the door, Elijah was changing into clothes I'd picked out, which were a bit less laid-back than what he normally wore. I had picked a camel-colored sweater that was very soft and charcoal gray slacks. He'd grabbed a belt on his way into the room.

I preoccupied myself by organizing my calendar for the following week. I'd have to be pretty productive tomorrow to make up for the time I took off today. Even though I was heading back to town with Millie soon, I still had some tasks to complete before my date with Elijah tonight.

I typed my to-do list into my phone until the latch on the door *clicked* and it swung open.

He stood there in the center of the dressing room with his chestnut waves tousled, scraping one hand over his short beard while the other was tucked into the pants pocket. I took him in from head to socked-feet, and then I did it again—and maybe one more time for good measure.

Holding his arms out to either side, he asked, "What do you think?"

I pinched my lips together and nodded. "It looks really good on you."

"Thank you. Is this what you wanted?"

Scanning over the broad set of his shoulders and the loose fit of the sweater at his waist, I hummed, "Mm-hmm."

Elijah turned his back to me, from my place in the hallway my focus instantly dropped to his firm, round ass. After a beat or two, I enjoyed the thin fabric of the sweater stretching across his shoulder blades.

He looked so good. The anticipation for tonight grew into something needy low in my stomach and an ache formed between my legs. The memory of him, naked and sweating, roared to the forefront of my mind. There were too many layers between us in this public space, though I would do unlawful things if he suggested them.

"What are you thinking about, Hazel?" His tone had dropped, the words scraping his throat.

"Huh?" I met his eye in the dressing room mirror where he watched me. My eyes were wide, as if I'd been caught doing something wrong.

"You're blushing."

The warmth that had already filled my cheeks spread to my neck and chest.

"That look on your face is going to get us arrested," he rumbled.

I couldn't believe I could speak, even if my voice was weak and airy. "I believe in your self-control."

"But not yours?"

"I don't have much faith in mine right now."

In slow movements, he turned and gripped the doorframe over our heads in one hand. He tilted his head down, capturing my gaze in his. I was trapped in his snare, without any desire to struggle free from it. He was so close, but we didn't touch. He smelled like cinnamon, and my mouth watered, wanting to taste him.

He looked to either side of the hallway, ensuring that we were the only two people nearby.

We aren't really...?

Because if he touched me, kissed me, pulled me into the dressing room and closed the door, I wasn't sure I would stop us. The way my heart was pounding in my ears drowned out all my rational thoughts.

He stared at my mouth, his tongue moistening his lips, and I swayed toward him. His grip tightened on the doorframe and his bicep flexed. His hand skimmed the thin skin of my throat, and his thumb drew a line across my lower lip.

I was a pile of desperate skin and bones. I wanted his mouth on me so badly, every nerve in my body thrummed for more of his touch.

Somehow, I didn't groan when he removed his hand and straightened, putting distance between us. There was a dark, dangerous tint to his eyes I'd never seen before. The rattle of his belt buckle startled my gaze to his waistband. I darted a look over my shoulder, but there was still no one there.

Only us.

"Just look," he growled.

He sounded as desperate as I felt. As if there was a part of him clawing to be released, and it belonged with the part of me I could hardly hold back. The part of me that itched to run my hands over his body, that wanted to climb him like a goddamn tree.

He whipped the strap out of the loops with the sharp sound of leather on fabric, then let it fall to the floor. My jaw slackened as he stroked the heel of his palm along his hardened length, straining along the front of his pants. Then he took hold of the hem of his sweater and pulled it over his head. His curls fell into his eyes, and he shook them back. The white undershirt he wore clung to his rounded pecs and long waist.

I had to cross my arms not to touch him.

Slowly, he took hold of the top of his pants and eased the button undone, and a sliver of his black boxer briefs peeked through the tri-angle. His fingers were long, and the rounded pads of his thumb and index pinched the metal tab of his zipper. Metal scraped on metal as he deliberately drew the zipper down. Inch by inch, he opened the triangle wider until I could see the base of his thick erection outlined in the thin fabric of his underwear.

I shifted my hips with my thighs pressed together, but it wasn't enough. I was uncomfortably wet.

We stood there, frozen. The need in him ricocheted off the need in me—expanding, stretching, swelling. It strained against the few feet between us, pulling us closer. Urging us to stop thinking and just give in.

The buzz of my phone in my back pocket made me gasp.

I sighed as the spell whispered away, the intensity broken.

Elijah ran his hands through his hair and clasped them behind his neck. His jaw set firm.

Looking down at my insistent phone, I saw Millie's name. The time on the screen revealed that I was supposed to be at her car for us to make the drive back to town. "Shit, I'm so sorry," I said to Elijah. "I have to go. I'm late."

His Adam's apple worked on a swallow. "I'll see you in a few hours."

I backed away from him, not trusting myself to even kiss him goodbye. Not when he was standing there half-dressed like the manifestations of all my fantasies.

Chapter 11

Elijah

I set the cooler down on Hazel's front porch and knocked on the door. Shoving my hands into my new pants pockets, I heard a chair slide on the floor on the other side of the door. I checked my watch to confirm I hadn't shown up early—I was punctual, though.

My anticipation built as she neared, until the door finally opened, and she was right there in front of me. She'd traded her jeans for a dress I hadn't seen yet. It was burgundy, with a high lace neckline and long sleeves, cupping her full breasts and cinching at the waist. The scalloped hem was closer to her waist than her knees, revealing pale skin stretching across her thighs and calves.

After the lustful way she'd watched me undress, I'd been struggling with a semi since that damn dressing room. Then Hazel opened the door wearing a dress that played with sex and modesty in the same way she did.

This was supposed to be our first date, but I didn't see how I could cook *and then eat* before we gave in to the sexual tension between us.

I wanted her to see me as a potential boyfriend, but the chemistry between us was the same as it had been the year before—persistent, hot, demanding.

A pleased smile played on her lips as she took in my appearance. "You bought the outfit."

I ran my palm over the soft light tan sweater. "I did. I like it."

"I do, too."

Taking a step closer, I laid a hand on her hip, the lace delicate under my palm. "I have a problem."

"What's that?" She rested her palm on my chest.

"I really want to make you this meal, but you look so good in this goddamn dress, I've forgotten everything I've ever known."

She giggled. "That sounds serious."

"It is."

Lifting one shoulder, she said, "We should probably get me out of it, then."

Leaving the cooler on her porch, I kicked the door closed.

I pulled her to me. Arching her spine, she wrapped her arms around my shoulders. My lips met hers, and the constant noise at the back of my mind quieted. There was only Hazel, and the taste of her tongue, and the feel of her heart pounding on my ribs—the texture of the fabric of her skirt over her full ass. There was only her soft moan as I pulled her tighter and scraped my teeth along her jaw.

"I love the sounds you make." I groaned into her neck. "They've haunted me this whole time."

This was good. So fucking good. If all we were was a couple of weeks—a firework blasting bright and beautiful in a dark sky—then at least it was this perfect.

But my arms felt like they belonged around her. The sweet taste of her mouth satisfied a craving I'd searched for my entire life.

This was not the kind of relationship I'd walk away from unscathed.

She pulled my mouth to hers, urgent and hungry. Her words were breathless, and so quiet, I almost didn't hear her. "I thought about you so many times..."

My hand flexed, squeezing her harder, pressing her heat to my throbbing cock. "Are you telling me you made yourself come thinking about me?"

She bit her lip and nodded. Her brown eyes pleading and needy.

"With your hand or a toy?"

"Both."

My cock twitched. "Fuck, baby."

Her hips shifted, rubbing her cunt along my length. "God, you calling me that… Why is it so hot?"

She provoked something primal in me as a shiver ran over my scalp. I wanted to bite her neck and take her hard. I needed distance; otherwise, I was going to lose my fucking grip. I pressed her to the wall, putting a couple of feet between us.

"Show me." I didn't think I'd ever sounded so rough in my life.

Her hand twitched toward the hem of her skirt, then stopped. She chewed on her bottom lip and shook her head. "I can't."

It took everything in me not to tell her she could. And she fucking would.

That she'd done it unconsciously for me once.

But I wouldn't push her without her permission.

Instead, I fisted the delicate lace in my hand. "Feeling shy, baby? Do you want me to show you? You wanna see how I fuck my hand thinking about you, remembering the feel of your cunt?"

She slid on the wall, her knees buckling, before she straightened again. "Yes. Yes, I want that."

I straightened and pulled my sweater over my head. She watched as I undressed, just like she'd done at the store, but this time it wouldn't be a tease. I wouldn't stop. This time it would end with both of us satisfied.

Pressing a hand to the wall over her shoulder, I supported my weight and took hold of my aching cock. She shuddered out a breath, her breasts strained against the fabric of her dress.

"I like to start slow." I stroked from my base to my tip. "I don't want to come too quickly. I want to savor the memory of you, and I know I'm going to come hard, anyway."

I kissed just behind her ear and slipped my teeth on her earlobe.

She squirmed, her upper legs rubbing together.

As I rubbed my hand up and down my erection, she fed her skirt into her fists, inch by inch, until I caught a glimpse of her red satin panties. My hips jerked, and I knew I had to pause. I gripped my base, desperate for control.

"Keep going," she whispered.

But I was too transfixed by her fingertips gliding down her mound and between her legs.

"Elijah," she said, her voice throaty.

"Fuck." I started rocking my hips, screwing into my hand.

Her whimpers and moans were gasoline on a flame already burning through me.

I fell to my elbow on the wall, kissing and sucking the sensitive skin of her neck. I couldn't see what she was doing, but her arm brushed my stomach rhythmically.

The fingers of her free hand drove into the hair at the base of my skull, pulling me to meet her mouth.

I ran both hands up her ribs and found her hard nipples. I flicked and circled my thumbs over them. She arched her back, pulling on my hair hard. It was a good thing I'd stopped jerking off when I had, or I'd be spilling all over her thighs.

I almost did just watching her as her orgasm washed over her.

Fuck, she's beautiful.

Open and vulnerable. So goddamn sexy.

Her hand slipped out of her panties, and she sucked in deep breaths, her long dark eyelashes resting on her cheekbones.

I wanted her so fucking badly.

With her eyes still closed, she whispered, "I can't believe I just did that."

Nuzzling my lips down the slope of her neck, I asked, "Do you feel okay?"

She wrapped her arms around my neck, hitching a leg on my hip. "I feel incredible."

I gripped the back of her thighs and picked her up. Even with the thin fabric of her underwear still between us, I could feel her wet heat against my aching erection. My grip tightened, my fingers pressed into her flesh.

"Point me toward your bedroom or I'm taking you on this wall," I ground out between clenched teeth.

Still rubbing and teasing me with each rock of her hips, she practically purred, "Don't threaten me with a good time."

"Hazel," I warned.

Lazily, she flicked her wrist toward the hallway around the corner. "That way."

"You're gonna want to get more specific or I'm kicking down doors," I joked—mostly. "And I cannot swing a hammer, so I won't be able to fix the mess I make."

Her laugh was throaty. "End of the hall, door on the left."

The slip of her tongue on mine had me needing that bed more than ever as I took clumsy steps toward her room. The door was unlatched and thudded off of the wall with the push of my hand.

Her legs stayed around my waist as I found the tab of her zipper at the nape of her neck. It got stuck a couple of times as I tugged it down. I'd normally like to be more composed, more in control, more careful not to rip her clothes, but none of those things mattered at the moment.

I set her down, and her hands ran over my pecs and abs and lower.

I caught her wrists before she could continue her path. "I'm about to tear your dress apart."

"Do it—" But her words were cut off by my taking her hips and turning her around. Less than a second later, I had the zipper down the rest of the way and was pushing the garment off her shoulders and down her hips.

Her red panties curved up at the bottom, exposing the pale skin of her ass cheeks. I cupped her, kneading her soft flesh.

Slipping my fingers under the thin fabric, I brushed up and down her slit. "So fucking wet."

She leaned back, pressing her shoulders to my front, and my erection was caught between her spine and my stomach. Her arms circled around my neck, giving me a view of her swollen tits practically spilling out of her strapless bra.

"Tell me there's a condom in here. Mine are in my pants by the front door."

"Top drawer."

I stepped away, and even though I'd be back in a few seconds, it felt too long. By the time I turned around, her underwear was a crumpled scrap of fabric on the carpet, and she'd reached behind her back to undo the clasps of her bra. Her breasts fell free, full and heavy.

My balls drew tight.

Her naked body brought me to a full stop with the condom pinched in my fingers. The dark curls on her mound, the round curve of her belly, the dimpled flesh of her thighs. She was so soft, and I wanted nothing more than to sink into her.

When my gaze finally trailed up to her face, there was a playful smirk tugging at her lips.

"I love how you look at me," she said, her voice thick.

I strode back to her. "As much as I love the sight, I need to do more than look at you."

She let out a surprised squeal as I wrapped my arm under her ass and tossed her onto the bed. Her tits bounced before settling into her armpits. She gripped the light purple comforter on either side of her hips, her back arched.

I was a goner, completely crazed just taking her in. It was physically painful to not be inside of her.

I bit the foil wrapper and tore it open.

She groaned as I rolled the condom on my hard length.

I wanted to tell her how badly I wanted her, how much I'd needed this, but the words were trapped in a hazy, lust fog. I felt drunk or high, time lapsed and stretched. None of my thoughts were clear—just the insistent beaconing of her body calling to mine.

I pulled her into my lungs, and she coursed through my veins. I floated, I sank.

She reached for me, pulling me in without saying a word.

I held her gaze in mine, and went to my knees on the bed. She hooked a leg around my hip, and I slipped inside of her.

She gasped.

I groaned.

Buried completely inside her heat, I waited for my control to return. Her walls flexed around me. I needed something to hold on to, something to ground me. Gripping her palms in mine, I pressed them to the mattress over her head.

Her mouth gaped open, and all the things I wanted to do to that mouth raced in my brain faster than the blood rushing through my veins. I lowered to kiss her and began rocking my hips.

My knuckles were white, holding on to every ounce of restraint I could find.

Her back arched, and I took one of her nipples between my lips. She held her breath when I found the spot that made her thighs twitch. Her pulse throbbed against her throat, fast and frantic.

She spasmed around my cock, and I lost all sense of finesse. I pounded into her. Lost to anything but the soft warmth of her body taking me in, I thrust over and over. The smack of our skin joined the half-formed words of praise I muttered through my clenched teeth.

I speared as deeply as I could inside her as I came into the condom.

At some point, I'd bit down on her shoulder, leaving little red imprints from my teeth. I brushed my lips over them.

Rolling onto my back, I sucked in air and stared at the white plaster of her ceiling.

"Fuck." I sighed. "That feels so much better."

She giggled, curling into my side.

Chapter 12
Hazel

For the first time in...I didn't know how long, probably since the last time Elijah and I had slept together, my brain was silent. My head rested on his shoulder. His chest rose and fell in deep breaths, and his heart pounded a quick beat in my ear. Breath by breath, his heart rate slowed.

I must have been falling asleep because he ran a hand down my back, and I startled.

"Are you okay?" he asked the top of my head.

I snorted. "Yeah, I'm good."

"I wasn't too rough with you?"

Turning my head, I propped myself up to meet his eyes. "No."

"Good." With his middle finger, he pushed a few strands of hair behind my ear. "Are you as hungry as I am?"

"I'm pretty hungry."

A few minutes later, I stepped out of my bathroom and found Elijah March in only his slacks, taking a pan off of my rack. The lean muscles in his stomach flexed under his skin, and I thanked *every* decision that had led me to this moment.

There was a saucepan heating on the stove already.

I pulled my messy hair over one shoulder and sat in a chair at the kitchen table. The sweatshirt and shorts I'd pulled out of my drawer suddenly felt very unsexy compared to Elijah.

"Dinner and a show, huh?" I joked.

One side of his mouth lifted. "You almost missed it. I'm putting my shirt on as soon as I start heating the olive oil."

"What are you making?"

"Nothing fancy. Sauteing some veggies, Parmesan couscous, and there's salmon in the oven." He shrugged. "I figured a simple dinner, and then we could put our attention to other things."

A thrill shot through my stomach. My body already ached pleasantly from our earlier *things*. "Felt pretty confident about how tonight was going to go, hmm?"

His green eyes flicked to me with promise. And it all felt so natural, having him here. I couldn't believe I hadn't built up the courage to text him for all those months. My memory had created a monument out of him. My unattainable first crush, and then the title of sex god—which, to be fair, he deserved—but also, he was just a really kind man.

"We've already proven my confidence to be correct." He reached for his white undershirt draped over the back of the chair next to me. The fabric stretched as he pulled it on.

"Well, I'm happy not to prove you wrong on this one."

Grinning, he drizzled olive oil on the heated pan. "Did you get everything done you wanted to when you came back today?"

I slouched and rested my cheek in my palm. The events of the past couple hours came back to me. I had hoped it wouldn't come to this, but I had figured it would. Anxiety slithered in my stomach. "No, I kinda got wrapped up in something I should have just ignored."

A crease formed between his eyebrows. "What's wrong?"

"The churches are creating an uproar around our auction."

"Why am I not surprised?" He shook his head. "I don't want to come off cynical, but my dad's at the top of this, isn't he?"

With an exhale, I nodded. "Yeah."

I'd read a couple of his posts on the community's page, and it hurt. He had struck at my character. Citing past moments where he'd supposedly gone against his gut and believed me to be virtuous—whatever the hell that meant. The venom in his words was hard to swallow, causing my stomach to twist and my head to swim. My vision had darkened around the edges as my blood pressure skyrocketed reading my neighbors' battle in the comments.

I knew my relationship with my mentor had been tarnished, but for him to openly condemn me made me want to hide. But I wouldn't.

I had a mess on my hands, and a way to clean it up. I would see this auction through. I would raise the money the humane society needed, and I would not cower in front of a bully.

No matter how badly I wanted to.

Elijah pressed his lips into a thin line and swallowed as if it was the only way to keep his anger in check. "I'm sorry, Hazel. You know you have a lot of support around you, right?"

I breathed in deeply. "Yeah."

"You wanna keep talking about it or something else?"

"Something else. I don't want to get bogged down with it."

He poured a plastic container of fresh veggies into the heated oil. "Have I ever told you about my friend Seb?"

"I don't think so."

"He's my business partner, and the reason we started the company. He got it in his head that we could do it for ourselves, and when he's determined about something, he doesn't let it go."

"Kinda like Nora?"

He stilled, considering the comparison, before a smile spread across his face. "Yeah, but way less calculated. He is just action. If he's working toward something and hits a block, he either breaks through the block or finds a way around it. He just never anticipates the block."

I rolled my eyes. "Nora anticipates every block, which makes her impossible to defeat."

His laughter, warm and easy, burst into the kitchen. "*Defeat*. You make her sound like a supervillain."

"She would make a spectacular supervillain."

"She really would."

"What is it exactly that you do?"

"Network securities."

I blinked. "That explains nothing to me."

He smiled and nodded. "I get that a lot. So, if a business' data is compromised, or ransomware is installed in their core infrastructure, we go in and take care of it."

"Ransomware?"

"Yeah, hackers will shut down websites until they receive funds."

"That's so mafia."

He snorted. "It is."

"That's an interesting job, though."

"It can be."

After just a few more minutes and conversation, Elijah carried our plates to the table. It looked and smelled delicious—the aroma of garlic and herb wafting in the air. Before sitting next to me, he reached behind him for a lemon he'd quartered off the counter.

"I hope you enjoy it." He shifted his shoulders with jerky motions.

"I'm sure I will. No one's ever cooked for me before."

"Really?"

"No. It looks really good."

Out of the corner of his eye, he watched me bring a bite of salmon to my mouth. I closed my eyes as the flavors mixed, bright and savory on my tongue.

I held my fork in front of my lips. "This is delicious. Thank you."

"You're welcome." He looked around as if he was searching for something. "You don't have a pet?"

Disappointment sank in my stomach. "No. I don't have the time to devote to a pet right now. Maybe when I don't have to work so much…"

We sipped white wine as we ate, and I was looking forward to having a second glass halfway through my first one, when my phone rang. I intended to ignore it, but Chelsea Thelen's name lit up my screen. Her son, Brock, was overseas, and she was watching his dog.

It can wait, I told myself, even as a crease formed between my eyebrows.

"Do you need to get that?" Elijah asked.

I chewed my lower lip and shook my head. "I just don't know why she'd be calling. She's not an after-hours caller like some pet owners."

"It's okay. You can answer it."

"I don't want—"

"It's okay. I get it; I have a job that has emergency hours. You should answer it."

"Okay, thank you. I'm so sorry." I waffled between apology and gratitude as my phone continued to buzz. Answering it, I pressed it to my ear. "Hey Chelsea, what's going on?"

Her voice came through strained, as if she was trying not to cry, and I was instantly more nervous about what she was going to say next. "It's Echo, Brock's dog…"

"Okay, what's going on with Echo?" My tone had assumed the assertive professional detachment I tended to use during high-stress vet visits.

"He seems like he's in a lot of pain—"

In the background, I heard one of her younger kids say, *"Mom, he's throwing up."*

"—He's been in this position where his butt is in the air, and his face and front paws are on the ground. At first, we thought he wanted to play, but his tail wasn't wagging. And he's been in that position for a while, and now he's throwing up."

"Mm-hmm, can you get him to the clinic?"

"He doesn't want to move, and he's too big for me to pick up."

"We'll go get him," Elijah said from behind me—clearly, he could hear the conversation happening on the phone.

"Send me your address, Chelsea. We'll get him in your car and you can follow us to the clinic."

"I don't even want to ask, but how much is it going to cost?" Through the phone, I could hear one of her kids let out an appalled, *"Mom, who cares about* money? *It's Echo."*

But both Chelsea and I knew just how much money played a factor. She was a single mom, with her oldest son serving in the military, and two younger kids between twelve and fifteen. And I didn't know how I would pay for this dog's care if she couldn't contribute any funds, but I also couldn't stand to think of Echo being in pain, knowing I could help him.

I sounded more confident than I felt as I said, "Let's take care of Echo, and we'll discuss payment later."

"I don't have much." Her shame came through the speaker, as if her lack of wealth was a character flaw.

"If it comes down to the clinic taking care of it, that's what we'll do."

"Thank you, Hazel."

"Send me your address; we'll be right there."

I stepped out of the examination room while Remi gave Echo fluids through an IV. Remi had agreed to assist me, even after I'd told him I didn't know if I'd be able to pay him.

He'd paused, then said, "I'd pay you for the distraction today."

I'd tilted my head.

His chest had fallen with a sigh. "Five years ago today, I got divorced…"

"I'm sorry."

"It's okay. It probably shouldn't fuck me up like it does. Anyway, I appreciate the distraction."

In the waiting room, I found Elijah reading on his phone. His ankle was crossed over his knee, and one hand hung loosely toward the tile floor. He'd insisted on staying until I was done, promising we could continue with our date, or he could drop me off at my house if I needed to rest instead. But seeing the way he looked like a GQ model in my uncomfortable vinyl waiting chairs, I was feeling less tired.

Chelsea sat at the other end of the room with her two daughters, looking anxious. She was only about ten years older than me, but with a kid sitting on each side of her, and another one old enough to serve overseas, those ten years seemed like a larger gap. She was beautiful, but exhaustion was deep-set in the slouch of her shoulders and heaviness of her eyes. The kind of weariness that needed more than a nap to stave away, as if it was a constant pressure clinging to her piggyback-style.

Her oldest looked up, her eyes the same gray shade as her mom's. "She's back."

Chelsea blinked, then met my gaze.

"Echo is okay." I held up my hand in a comforting gesture.

She deflated with a sigh. The tension left the stiffness of her spine, and she fell back into the chair, her head resting against the wall. I looked down at my sensible sneakers, giving her whatever privacy I could as she blinked back tears. I couldn't imagine having a son on the other side of the world, and then how terrible it would be to consider telling him that his dog wasn't well... or worse.

When she sat up straight again, I could still see her raw emotions. She swallowed and nodded for me to continue.

I sank into the seat across from her, and I felt more than saw Elijah's gaze on me—as if he was looking for any vulnerable spots I might need protecting. "Echo suffered from acute pancreatitis. It is not breed specific; sometimes it can be triggered by a fatty meal—"

"He only eats dog food," the oldest daughter interrupted.

The youngest sank deeper into her chair, and I worried she'd been slipping Echo human food. Not because it could have caused his condition, but because it likely didn't, and the little girl didn't deserve to feel guilty for it.

I smiled at the oldest, hoping to ease her defensiveness. "That's awesome. That's exactly what he should be eating." I shrugged. "Honestly, this just happens sometimes. He is not likely to suffer from this again, and it is very treatable. Are you comfortable talking about money here, or would you like to step into my office for more privacy?"

Chelsea's eyes flickered to her daughters, then to Elijah, who was already standing and moving to the front door.

"Can the girls go see Echo?" she asked.

"It's best that they don't. He's groggy right now and needs to rest."

"We can stay, Mom," the oldest daughter argued, her tone petulant in the way a teenager could produce. "Maybe we can help."

Chelsea shook her head.

The youngest daughter watched the power struggle with wide hazel eyes.

"Mom," the oldest begged, the word bound up tight.

Chelsea sighed. "Fine."

I lifted a questioning eyebrow. It wasn't until she nodded that I continued, "I'd like to keep him for two nights as I need to monitor his progress. Remi—Dr. Skogman," I corrected, "has already volunteered to take care of Echo until Monday. I can cover the cost of his treatment today, as well as the hospitalization."

"Hazel, that's too much. You have to run your business."

She wasn't wrong, but I lifted my chin and rolled my shoulders back. "We'll be okay. He's going to need special medicinal food for the next six months, and it is expensive." I handed her a piece of paper I had folded in my palm. "This is the wholesale price per bag, and how many bags I expect you'll need over the next few months. The total is at the bottom. Can you cover this expense?"

Chelsea's features remained blank as she looked at the amount. "I can."

I believed her, even if I could see her calculate the sacrifices she'd make to afford it. I crossed my legs and leaned forward. "Do you have any more questions?"

"Can I work here?" The oldest caught me off guard.

Chelsea's head hung toward the floor. "Baby, how many times do we have to go through this? I don't want you to have a job. You should be worrying about school. Let me worry about the money."

"Worry about the money? *All* you do is worry about the money. Let me help... I can get a job."

I interrupted before their argument could go any further. "I don't have a position you can do right now. Did you ask because you're interested in animals?"

She nodded sullenly.

"I always loved animals, too. You can always volunteer at the humane society."

The corner of Chelsea's mouth quirked up in a prideful smile. "Both girls do actually, a couple of times a month."

I beamed. "That's great."

We went over a few more details before I waved goodbye to them, though they stayed with me while I let Remi know I was leaving. They remained in the back of my mind as Elijah drove to my home. And as I tried to think of a way to tell him I needed to go to sleep—a.k.a. cry in the shower because this family deserved better. This community deserved better.

I didn't know what else I could do.

"That was very generous of you," he said after a few moments of silence.

I shrugged.

"Can you afford that?" he asked.

No.

"I'll be fine," I answered flatly.

"It's great how much you care, but you need to take care of yourself, too."

"I'll be fine."

"Okay. Can I help with anything?" He put the car into park in my driveway.

I met his eye. "I don't need any help, but thank you."

At my front door, he wrapped me in his arms with his chin resting atop my head. It was all so tender, safe.

"Do you want to be alone?" he asked.

"I think I need to be."

He kissed my hair. "I get it. I'll bring you coffee tomorrow."

"Thank you."

I sank into him, my cheek resting against the soft fabric of his sweater. My shoulders relaxed away from my ears as the hair atop my head tangled in his beard.

But it was my heart that really fell.

Chapter 13

Eliah

"Oh my god, Elijah." I liked Hazel moaning my name, even if it was only because of the quinoa dish I'd made for her.

"I'm glad you like it." I lifted a forkful to my mouth.

Her braid was frizzy and loose, and her mascara was flaking under her eyelashes. She'd taken off her white lab coat when she'd washed her hands, removing most of the pet fur from her body with it—even though there was still plenty on her dark slacks.

And I couldn't get over how beautiful she was.

Her eyes were lit with excited energy as she spoke. "It's delicious. Anyway, Brooks has to be so rung out. He was at three different farms today, and each of them had additional unexpected ailments. And seriously, cows and horses are so big, it can be exhausting to work with them. I don't know how he does it all the time."

"He's not that big of a guy, either."

She took a drink of water, her lips pursed around the straw. "He's not, but he is freakishly strong. It's crazy."

I snorted, wondering what that even meant, but she didn't elaborate.

"What'd you do today?" she asked.

"Nothing exciting, just a couple or hours of work. Then I made this," I gestured to the food on the table, "and came here."

"I feel so spoiled." She bounced in her seat, taking another bite.

In the past week and a half, I'd gotten used to seeing her more relaxed. The air around her felt lighter. I didn't know if it was because I made her feel that way, or if she was more confident around me, but either way, I loved it.

"Nothing could spoil you."

The break room was just big enough for a table for two, a mini fridge, and a microwave. It was a shame it wasn't a bigger space. The basement had been untapped real estate while my dad owned the clinic—he'd never cleared it from when my grandpa owned the business. Maybe one of the weekends I visited I could help Hazel clean it out. Who knew what the space could be used for?

I only had three more weeks until my vacation was over, and I was already missing all the little ways we spent time together—these lunches, cuddling on her couch until she fell asleep, and waking up together each morning.

My leaving had become a conversation we needed to have, but I hadn't figured out how to bring it up. I kept reminding myself that we were only a few hours apart, but the more I fell for her, the more those hours—the distance—seemed to grow.

I was staring into space when she pressed her thumb between my eyebrows. Blinking, I watched as a satisfied smile spread across her face and she let her hand fall back to her side. She considered me for a moment. "Better. What had your forehead all creased up?"

Well, this is as much opportunity as I'm gonna get.

"I don't want to leave in three weeks," I answered.

"Hmm. Yeah, all right, the creases make sense."

"You'll allow it?"

"I'll allow it."

I ran my hands down the tops of my thighs. "Do we talk about how we continue *this* when I'm gone?"

She paused for a minute. "I don't want *this* to end."

I grinned down at the tabletop. "Good. Me, either."

"So..."

"I think I could make the drive here three out of four weekends—"

"Oh my god, you'd be willing to come here that often?"

"Could you drive to me on the fourth weekend?" I still couldn't meet her eye. It felt like I was telling her just how much I liked her without actually saying the words, or knowing if she felt the same.

"Yeah. I can do that."

It wasn't exactly a declaration of love, but all the tension in my body released in a single breath.

She tapped her fingertips on the table between us. "It feels really weird to ask, but like, how long do we do that? We've only been dating for a couple of weeks, but would you even consider..."

"Moving back here?"

She nodded.

Leaving this place had felt like a new start, as if chains had been released from my body. And I had needed it at the time—someplace new, where I was more than the sum of my past written in scandals. But I had always known an end game with Hazel would mean moving back here. I hadn't realized considering it wouldn't feel like slipping those chains back on.

I laced my fingers in hers, running my thumb across the hills and valleys of her knuckles. "If we're good, and we know what we want from each other, I would move back here."

A smile tugged at the corner of her mouth. "Okay."

"Okay?"

"I like this plan. We can FaceTime, and text throughout the day, and I'm gonna miss you a lot, but..."

I waited as she chewed on her lower lip.

She swallowed. "I would be pretty heartbroken if we just stopped."

I squeezed her fingers, and when she met my eyes I said, "I would too."

We sat there, grinning at each other, making promises without saying a word.

Ransom's garage smelled like motor oil and lumber. He and Sterling leaned against the workbench, talking about their grandparents and sipping beers. I'd switched to water a few hours ago, making sure I'd be able to drive to Hazel's when she got out of work. Sitting on a metal stool, I silently hoped to not get grease on my jeans. I wasn't the work-toughened kind of man Grand Ridge usually turned out. Most of the guys I grew up with would consider it a waste of time to care about the condition of my clothes, but then again, I'd helped most of them look presentable for the upcoming auction.

It was The Sterling Show, as Ransom and I had dubbed it when we were kids. He was telling stories and cracking jokes, and we were his avid audience and hecklers. We were about to enter into one of my favorite tales about the time he'd gotten a terrible sunburn on some unfortunate places. Ransom and I shared a shake of our heads, but Sterling wasn't deterred.

My phone buzzed, and I pulled it out of my pocket, expecting a text from Hazel. Instead, it was my mom. *Is Hazel okay?*

Concerned, I lost the ability to breathe for a moment. *What happened? Why wouldn't she be okay?*

Pastor Lou did a service on the auction. They just posted it to the community page.

"Shit." I groaned. I remembered being the "inspiration" of sermons given by the pastor of my dad's church. Even if Lou didn't call anyone out by name, the town was small enough that everyone knew who he was talking about.

They had known it was me, and his personal vendetta against me, when he'd pounded on the pulpit, warning all of the young women to guard their virtue from serpents in the grass.

He had sway in this community—even more than my dad—and I knew firsthand how he could ruin a person's standing.

It'd happened to Mom, too. I didn't want her to think Hazel would be alone the way Mom had been.

I'll make sure she's okay. Thanks for letting me know, I texted.

"What's up?" Sterling asked.

"Pastor Lou did a service against the auction, and there's a recording. That old bastard."

"Fuck." Ransom's face typically rested at stern, but it turned dangerous with the slightest twitch of his mouth.

Pocketing my phone, I didn't bother searching for the video. "I gotta go find Hazel."

"Yeah, man. I'm texting my sisters for help to turn the narrative. I'll get this fixed up." Sterling looked down at his phone as he typed out messages.

"Thanks."

I drove to the clinic first, where her car was parked in the lot. There was still a half hour before close, so I walked through the front door.

Relief washed over Nora's face when she saw me. "She's in her office. She made me come out here, or I'd be back there with her."

I could practically see Hazel telling Nora she was okay, and Nora should do the closing tasks.

"Yeah, I get it." I walked through the door between the lobby and the front desk.

It only took a few long strides down the hallway to get to her. The doorknob for her office wasn't latched, and I pushed it open. She had her hands pressed to her chest as she sucked in deep breaths. Her eyes were wide and watering when they landed on me.

"I'm fine." She gasped.

"I know." I didn't argue with her as I took a step closer, prepared to hold her or give her space, depending on what she needed.

"I'm fine," she repeated.

"Yeah."

"It's just they're…" she had to stop to catch her breath before she continued, "saying so many things about me. That I took advantage of your dad. That I'm sinful and disloyal. That I can't be trusted because of the company I keep, but like, what the fuck does that mean?"

Me.

Did she really not know? Or was she sparing my feelings?

"It's fine, baby. Just breathe. I know it feels terrible, but it'll pass. Just breathe." I held my arms out, and she fell into them. Holding her, I rocked back and forth, making shushing noises. Her tears leaked onto my shirt. Little by little, her lungs filled with air—expanding a little more with each inhalation. "Good job."

"I don't know what to do," she whispered into my chest.

"Keep doing what you're doing. It doesn't feel like it now, but this community is changing. This bullshit might not be eradicated, but you're not alone. And that alone is progress. Sterling, Bet, and Lola are already on the defense for you. Hell, my mom told me about all this. She was looking out for you."

She squeezed me tighter. "You're here."

"Yeah, baby. I'm here. I've got you."

And god, she had me. I was so wrapped up in her. Tangled in her threads. Weaving into me, pulling out my better fibers.

After one more slow exhale, she pulled back. "Oh no, I ruined your shirt."

I looked down to see black mascara smudged on the loose cotton. I cupped her cheek and lifted her chin to meet my eye. "Who cares?"

"I really liked it."

"You can have it to sleep in. You'll look cute as hell."

She snorted. "Maybe after I clean up."

I pressed a kiss to her forehead, taking in her pinkened nose and cheeks. "You're cute as hell now."

She leaned her forehead on my shoulder. "What if the backlash continues to grow, and people start canceling their appointments?"

Her concern was legitimate. "Cancel culture" had been a long-standing tradition here, well before it was acknowledged and named by society as a whole. *Conform to our beliefs, or else*, had been the reigning unspoken threat.

"You think Nora would stand for that?" I asked.

Hazel let out a watery laugh. "Thank god, she's on my side."

"She is."

Turning her head, she rested a cheek on my chest. "I just wish everyone would stop talking about me, you know?"

I snorted. "Yeah, I know."

I didn't know a solution, and all of the comforting words I could say felt trite, so I just held her as her heart rate continued to slow to its normal pace. I hoped that the world faded away for her, the way it did for me, when she was in my arms.

Chapter 14

Elijah

"You've been busy," Mom commented with a lift of her eyebrow. It was a strange déjà vu to be in this town, with my mom insinuating she knew something about me I hadn't told her. Only this time, I wasn't in trouble... and I was a grown man.

The espresso machine sputtered, steaming milk for someone else's latte. A mom and dad with two small children sat on two teal loveseats, their North Face coats marked them as tourists. On the coffee table between, their drinks were forgotten in a mad dash to clean a hot chocolate spill. Warm and colorful, it was the kind of cafe that felt lived in—someplace a spill would be cleaned up and nothing was forced to be pristine.

"I guess so. Just hanging out with Hazel before I have to go back to Detroit in a couple of weeks." It was true. But it didn't express how I was constantly preoccupied thinking about her. Or how being with her felt... *right*. I didn't know how to explain it—and I wasn't going to try.

How two weeks was too short a time to have left of these moments.

The past few days, had been hard on her. But the sermon was already growing distant—much to Sterling's efforts.

I lifted my latte to my lips and looked out the cafe window at the dark blue waters of Grand Ridge Lake. Autumn leaves floated on its flat surface, and a teenage couple sat on a bench by the beach. Their mannerisms were jerky and awkward, the way young people were when they didn't know how to behave with someone they liked. It was sweet.

I could see how people fell in love with this place. I was beginning to feel like it was possible for me, too.

"Oh, I don't mean your time spent with our lovely veterinarian."

We both knew exactly what she was insinuating, but I was working very hard to keep that a secret.

This town was not made for secrets.

I needed my plans to remain quiet for one more week, that was it. At that point, I'd have it all set up and I could tell Hazel about the community fund I'd established with the help of the town clerk and head librarian. It would benefit households that weren't able to afford vet care. It'd require charitable events or crowd funding from time to time, but it would take some of the burden off of Hazel.

Mom squinted at my blank expression before flicking one hand. "Okay, don't tell me. But I still think it's very sweet."

"You know this rumor mill goes in both directions. You're renting the cabin for another month?"

"I am." She beamed. "I'm really enjoying myself. I figured, why not? I wanna remember what November is like up here."

"Did you also rent a four-wheel drive vehicle with snow tires?"

"I did."

"Okay, then I'll worry less."

"Oh, son, you don't need to worry. Turns out, there's a lot of people up here that will help me if I get stuck in a ditch." Her eyebrows twitched, and she got a faraway look in her eyes. "I forgot how much I liked being a part of this place."

I made a "Hmm" sound of understanding.

She looked up at the clock above the cash register. "Well, I should get to Bettie's Pour House. Ginny is driving me to Deb Creger's for Euchre Club."

I narrowed my eyes in mock suspicion. "Now I see where you're getting your intel."

Mom leaned forward and whispered, "Those women know *everything* that's going on around here."

Laughing, I stood to give her a hug goodbye. "It's about time I head out, too. Gonna go for a walk on the beach with Hazel before we get dinner."

"It's a great day for it. She seems wonderful; I can't wait to meet her. I only vaguely remember her as a kid."

"It's still new."

Didn't mean I wasn't in over my head.

"You seem…" Mom tilted her head, considering me. "Committed."

"I've been committed before," I argued.

"Of course. It's just different."

A twitch of my eyebrow was my only acknowledgment.

"Okay, well, I'm off. Be safe. I love you."

"I love you, too. Have fun."

I ordered a vanilla latte with an extra shot of espresso for Hazel, and promised to tell her that Millie said hi. She was a tall woman, with an easy smile. And then, I left Country Grounds a few minutes later.

Taking in the beautiful fall day—my breath coming out in swirling steam—I turned the corner toward the vet clinic. A man just a few feet away made me come to an abrupt stop. He was almost exactly my height and stature.

I knew I'd run into him eventually, but seeing my dad without a warning shot anxiety through me.

When I'd cut my visit short last summer, he and I had not ended on good terms. I couldn't remember a time we ever had been.

His venomous, harshly whispered words, "How did you come from me?" had me, on more than one occasion, considering going back to therapy. It couldn't be healthy to imagine cutting him just as deeply as he had me. I probably shouldn't circle back in my memory to the disgusted way he looked at me.

"Don't make her pay for your sins," he'd warned. And I was pretty sure Hazel was paying for what he perceived as my sins. In fact, his smear campaign against the auction was probably done in an attempt to hurt me, and not necessarily Hazel.

Unfortunately, I wasn't catching any of that heat.

But Hazel certainly was—on the internet, in haughty side-eyed glances at the grocery store, and with a dip in appointments at the clinic.

She just wanted to raise money for the humane society. Money she needed because Dad loved control more than he loved anything else.

"Son." A muscle jerked in his tight jaw.

"Dad." My voice was void of all emotion. I didn't have anything else to say to him, and I moved to walk around him.

He stayed where he was, not blocking my way, but not making it easy for me to go around him, either. "I told you to stay away from her."

I willed myself to keep going, to not give him the satisfaction of a response.

"I knew you'd take her down to your level. I should never have let you come here last year."

I had taken a step past him, but despite my better judgment, I turned to face him.

"What exactly *is* my level? I don't pretend to be anything but who I am. You're the one hurting people, not me. I've been a grown man for a while now. You don't tell me what I can do anymore—and *that's* what you hate about me."

"No, son, I hate your sinful ways, and the way you draw good people to sin. You make good people do bad things."

It took a force of will not to crush the paper cup containing Hazel's latte. Memories from my past rushed to the surface, rippling out old shame I still struggled to rebuke.

"I didn't make anyone do anything," I stated, reminding me just as much as telling him. Despite the way I had been depicted, I hadn't been the devil tempting Eve to taste from the Tree of Life; I'd just been a boy with a crush on a girl.

He shook his head, disappointed as ever.

"But are you really mad at what I did? Or are you mad that when I got caught, it threatened your image?" I demanded.

For a moment, I thought I'd struck a nerve, because he looked over my shoulder. I got sick pleasure from it.

Then his lips twisted into a sad smile. Jerking his chin toward something over my shoulder, he said, "That's the kind of man she deserves."

I twisted my neck and saw Hazel walking with Dennis to his truck. His dog trotted next to him, the leash held loosely in his hand.

They looked good together. Easy. Natural.

I was grateful my dad couldn't see my face as his words hit their mark.

"Give her time, and she'll see the truth of it for herself," he commented sagely, as if passing on some fatherly wisdom.

With my shoulders back and my head up, I walked away from him. But I'd hesitated too long, and I knew that he knew he'd hurt me.

Being weak in front of him was worse than the pain.

"Are you cold?" Hazel's voice near my right shoulder pulled me out of the recesses of my mind. The wind whipped around us, sending the loose hair at her temples across her face. The evergreens and gray sky behind her gave the concern in her brown eyes a solemnity. Instead of her usual warm smile, her beautiful lips were pursed.

I glanced behind us at the long lines of shoe prints in the sand and wondered when was the last time I'd spoken as we walked Lake Michigan's shoreline. "No, I'm not cold. Are you?"

The corner of her mouth twitched up. "You saw how many layers I put on before we left my office."

My laugh came out in one puff of steam.

"I'm not cold," she went on. "You've been quiet."

"Yeah, sorry. How was your day?" I took her gloved hand in mine, and we continued down the beach. To my left, the stone-colored water crashed with wave after wave—white bubbles against the darkness, stretching as far as the eye could see. The surface was rougher than normal, but it didn't have the large curling waves of the ocean.

Her shoulders fell. "Busy. It's always busy. Not with patients, unfortunately, but with stuff to do. I'm falling behind."

I stopped and tugged her arm so we could speak face-to-face. "Can I help with anything?"

"I don't want to bother you with it."

"I *want* you to."

"I don't even know what you could do... I don't... I don't know how to give any of these tasks to someone else."

I nodded. "I get that. I think it'd be good if you did, though."

She tightened, her shoulders drawing back up and her spine straightening.

I kept my voice gentle, hoping my words wouldn't hit a sore spot. "Hazel, you can't keep this pace up. It's taking so much from you."

I knew she was sleeping more than she had been before we'd started dating—taking more time outside of the clinic in general. But even this much work wasn't healthy. The dark circles under her eyes were still there, even if they were lighter. The reason she was spending less time working was because of me. Would she go back to overworking at the rate she had been before I'd arrived?

If she could just share the load with her staff... I could see all the weight carried on her shoulders—and it was a lot.

"What am I supposed to do?" Her tone made it clear I should tread carefully.

"You're doing cleaning, and stocking, and ordering. Give those tasks to someone else."

She scoffed. "I can't do that. Everyone's working fifty-plus hours a week, and then I'm going to be like, 'By the way, here's more work that was *not* in your job description. Enjoy.'"

"How many hours are you working, Hazel?"

"Less than I need to be because I'm spending time with you," she bit back. Shaking her head, she took a calming breath. "I'm sorry. I want to be here."

She shook her head again. "I'm really sorry. I'm just overwhelmed and tired, and I don't know how to make everything work."

Feeling like she might need to move again, I turned us back the way we came and started walking. "What about that woman's daughter? The one who wanted the job?"

Her lifted eyebrow could only be described as annoyed. "You mean, the woman who said her daughter couldn't have a job?"

"There are other high schoolers. You could hire someone for two, three-hour shifts a week. There are things that only you can do, but things like advertising or community outreach—things that actually bring in more business—can be given to others. Unloading that work could pay for itself." After a moment of silence, I asked, "Do you want to keep talking about this or do you want to let it be?"

"Let it be."

"Okay." I lifted our joined hands and kissed the back of hers. Her glove was warm against my cold lips.

"You said you ran into your dad?"

And he drudged up old memories better left in the past.

I hummed confirmation, but didn't elaborate.

"Is that why you were being so quiet?"

"Probably."

"Wanna talk about it?"

The knot in the pit of my stomach tightened. "It was just a playlist of all his greatest hits."

Now it was her voice that was gentle. "What are those?"

I kicked at a clump of frozen sand, which flew in every direction. "It all boils down to the fact that he thinks I'm not worthy. That I'm not good."

That you *would be better off with someone else.*

"Not worthy of what?"

"Acceptance, forgiveness... love."

She stopped, the toes of her shoes planted in the sand, and I turned to face her. The firm set of her jaw, and the conviction in her eyes, made the center of my chest feel tender, and I looked out at the turmoil playing across the water's surface.

"You are good," she said simply. "You are worthy of love."

"I know," I mumbled. Needing to move, I began to walk again, and she joined me—her feet falling in rhythm next to mine.

Her tone was softer, almost swallowed by the wind. "I'm falling for you."

My step stuttered before I brought us to a stop again.

"Is it too soon to say that?" She tugged her hand from mine and ineffectively smoothed it over her hair.

I shook my head. The words were trapped inside my throat, caged in tight behind years of hurt, blocked by wounds I thought I'd healed in therapy. I wanted to tell Hazel, but my pain had been dredged up too recently.

My expression felt hard, my features set to portray impenetrability—jaw firm, eyebrows drawn, eyes narrowed at nothing over her shoulder. "Are you really?"

"Yes." She wrapped her arms around me and pressed her cheek against my chest.

I hugged her closer, resting my chin atop her head. It was easier to tell her than it was to accept her statement. "I'm falling for you, too."

Already fallen, actually.

The air around her felt charged, shifting with new energy.

The waves continued to clap, and the wind continued to rush past pulling and pushing us. But I could have sworn that the sun broke through the dark gray blanket of clouds, making everything warmer and brighter.

Tilting her head up, she stretched to her toes. Her mouth was soft as it brushed mine. I drew her in, as if everything I needed could be found in the delicate skin of her lips. She sighed and melted into my arms, and I was helpless to her silent demand. My cage's doors curled open, and the steel barriers that had protected me gave way under the slightest urging from Hazel.

I wanted to open to her completely. Draw her in. Lay bare. All of my wounds in full view.

I just hoped she would still want me after she saw them.

Chapter 15

Hazel

Benji's was quieter now that tourist season was nearly done. There was maybe a weekend for color cruisers—people who drove around, looking at the changing leaves clinging to the trees. The autumn chill had grown too frigid—my cheeks were chapped and raw after our walk—but the cold couldn't touch the hot flurry of emotions inside my chest.

It was even enough to quiet the constant "to-do" list that was always growing larger. But maybe Elijah was right; maybe I could pass some tasks on to others... Maybe.

He sat across the table from me, his body relaxed in the booth. He looked down at our joined hands.

We hadn't spoken much through dinner. Every time I opened my mouth, his eyes locked onto mine, conveying a promise that stole my breath. Instead, we waited for his credit card to be returned so we could go back to my place.

I was so deep in my anticipation that I didn't notice Tara Nelson until she was standing at the edge of our table. Surprised, I blinked up at her stern, round face, surrounded by bleached blond curls held in place by a matting of hairspray.

"Hi," I said. She was my parent's age, and I didn't know her well. Mostly, I knew her from when I went to school with her daughter, Lily. I remember Tara was always calling the school to argue about a poor grade she thought was undeserved.

She fixed her icy-blue gaze. "Hello." Shifting her attention to Elijah, she spat out, "You should never have come back here."

The man at the table next to us glanced over his shoulder.

I sank deeper in the booth. Blood rushed in my ears, and I felt my cheeks warm. My stomach instantly felt too full and queasy.

Elijah's fingers flexed, tightening his grip on my hand. Outwardly, his demeanor didn't change—his arm casually draped across the back of the booth, his shoulder lounged against the wall—but his green eyes took on a sharp focus I hadn't seen before.

His tone was almost bored when he said, "Okay."

"You're trouble, and you don't belong here," Mrs. Nelson growled.

"Noted. Are we done?"

I didn't know how he could seem so calm, especially when I was stuck in the freeze mode of fight or flight.

She shook her head—and not a single hair moved. "Your father is a good man. You have always been a bad son."

Again, only the slightest twitch of his fingers betrayed any agitation he might have felt.

My spine straightened, and my chin jutted out. "That's not true. He's *good*."

It wasn't exactly an elegant speech, but the corner of Elijah's mouth lifted.

"And *you*." She focused her narrowed eyes at me, her mouth pinched in distaste. "*You* took advantage of him."

"What?" I sputtered. I wasn't used to doing anything that drew negative attention; in fact, most people didn't even notice me. And just then, I wished I could fly back under the radar.

Go back to being unnoticed.

"You swept in and *stole* the clinic from him."

"Stole? I *bought* it."

"He built that business—"

"No," Elijah interrupted. "My grandpa built that business. And while my dad ran it okay—not great—he certainly didn't build anything, he coasted. I'm guessing what you're actually upset about is the upcoming auction."

She scoffed. "I've heard about your *auction*."

"Good. Sterling has been working really hard getting the word out."

"Our town used to be better than this. It's shameful how quickly you've tainted us, but I would expect nothing less of someone like *you*."

From the bar, Ben's head jerked up at her raised voice, and he took unhurried strides in our direction.

Elijah sat up and crossed his arms on top of the table. "Every single one of the men involved volunteered their time to help someone in this community, while also raising money for the humane society. None of them asked you to be the morality police or fight on their behalf. But you're still welcome to participate. Bring your money; I hear Brooks is auctioning off gardening. *Scandalous*."

"Everything okay here?" Ben leaned a hip against our booth, taking in the scene.

Picking up his water cup, Elijah raised it to an inch from his mouth. "Yeah. Tara was just leaving."

She clenched her jaw. "You are defacing your business by hosting that *auction* here."

Ben shrugged. "Well, if you feel that strongly about it, I guess we won't see you on Taco Tuesdays anymore. Have a good night."

"No, you won't." She glared at me.

"That's too bad." But the neutral expression on Ben's face did not convey the same message as his words.

She opened her mouth again, but he cut her off, "It's really best that you just leave." Setting our receipt and Elijah's credit card down, Ben blocked Mrs. Nelson from continuing to berate us. "Keep the table as long as you'd like, no rush."

For a couple of moments, nothing happened. She didn't leave, and he didn't move from our table. I could feel all eyes fixed on us, pricking like needles on my skin. Then, finally, she huffed and turned away, ranting the whole way to the door—using language she would never say in church.

"You two okay?" he asked.

"Yeah," Elijah answered, his voice steely.

I nodded, but my wide eyes must not have been convincing because Ben's eyebrows drew down in concern.

Elijah leaned closer to me. "You want me to take you home?"

I nodded again, not sure I could trust my voice. My embarrassment was sharp, and my eyes stung with unshed tears—which was humiliating all on its own. He wrapped a protective arm around my waist, but I couldn't help thinking that it'd be easier for me to hide if he wasn't right next to me.

Elijah was the source of attention everywhere he went, without his ever trying to be. Just being near him brought me under more scrutiny.

Elijah's chest was firm and warm against my cold cheek. We were watching a TV show I wasn't paying attention to, my mind wandering.

Wander might not have been the correct word. It implied that my thoughts meandered, took multiple routes, contemplated many things, and that wasn't true. I had one thing on my mind—would my reputation be so tarnished by the auction that the clinic would fail, and I'd be buried under a pile of business loan debt as well as school loans, and I'd ruin the lives of my employees because of it?

Elijah's fingers paused in my hair. "Care to share your thoughts with the group?"

"I'm fine," I lied. We'd already talked about Mrs. Nelson, and I just wanted to move past it. I didn't want my anxiety ruining any more of our night.

"Baby," he murmured against the top of my head, "you're thinking too loudly for me to hear the show."

My lips twitched on one side in something like a smile. "Sorry, I'll think quieter."

He lifted the remote and the TV screen went black with the click of a button. In just a few awkward shifts, I was seated half on his lap, half on the sofa cushion, and he was looking directly into my eyes. "Talk to me."

"I'm just spiraling a little."

"Where are you spiraling to?"

I opened my mouth, but then closed it, too humiliated to tell him. Wasn't I supposed to be above anyone's opinions of me? Especially someone as mean-spirited as Mrs. Nelson?

"The town feeling too small?" he offered.

I nodded.

"You can talk to me about it."

Biting my lower lip, I shook my head. "I already have."

He rubbed the back of his neck with one hand. "I told you about running into my dad earlier."

"Yeah."

"He insinuated something from when I was a teenager. It... You probably heard of it."

I cringed, knowing exactly what he was talking about. It was the top moment mentioned whenever Elijah's name was brought up in a group.

Remember that time... But the way he was leading into it now, with his shoulders tight and his eyes looking anywhere but at me, I suspected it'd gotten warped in the retelling.

It fit well with the trail of broken hearts narrative that followed Elijah.

"Pastor Lou's daughter and the church shed?" I asked.

"That's the one." His eyes didn't hold any of their usual light as he looked down at the floor. "So, I was seventeen, and my parents were recently divorced. There was so much shit being said about my mom, and I was trying hard to be a good kid and not draw any bad attention. That summer, my dad volunteered me to mow at the church—it's got that two acre-lawn."

He waited long enough that I hummed a confirmation.

His chest rose before breathing out in one big puff. "Anyway, Hannah—Lou's daughter—was doing flowerbeds and stuff. We'd been around each other a lot through church functions, but we never spent time together. It wasn't until that summer that I got to know her, and I started to like her. It took a couple of weeks for me to work up the nerve to ask her out. She said she liked me too, but she couldn't date someone like me."

My mouth hung open. "Someone like you?"

His eyes flicked to mine and then away. "Yeah, at that point I'd dated a couple different girls, and been caught partying. Hannah said we could date in secret, and I thought that was fine."

"Elijah." I waited until he lifted his head. "You didn't deserve that."

Something cold whispered down my spine, remembering how he and I had a secret affair. Had it made him remember that time?

"I know. I thought I did at the time."

"You didn't."

"Thank you. But everyone knew she was good, and I wasn't. What we did wasn't really *dating*; it was mostly just talking behind the shed. It was nice. Wholesome. It took weeks before we even kissed."

My stomach twisted, knowing that the rug was about to be pulled out. His story gave insight not only to the way the town could twist the truth, but also on the boy I'd idolized at the time.

"By the time we got caught... we were past the kissing stage. I don't blame Hannah for not speaking up when her dad started saying terrible things about me. She was scared."

He tapped his fingers on the armrest. "But it finalized everyone's idea of me. For months, it felt like everyone was talking about me. Like everything I did was proof that my mom didn't have control over me, and I was a bad influence on... *everyone*. It wasn't who I was, but it was what they thought of me. It was shitty."

Wrapping his arms around my waist, he held me. "If you don't want to talk about it, you don't have to, but I just want you to know that I know firsthand what's going on."

I pulled back to stare into his beautiful eyes. This close, I could see a ring of dark brown circling the green.

"I hate the attention I'm getting right now," I managed to say before my throat grew too tight.

His arms flexed—protecting me. "You have a lot of support, though. Ask Echo's owner what she thinks of you. Or Patricia over at the humane society. Have you noticed how loudly she's supporting this fundraiser?"

I shook my head, my eyes stinging.

A smile spread across his face, so beautiful and quick. "She's not holding back her two cents."

"No?"

"No." He lifted his eyebrows, the grin still on his face. "She's support-ive."

"It's hard to hear the good stuff when I feel so scraped up by the bad stuff."

He rubbed soothing circles on my back.

"I feel like I should be above it. Like, why do I care what they think?"

"Because you do."

I lifted a shoulder, still not happy with the explanation.

"I don't want to. I want to be bold like Nora, or at least apathetic like Brooks."

"You aren't them. You do care."

I hid my face in his shoulder. "It's embarrassing."

"I don't think it's anything to be embarrassed about." He pressed his lips to my temple. "It's okay to be you, Hazel."

His acceptance was a balm for my wounds. A safe place to vent my insecurities. He kept opening himself up to me, letting me see his vulnerability. I just wished he could see just how good he was.

I cupped his face in my hands. "It's okay to be you, too."

The tension rushed out of his shoulder, and his sigh tickled through my hair.

I lowered my mouth to his. I tried to pour all my feelings into the soft pressure of our lips. He held me closer, tighter, as if his arms alone could shield me from our small town. His mouth parted, and his tongue swiped over mine. I moved my hands down to rub gentle circles into his shoulders, and slowly, they eased.

The last thread of my defenses broke; the veil that I'd left as a fail-safe, the one I'd never unwrapped around my heart. The one that whispered, *Just in case*, was gone. And behind it, I was left unprotected.

It was terrifying.

It was overwhelming.

It was right.

The strong hold of his fingers on my thighs, and the way his mouth demanded more… it was all right.

I'd gone over the edge, but I'd gone over in his arms. I trusted him to not let me fall. If I ended up careening too fast into something unknown, I knew he'd be there with me.

He rolled, placing me under him on the sofa. Kissing over my clothes, he moved down my body, his touch reverent.

He bit the flesh of my thigh before looking up at me through his lashes. "Do you even know the little noises you make?"

I bit my lip and shook my head.

His grin turned devilish as he unbuttoned my jeans only to reveal wool-lined leggings underneath. "I miss your dresses."

Giggling, I said, "They'll be back in the spring."

"They better." He made a show of peeling my layers down my legs.

By the time I was in only my underwear, we were both laughing and hot. My laughter caught in my throat when he scraped his teeth along the inside of my knee.

His groan vibrated against my skin. "Like that fucking noise right there. I want more of it."

He hooked my underwear on his finger and pulled them to the side. He took in the sight of me—my legs open, my breasts rising and falling with each short breath. His eyes were dark and hungry when they met mine, and I whimpered. One corner of his mouth turned upward, and he licked his lips. My core clenched as he lowered, never taking his gaze from mine.

His breath brushed hot against my skin.

I gasped.

The grip he had on my panties tightened, pulling them tight against my ass. He licked my clit once and moaned deep in his throat as if I tasted good, satisfying. My hips jerked.

His free hand snaked up my sweater, and his fingers found my sensitive, hardened nipples over my bra. My back arched at his touch as my hands tunneled into his hair. His beard tickled my inner thigh as he flicked his tongue over my sensitive nub.

I lost track of everything except for the way he sucked and drew me closer to my climax. I wanted it; I wanted the waves of electricity washing down my scalp and spine.

But I needed him.

I needed to look into his eyes while he was inside me.

"Elijah," I pleaded. "I need you."

He opened his eyes and sat back on his heels. His lips and chin glistened in the dim light of my living room. He looked incredible, half-dazed with lust. "What do you need, baby?"

"Just you."

For a moment, he didn't move. He held me trapped in his eyes.

His lips formed the words, *Just me*.

Running a hand over his mouth, he swallowed. He reached down and undid the button of his pants. "Take off your sweater."

While I struggled to undress, I heard him stand and push his pants to the carpet. By the time I got the multiple layers of shirts off, Elijah was completely naked, laying a throw blanket on the carpet. The muscles in his back flexed with each movement. He was artful and lovely. Being able to see him like that made my chest tighten, as if my heart had grown too large for its cage.

Smirking, he asked, "You made it out of there?"

I giggled. I loved that even when our emotions and chemistry were intense, he could still make me laugh.

"It looked touch and go for a second there."

I reached behind my back to undo the clasp of my bra. "It was."

"Come here." He lowered to sit on the floor, resting an arm on his propped knee. He was draped in lights and shadows, and nothing else.

The blanket was soft under my bare feet. He ran a hand up the back of my thigh to grip my ass, urging me closer, before placing kisses low on my stomach. Desire throbbed through me carried on my pulse, but I wanted to be open to him. To be bare to him in a way I had never done before.

I buried my fingers in his hair. Gently, I pushed him to lift his chin and look at me. "Just you," I whispered again.

We'd already discussed our comfort with not using protection. His eyes never left mine as he leaned back on his arms, and I lowered to my knees. I hovered above him. Placing him at my entrance, I sank down. He slipped inside me, filling me.

I sighed, my head falling back.

After a few grounding breaths, Elijah took hold of my ankle to move it behind his back and then the other. Wrapped around each other, we started pulling apart and coming back together, over and over. His mouth sought mine as my hands memorized the path of his spine. Hugging him tighter.

Our hearts beat against our chests so closely, I couldn't tell which was his and which was mine.

I was shivering, my feelings too potent. They'd become something more than an idea—more than a possibility, more than an inclination. They were so real, I could practically hold them in my hand. Like cupping a fire that didn't burn, something I could pass from my fingers to his.

Tears stung my eyes as I came.

His forehead pressed into my sweaty neck as he shook and shuddered. He pulled in deep gasps as his fingers gripping my sides loosened one by one.

"Hazel," he spoke my name as if it was sacred.

I said his name in the exact same way, "Elijah."

Chapter 16

Hazel

I was running late.

So goddamn late.

I needed to leave *right now*, or I'd be tacky late, instead of fashionably late to *my* auction. I was just trying to catch up on some work. I set alarms on my phone, and as they alerted me to the dwindling time, I ignored them.

Now I had my hair in a messy bun, though I was pretending was messy in a cute way. The mascara I swiped on my lashes had smudged—something I hoped to fix in the car... When I found my keys.

I'd been in every single room of this clinic... they could be anywhere.

"Fuck." I hissed, dashing from the front office to my office in the back of the building. To my unbelievable good luck, my keys were sitting atop my desk. I snatched them and spun back the way I came in one movement. Swinging the door closed behind me, I strode half a step away when I heard the door slam against the interior wall of my office.

I had to figure out something. I needed that damn door to close. Hopefully, the doorknob hadn't dented the drywall. I was in too much of a hurry to check.

Practically flying out the staff entrance, I didn't grab the railing as I ran down the steps out of fear of splinters in my gloves.

It probably happened because I was pounding down the stairs like a stampede of wild horses, but when my sneaker hit the bottom step, it cracked. I plunged toward the cement walkway. Luckily, my other foot was already extended to catch me, and I jogged forward with my arms flailing until I caught my balance again.

The weatherworn wood was V-shaped, shards poking upward.

I stood there with my mouth open, shaking my head.

"You have to be kidding me," I whined.

Any feelings of anger or sadness were overcome by disappointment and being overwhelmed. I was trying so hard, but not hard enough. I'd allowed myself to become distracted, and because of that, I'd almost broken my ass—or more accurately, my ankle.

"Thank god it was me and not someone else."

Clenching my jaw, I didn't allow myself to consider the trouble I could have gotten into if someone else had fallen.

I tried to shake off the feeling on my way to my car.

Rounding the block brought Benji's Place's parking lot into view.

It was packed.

I had never seen it this full.

"Oh my god," I whispered to the windshield.

After parking in the lot of a neighboring business, I went through the employee's only entrance.

Emily, the bartender, lifted a case of something. "There you are! We've been looking for you."

"Uh... yeah, I—" I stammered, and shrugged. "I'm late."

She threw her head back, her blond ponytail swinging. "Yeah, you are. Girlie, it is crazy out there. You have to go and say, 'Thank you,' to start the show."

My stomach flipped sickeningly. I tripped on nothing as I followed her out. "I have to say something?"

"I think so."

That was all the explanation I got before she exited through the swinging doors. When they swung open, the sounds of people—mostly women, talking and laughing—carried to the backroom. The roaring cacophony matched the volume of my internal thoughts, which were screaming, *I cannot speak in front of all these people!*

Sweat beaded on my forehead, and I hadn't even been handed a microphone yet. It felt like a reoccurring nightmare, where I'd arrive to high school for my exams, and realize I hadn't been going to my math class all semester or know where the classroom was in the building.

I wiped my brow with the back of my hand. I swallowed, then squared my shoulders and plastered on a smile.

This was my nightmare, but all these people had shown up for a cause that really mattered to me.

A chorus of, "Hazel!" greeted me on the other side of the swinging doors. It started at the bar with the people nearest to me and fanned back to the walls. It drowned out Tim McGraw's "I Like It, I Love It," for a moment.

I had to force a small smile, but I lifted my hand and waved.

"There's the woman of the hour!" Ben moved next to me, throwing a heavy arm over my shoulder. "Everyone, raise your glass for our girl, Hazel, and the animals we're going to save together!"

The last part of his sentence was drowned out by whoops and hollers. I guffawed, absolutely in shock at the gathering in front of me.

His eyes were full of excitement as he looked down at me. "Moscow mule?"

"Yes, please," I yelled back.

"Double?"

"Triple!"

He laughed, the smile lines fitting into the corners of his blue eyes. Holding up a finger for me to wait, he moved down the bar to prepare my drink.

I scanned the crowd, looking for Elijah, but instead, I found Nora working through the mass of people. They parted for her with little resistance. There was a no nonsense set to her jaw. She was in her element, orchestrating this event and guiding all these people to her goal. Not for the first time, I thanked my lucky stars that she was on my side.

"Hey, babe." She leaned against the wall to our left.

"Hey right back. Look at all this." I gestured at the packed bar.

She shrugged. "I knew it was the right idea."

I rolled my eyes, but there was no fighting her logic.

It was then I noticed her twin sister, Olivia, trailing behind her, but unlike Nora, the crowd closed in around Olivia. Squeals of excitement marked her progress as people realized she was in town.

"I didn't realize Olivia would be here," I said.

Nora scoffed. "And miss out on the juicy gossip? Plus, I think she wanted to see everybody before she and Anton move to Denver."

"Is she excited?"

Nora tilted her head, considering. "You know her, she's always game for something new, especially if it's attention grabbing." Turning, she spoke directly into my ear. "They're touring wedding venues while they're here."

I gasped. "Is there a ring?"

Anton and Olivia had been dating for years, but neither of them was in a rush to get married—even though it seemed inevitable. They were so happy together.

"It's been purchased, just no proposal yet." With her gaze fixed somewhere in the middle of the crowd, she muttered quietly enough that I almost didn't hear her, "The window is closing."

"What window?"

"Nothin'."

"What do you mean?" Why was she being so annoyingly vague?

At first, I didn't think she was going to answer. But then her shoulders fell, and she looked sad in a way I'd never seen from her before. "Some people just... are too scared to try, you know?"

I hated seeing the resignation set in her mahogany eyes. "You okay, Nora?"

"*I'm* perfectly fine." Nodding toward the temporary stage constructed of wood pallets, she added, "Gonna get this thing started soon."

My earlier dread grew in my stomach again. "Do I have to give a speech?"

"What?" She looked at me with outraged disbelief. "No. Why did you think that?"

Relief flooded me so abruptly that I fell against the wall. "Emily said something when I got here."

Nora rolled her eyes. "Oh, Em. No, I would give you so much warning. I would never just drop that on you. Jesus, that's like the meanest thing I could do to you. I have an idea of what I'm going to say, so I'll give the opening speech."

"You haven't planned it?"

She lifted her drink to her lips. "What's there to plan? I'm just going to get started before handing the microphone to Ben."

As if conjured by her words, he showed up next to me and placed a copper mug in my hand. Jerking his chin toward the frenzy at the bar, he said to her, "Give me a couple of minutes' warning when you want to get started."

She yelled after his retreating back, "This is your warning."

He gave her a thumbs up in recognition before he leaned over the counter and took a drink order.

Scanning the bar again, I searched for perfectly tousled, chestnut-colored curls. "Have you seen Elijah?"

I wanted him, but after the first flood of attention, I was enjoying my usual anonymity against the rear wall. When he was with me, eyes darted in my direction. Observing. Assessing. Judging.

She pointed at the center of the dance floor. "Somewhere in there with Remi, Sterling, Bet, and Lola." Over my shoulder, Nora nodded, then joined Ben to go on stage.

I took a sip of my Moscow mule and winced as the vodka burned a bit as I swallowed. He had taken me seriously about that triple. Resting against the wall, I noticed a throbbing pain in my leg. I bent down to lift the hem of my dress. The pale skin of my calf had turned a dark shade of purple. Apparently, I hadn't taken the step breaking completely unscathed.

With the back of my head pressed against the wall, I took a gulp of my drink. This time, I welcomed the burn of alcohol.

Chapter 17
Elijah

A ***re you here? They're about to start.*** I texted Hazel. It sat beneath the texts I'd sent before, with no responses. The image of her still buried under work as *her* fundraiser started made me frustrated and sad. And wondering about our relationship when I went back home in a week. Would she keep to our plan? Would she make time for me?

Doubting her before it'd even begun wasn't fair. Even if my concerns seemed valid.

She was passionate about her work, and I wanted to support that. But there had to be space in her life for me, or none of this could work.

I lifted my hand to run through my hair, before remembering that I'd styled it and lowered my hand to my side.

By some miracle, my community fund surprise for Hazel had remained a surprise. The local gossips hadn't caught wind, and in just a few hours, I'd get to announce it. Maybe that'd take some of the pressure off her—knowing she wasn't alone in her mission. That this town supported her.

"Where's Hazel?" Sterling yelled over the crowd. He was taller than me, but judging by the way he kept swiveling his head, he couldn't find her, either.

"I don't know. She hasn't texted me back," I said. When I couldn't find the top of her head, I searched for Dennis, figuring he wouldn't be far from her. My stomach twisted with an ugly jealousy. I snapped my eyes forward, changing my mind. If he was with her, I didn't want to see it.

Nora stepped on the stage first. It only made her about two feet taller than usual, but it was enough that she was visible. Ben stood to her right as she picked the microphone off its stand.

Chatting had already begun to die down, but at her amplified "Hello, everyone," it ceased.

Never one to waste time, she continued, "Hazel and everyone down at Grand Ridge Animal Clinic would like to thank you for coming out. The fine men of our town have volunteered their time and expertise, and we are preemptively grateful. So, get your money ready, folks. We're doing this for the dogs, cats, and animals who need someone to take care of them. And the town of Grand Ridge, Michigan, does not turn away from anyone in need."

"We also don't turn away from a beer or two, now do we?"

Cups went into the air as the group called out in agreement.

Nora's smile was wolfish, knowing we were in the palm of her hand. "That's what I thought. My friends, my townfolk, my neighbors, I want you to be so loud tonight that my ears are ringing when I walk out of this building. And fellas," she cocked a playful hip, "don't be shy... let's see what you're working with! It's for a good cause!"

This time, when the crowd screamed, it was primarily female voices. Sterling laughed, gripping my shoulder. Even through my concern for Hazel, my smile spread.

Everyone was still losing their minds when Nora cooly handed the microphone to Ben. She descended the stairs and joined the rest of us.

Ben held up a calming hand. "All right, all right. I see our girl got you all worked up. Now, let's get our first bachelor up here. The order is random, so if there is anyone or," he lifted an eyebrow, "a service you're looking for, there's no telling when they'll be up. Just be ready."

I hoped the pattern wasn't too random, especially since some of our bachelors were already drunker than others. I found Shane with a drink in one hand, swaying his body to music that wasn't playing anymore.

"Shane Briar, will you join me on stage?" Ben swept an arm in welcome.

So, not too random.

"Hell yeah!" Shane hollered.

My phone buzzed. Pulling it out of my pocket, I found a new text from Hazel. ***I'm here. By the bar.***

Not bothering to text back, I made my way through the crowd. The music had started up again and hands shot into the air to cast their bids.

I found her with Nora. Hazel's long dress draped her body, brushing over her curves, and her blue jean jacket hit just above her hips. She was my girl next door dream come true, and just the sight of her thrilled me. A smile spread across her face when she saw me, even if it didn't quite meet her eyes.

My jealousy from a few minutes before was an embarrassment I wished I could forget.

I snaked my arm around her back and kissed her. I pulled back, and she rested her head on my shoulder.

"How are you doing?" I yelled, unsure if she could hear me over the noise.

"Um... I'm here. How are you?" She leaned more of her weight onto me.

"Great. Everyone's excited! There weren't any brimstone fires or pitchforks on our way in tonight, so I don't think any of us are going to go directly to hell."

She chuckled.

"Why were you late?" I asked.

Her shoulders tightened under my arm. "Working. Lost track of time."

This auction was important to her. She was under a lot of pressure to produce money for the humane society, and she was taking a risk getting that money this way. And still she had "lost track of time."

You gonna be late on your weekend you come to me? I didn't say the question out loud. It was shitty enough that I'd thought it.

"Sold," Ben's voice boomed, "for one hundred and twenty-five dollars to Lindsey Goodman! That is a great price for 18 months of oil changes!" He marked off something on the sheet on the stand in front of him. "Ladies, this next guy is going to look grumpy, but don't let that discourage you. Ransom, come on up, you surly bastard."

I laughed, big and loud, focusing my attention on the present, determined to have a good time.

This was definitely not Ransom's scene, and it just went to show how much he wanted to help that he was willing to be here. He stood front and center with his arms crossed over his chest, his feet planted shoulder-width apart. His auburn hair gleamed in the light, and behind his beard, he scowled.

"Ladies," Ben began, "I know he seems feral, and he possibly is—there are rumors he was raised by wolves—but he's offering up ten hours of masonry work, including a one-hundred-fifty-dollar budget toward supplies. Let's start the bidding."

It shot through the starting bids quickly.

"Do you need any masonry done?" I asked Hazel. "That could be a hell of a deal."

She lifted her head from my shoulder. "You don't mind if I bid on other men?"

"When you put it that way, I don't love it," I joked. "But if you need something done, throw your hat in the ring. And you shouldn't bid on me. If you need IT work, I'll just do it."

She brightened. "Okay."

An intense battle raged, until elderly Mrs. Peters, who owned the town's flower shop and greenhouse, punched both of her dark brown arms in the air victoriously. "I told you I'd get a better price on that quote!"

The whole bar broke into laughter, except for Ransom, whose demeanor didn't change. He jerked his head in acknowledgment and exited the stage.

"We have over eight hundred dollars, and it's just been two people," Hazel said to no one in particular. "If we average this for the rest of the auction, we're gonna meet our goal."

Nora scoffed. "Oh babe, we're gonna beat the shit out of our goal."

"We're gonna beat the shit out of our goal!" Hazel beamed, her brown eyes so bright, they could have lit the stage.

I hugged her tight, her excitement and relief palpable.

The energy in the bar was still high forty minutes later. There were only a few more men, including me.

Remi had caused quite the uproar. Judging by the zeal in which three final women bid, it had more to do with Remi than the veterinarian work he was offering.

When Lily Nelson won, Nora leaned forward with her eyes narrowed. "Does Lily even have a pet?"

Hazel shrugged. "If she does, I've never heard of it."

Alcohol buzzed in my blood. I held Hazel in my arms, her back to my front, and she let me sway her side to side. "This isn't too close to dancing, is it? I know how much you'd hate that."

Her giggle sounded distinctly drunk. "If it was dancing, I wouldn't allow it. Not on my watch."

"Can I call it dancing?"

"You may not."

"I've danced before, and this feels a lot like dancing."

"This is *swaying* or snuggling; *definitely* not dancing."

My chest bounced against her back as I laughed. This was good. *We* were good. Even if I had to quiet my lingering insecurities. It was just because I was leaving soon, and our fresh relationship was going to change. But that didn't mean it would fail.

Ben took a drink of water. He was doing a good job of remaining enthusiastic, but he was beginning to look a bit frayed at the edges. "All right, ladies, let's all welcome our man Brooks!"

With cool, easy confidence, Brooks stepped onto the stage, a long neck bottle pinched between two fingers. An audible gasp rippled through the crowd. Of all the transformations, his was the starkest. Instead of the baseball cap he usually wore, his hair was swooped back on top and the sides were in a tight fade. He'd shaved his beard, showing off a strong jaw. The outfit we'd chosen fit nicely. He was still Brooks, just a more fashionable and better maintained version.

"Holy shit!" someone yelled.

"You are looking like a drink of water, and I am *thirsty*," Ginny, the waitress from the Pour House, called out.

It took a moment for the noise to calm down before Ben was able to begin the auction. "Standing here in his new digs is Jack Brooks. This strong, silent man is offering to," to himself Ben muttered, "I can't believe I'm about to say this"—he cleared his throat—"tend your garden."

Hazel and Nora clung to each other, both laughing too hard to support their own weight. Cat calls erupted, which varied in levels of decency. Brooks weathered it good-naturedly, seemingly unembarrassed. He sipped his beer and waited, with only a slight smirk on his face.

Nora's twin sister, Olivia, called out, "If you promise to work shirtless, I'll bid."

His head turned in her direction, his eyes laser focused on her.

"Oh shit..." Nora muttered to herself. "God, can she stop leading him on?"

"What? No one's gonna take her seriously." Hazel reasoned. "Her and Brooks, can you even imagine?"

An irritated lift of her eyebrow was Nora's only response.

Holding up a hand to slow everyone down, Ben said, "Bidding hasn't even begun."

Without shifting his focus, Brooks passed his drink to Ben, then took hold of his belt buckle. My eyes widened.

Shocked. Floored. Incomprehensible.

"No way!" Hazel screamed.

The crowd between us and the stage moved like particles heating up, spastic and frantic. With one quick pull, Brooks freed the leather strap from his belt loops.

"Jesus Christ," Ben exclaimed. "No one had money on Brooks taking his clothes off tonight."

Still focused on Olivia, Brooks' belt clattered to the stage.

Someone just started bidding, without being prompted. "One hundred dollars!"

Amounts continued to climb as he started with the button at the base of his neck.

"One hundred and seventy-five dollars!"

"What the fuck is happening right now?" I asked in disbelief.

With her face pressed into her hands, Nora groaned. "How does she not know? Sometimes she is too dumb to live."

Brooks pulled the tail of his shirt out of his slacks, letting it hang open over his white undershirt for a few seconds before freeing one arm, then the other.

Bids were shouted in a frenzy, and the numbers piled on top of one another.

Pinching the bridge of his nose, Ben said, "Brooks, you move your hips *at all*, and I need a cabaret license."

Brooks bundled his shirt into his fist and let it fly over the crowd. It landed on Olivia's shocked, blushing face. He hooked his thumbs into his pockets and lounged while standing.

She peeled it off her eyes and screamed, "Four hundred and fifty dollars!"

"Sold," Brooks' voice called out loud and clear, cutting off the bidding. A second round of gasps rippled through the bar.

Hazel's draw dropped. "Brooks and Olivia?!"

"Looks like it," I agreed.

Nora just shook her head. Throwing her hands up in disgust, she proclaimed, "Too dumb to live."

Chapter 18
Hazel

"I'm gonna... I'll be back." Nora pushed off the wall and disappeared, moving toward her sister.

Elijah lifted an eyebrow toward me and I shrugged.

"Elijah March," Ben spoke into the microphone, "get on up here."

Pressing a quick kiss to my cheek, Elijah stepped away. Unlike when Nora moved through the crowd and it opened for her, everyone squeezed in on him. He inched toward the stage with a smile on his face. I shook my head at how his smile sparked responses in the women on all sides of him—their eyes dreamy, their hands...*touchy*.

I didn't consider myself the jealous type, but I really wanted them to take their hands off him.

"Let the man through," Ben said. After a few beats, it was clear no one was interested in "letting the man through." Ben shifted his weight, then threw his hands in the air. "This is clearly going to take a while, so I'll tell you the services Elijah is offering."

Ben went on, but I was too distracted by Elijah's laughter as he made slow progress to the front of the room. He was beautiful, and nice.

Depending on the crowd, he was very popular. It must give him whiplash how quickly people went from shunning him to coveting him. Before buying the clinic, I could fade into the wall, but the spotlight on me grew even brighter when I'd started dating him. He was so noticeable, it rubbed off on me. He knew just how to navigate it, while it made me feel clumsy and awkward in comparison.

Their attention fit like a too tight outfit. Making me aware of all of my flaws and any seams that could tear, any threads barely holding me together.

He had just stepped onto the stage, his clothes a bit less put-together than they had been. His wavy hair was a bit rumpled, falling over his eye. Combined with the stubble on his jaw, and the lopsided grin on his face, he looked exactly like the roughish playboy I'd always thought he was. My heart thundered in my chest, and I couldn't look away from his beauty. Just like when I was a teen, watching him from the fringed edges of the group, I was overwhelmed with how lovely he was.

But there was also my quiet insecurity with him by my side, would I always be under fire?

Maybe it was the way everyone was fawning over him, or because I was all too aware of how strongly I'd fallen for him. But that question began bouncing around, gaining volume. I wiped my clammy palms on my skirt. Voices called out amounts, and I wanted to be excited about the money being added to the donation, but I was too busy being wrapped up in my head.

And good god, didn't that make me horrible?

He was so much more than the sum of their whispers. He didn't deserve to have me feel ashamed to be with him. Even if my shame had nothing to do with him and everything to do with my fear of negative attention.

I didn't even hear how much the final amount was when Ben called out, "Sold!"

Elijah jumped down from the stage and was instantly surrounded by women again. I could only see the top of his head, but judging by how tightly packed the group was, he must have someone pressed to each side of his body.

"How did you snag a man that dishy?" Emily asked, wiping the bar top clean.

"I didn't snag him; he came to me." I wished my tone sounded less defensive.

"Girl, I'm just joking around. I don't think you went out with, like, a butterfly net and caught him." She shrugged. "It's just kinda surprising."

"Why's that?" I asked, even though I knew the reason. But I had an open wound just waiting for some salt to be poured into it.

"Because you're you, and he's him. You aren't an obvious match."

Inwardly, I winced.

"But you look good together. You both look happy," she went on. "But like, everyone in town has been talking for weeks about how weird it is."

I looked down at the toe of my shoe—my throat tight.

Everyone in town talking about me.

Pressing a hand to her sternum, she said, "I mean, I think it's great. Just, ya know, be careful."

Emily strode down the bar, saving me from responding.

Dennis stood next to Ben on stage. The bidding had started, and I was already a couple of bids behind. I needed to swallow the ache in my throat. I needed to appear unfazed, unburdened, and unhurt.

I needed to win that carpentry work.

"One hundred and seventy-five dollars! Do I have one hundred and seventy-five dollars?" Ben asked into the microphone.

Throwing my hand high over my head, I proclaimed, "One hundred and seventy-five."

"I've got one hundred and seventy-five. Can I get two hundred?"

Linda Hengsbach lifted her arthritic hand from her seat at the front. She was a friend of my grandma's and had baked the cake for my graduation party. I really adored her.

But my clinic was falling apart—it should have been fixed yesterday—and I couldn't just back out.

"Two hundred and twenty-five," I called out.

"Two hundred and fifty," her weak voice cried out.

"Two hundred and seventy-five."

The group's attention had shifted to Linda and me battling it out. She'd switched to ten-dollar increments, so when it was my turn, I yelled, "Three hundred and sixty dollars."

I hoped the bidding would end soon, since I had a bit more I could spend—but not much. I'd put a lot of my own funds into Echo's care over the past few weeks, and my bank account was seriously depleted.

She bid three hundred and seventy.

I shouted out, "Four hundred and twenty-five dollars," hoping it would scare her off.

Her hand lingered at her shoulder, jerked up, then went back down. She shook her head.

"Sold for four hundred and twenty-five dollars!" Ben confirmed.

I punched my fists in the air and jumped before I remembered that I'd just beat out a sweet old lady. Smoothing my hands down the front of my dress, I cut my celebration off early. When I looked up, Dennis strode through the crowd. Everyone was watching me, and their scrutiny pricked at my skin.

His arms went around my waist, scooping me up. I clung to his shoulders—the ground felt very far away. Setting me down, he beamed. "That was exciting!"

I forced a smile to match his. "It was!"

Chapter 19

Elijah

Hazel fit well in Dennis' arms.

And I hated it.

The past few minutes were frayed at the edges. A blur of attention so tightly focused on me—giving me flashbacks of being loved by this community, only to be shunned by it. I wanted my quiet corner back. I wanted Hazel back.

Then... the adoring expressions around me turned pitying as she bid for Dennis.

I clenched my jaw tight, grinding my teeth. I'd told her she could bid for work she needed done. But even as my rational brain spoke reason, my gut twisted.

They looked good together. That was the kind of man she deserved, not someone like me. Not someone who couldn't do the work she needed help with. Not someone whose own father couldn't love him.

Years of therapy whispered, *That's not your fault.*

I'd been a wounded, unloved child begging to be seen. But I wasn't that kid anymore. I'd worked through my shit. If she chose Dennis over me, that didn't make me undeserving.

It was a struggle to relax the anger from my body.

"They're cute, aren't they?" Lily looked up at me through her lashes as she took hold of my bicep.

"Excuse me?" My expression must have gone too sharp because her hand dropped from my arm.

She lifted her chin, and I could practically see her incoming barb. Whatever she was about to say, she was aiming to hurt. I remembered this back-and-forth from when we dated in high school, but I didn't have to do it anymore.

"Excuse me," I repeated, moving away from the conversation. My first step took me toward Hazel, but I hesitated before taking the next. She was still with Dennis. They weren't doing anything inappropriate—he'd taken a step back, and so had she—but it was him. And despite how much I wished it wasn't true, I felt threatened by him.

He clearly knew how to fix the things that were broken around her. He wasn't needy like me; he didn't ask her to work less, to give less of herself to others.

I hoped it didn't look like I was being possessive when I wrapped my arm around Hazel's waist. She blinked up at me, surprised, as if she was shocked I was still here.

"Hey." Her smile looked tight.

My stomach twisted, and I felt sick. Whatever had changed since the time I left to getting back to her had changed in a big way.

I focused on appearing relaxed as I felt people pretending not to watch us.

"Hi," I said, then to Dennis, I lied, "Good to see you again."

"You too, man." He held his hand out for a shake, and I had to let go of Hazel to take it. "You really worked the crowd out there."

I opened my mouth to reply, but she cut me off, "That's the Elijah effect."

Her words sounded hollow. I couldn't quite place why her words were biting, but they stung.

"I don't know about all that." I gripped the back of my neck, my shoulders taut.

Dennis nodded. "Yeah, I get mixed reports about you."

My eyes narrowed, and my jaw clenched. Memories were long, and there were mountains of dirt on every person in this town. But having him blatantly acknowledge mine set my defenses up.

Next to me, Hazel had stilled, her brow furrowed. Was she beginning to realize the kind of backlash that could fall on her and her business if she stayed with me?

Any of the bystanders in earshot had to be salivating to repeat the whole encounter.

His lopsided smile was affectionate as he looked at her. "But Hazel is the best judge of character I know, so if she says you're good, that's who I believe."

"Thanks." I shoved my fists into my pockets. "You're gonna do some carpentry for her?"

The carefree grin was back on his face. "Sure thing. Apparently, a stair broke on her tonight... nearly broke her ankle. I'm sorry I let it get that bad."

"*I* let it get that bad," she insisted.

"A stair broke?" I asked.

She breathed in deeply, opening her mouth, but Dennis explained, "Right before she got here."

"Are you okay?" It was really hard to not read into the fact that she had told him and not me.

"I'm fine, just a little bruised." Gesturing to him, she added, "Dennis will fix it for me. It'll be fine."

"I'll fix whatever I can in the next couple of weeks, and then the rest of it when I get back, I promise."

It didn't slip past my notice that he was making plans for the future, and she wasn't doing anything to contradict him. What had happened?

Hazel and I were not in the same place we had been just a few moments ago.

Or was this the direction we'd always been heading? Had I been fooling myself every time I imagined Hazel being with me long-term? So long that our hair grew gray together. So long that the hands we grasped together were wrinkled from the wear of time. So long that we looked back and saw a lifetime spent together.

"I appreciate it." She looked around. "It looks like people are starting to head out. I should probably see if they need help cleaning up. Have either of you seen Nora?"

"She left with Brooks a little bit ago," Dennis answered, then he pushed both of his hands in his hair with his eyebrows raised. "Wasn't his bidding wild?!"

I nodded, my teeth squeezed too tight to say anything.

Hazel's eyebrows rose. "It was."

"You beat your goal, though. Way to go!" He reached his arms around her in a hug. I went completely rigid as she hugged him back. They rocked back and forth once before letting go.

"Thank you," she said to her shoes. "It's a huge relief."

"I bet. I know how much you care." To me, he explained, "She's always working so hard. She sees every animal in need like it's her responsibility."

I nodded again, it was the only response I could manage. The man was talking to me like I didn't know. Like I didn't know *her*.

Concealing my aggression was getting more difficult, but the eyes watching our little chat were growing.

"I'll help with clean up, you get home," Dennis said to Hazel.

"I'm fine," she argued, even though she looked exhausted.

I hadn't told her my surprise yet, but I could do that tomorrow. It wasn't the right time.

I kept my balled fists in my pocket and nudged her with my elbow. "Come on, I'll drop you off at your place and come back to clean."

She searched my face for a beat before she looked down at the floor.

I wanted her to ask me to come back when I was done, or to just stay with her. But all she said was, "If that's what you want to do..."

It wasn't at all what I wanted to do, but I did it anyway.

The bar's parking lot was mostly empty when I parked again. I was even more confused after the drive. Hazel's mood was a bit off—happy about the funds, but she wouldn't look at me. Or I thought she wouldn't. She was really tired.

I felt insecure. I tried to coach myself out of my shitty thoughts. People had off moments every now and then, and this was just one of ours. Our first. It was bound to happen eventually. Now that it was done, we could go back to having fun. Back to falling in love.

But when our kiss good night was all heat and no heart, I wondered if it was because she wanted to be kissing Dennis.

Dennis. The park ranger, who would wax poetic about mosquitoes in all their life stages, was the guy Hazel was choosing over me.

Entering through the back door, Sterling's voice carried over the sounds of the dishwasher. "She looked like she was into it."

"But she's in a relationship. You don't think she'd..." Ben let his voice trail off, making his point by leaving his words unsaid.

I filled in all he wouldn't say, and a series of heartache-inducing scenarios slammed into my mind. I half-heartedly tried to shove them out, but the more they rested there, the more they made a home, and the more they made sense. Why would she pick me over Dennis? They shared interests and a town.

Would she keep me around while he was on his research trip or break up with me and put me out of my misery?

Okay, that's enough, I argued with myself. *She hasn't said anything. They hugged. People hug. Dial it back.*

But I couldn't fully push the thought away.

Sterling and Ben walked through the swinging doors into the public space. I rolled my shoulders and neck, trying to loosen the knots there. Maybe if I could ease them away, I'd clear my mind.

I was ready to go back to my cabin, but I'd committed to helping with clean up.

In the dining area, tables had been arranged back into their places. Remi and Ransom were setting chairs around them, neither of them speaking.

I took a step in their direction, already appreciating their silence, when Shane Briar called, "Hey Eli, come help us carry these out."

God, I hated the sound of his voice.

There was a pile of wood pallets stacked next to where Dennis pulled nails out of the stage with the back of a hammer. Taking a step in their direction was the last thing I wanted to do, but arguing would just create a scene.

In a few strides, I was at the pile. "Where are they goin'?"

"By the dumpster outside," he said.

Not wanting to snag my clothes, I shrugged off my coat and flannel.

"Don't get naked, Eli; your female fans aren't here," Shane joked.

One corner of my mouth curled upward in what I hoped looked like a smile and not a grimace.

"You did get them worked up," Dennis added.

I hooked a couple of pallets under my arms, looking for an escape.

Shane jerked his chin in my direction. "He's always had that effect on girls. He's a fuck 'em and leave 'em type."

I knew I should have helped Ransom and Remi instead. "Still pissed about Missy Roberts? I don't know if you know this, but high school was a long time ago."

Missy had broken up with Shane to date me during our senior year. It didn't last long, but it was just another reason for Shane to resent me.

"I'm just wondering how long sweet Hazel has before you're off to someone else. Even the whole shed thing didn't slow you down."

I clenched my jaw so hard my teeth hurt.

"Is that true?" Dennis set down the hammer.

I didn't even try to veil the aggression in my voice. "Is what true?"

"Did you fuck Pastor Lou's daughter in the church's shed?" Shane grinned from ear to ear.

"None of your business, and her name is Hannah." I turned, eager to walk away from the conversation.

There was the *thunk* and clatter of wood being manhandled, then Shane's footsteps followed me. I picked up the pace. If I timed it right, there wouldn't be a pause long enough for him to start the conversation again.

Small snowflakes melted on the ground as I exited through the back of the building. It was rude, but I didn't hold the door for Shane. Unfortunately, maneuvering the door open didn't keep him from coming outside when I pivoted to grab my next load of pallets.

"You pissed?" he asked with mock concern. "You seem pissed."

Instead of responding, I strode past him.

"I'm sorry, man. They're like, meant to be together or some shit."

Stopping, I faced him. He was still stacking his pallets atop mine.

"What?" I demanded, even though I knew I should just keep walking.

He put his hands in his pockets and shrugged.

"It was just a hug," I dismissed.

One of his thin eyebrows rose. "If you say so."

"I do."

"Are you really that into her?"

I took an involuntary step closer, my fists clenched.

"She can't be that great," he went on, clearly aware I was hanging onto my temper by a thread. "I mean, she was fucking Dennis before you. Gotta be a lot of missionary. At least she's not too embarrassed to be seen with you. I heard Pastor Lou's daugh—*Hannah* didn't want anyone to know about you."

"Shane, shut the fuck up."

He glared, taking in my tight shoulders and clenched fists. "I'm trying to make you feel better."

"Fuck you."

"Jesus, you're touchy." His shoulders squared and his weight shifted.

In theory, I didn't *want* to get in a fight with a drunken backwoods townie. But into reality, I actually *really* wanted to. The will it took for me to shake my head and walk away was almost more than I could manage, but I did it anyway.

"You're just gonna be a bitch about it?" Shane shouted at my back.

"Sure." At least I sounded like he wasn't getting under my skin.

"No wonder she's looking for new dick."

Keep walking.

His footsteps came up, fast and angry, behind me.

I was almost at the door when he shoved my shoulder, hard.

The contact broke through my logical mind. I whipped around, fists up, and narrowly blocked his punch from landing on my nose. His knuckles grazed my cheekbone, and my vision blurred. Blinded by my rage, I lunged. My shoulder hit his sternum, and we both went down. He scrambled to roll me under him while I threw sloppy strikes. I coughed and grunted every time one of his blows landed, but the pain wasn't enough to cool my blood.

I attacked the hands that grabbed my shoulders and pulled me off Shane. I didn't stop when those same hands locked around my arms, their hands interlocked behind my head. I rocked from side to side, trying to get to my captor. It was no use; I was trapped.

"You're okay," a calm voice said at my ear. "You're okay."

Shane got to his feet, and I kicked and pulled in his direction. The mountain behind me lost his balance for a heartbeat, but held firm again.

"Fuck you!" Shane yelled.

"You don't know shit!" I yelled back.

Ransom moved between us, his arms held out to either side, blocking Shane from moving around him. "Walk home."

"Fuck you, man." Shane spat at the asphalt, blood mixed in the saliva.

"Walk home," Ransom commanded.

I struggled less against the hold on me and it began to loosen.

What the fuck did I do?

I had to close my eyes as blind hatred left my blood, replaced by shame. It washed over me, grimy and filthy. I was supposed to be better than this. *Shane Briar* was the guy who got under my skin? He had the finesse of a rhino. He knew nothing about me and meant nothing to me.

How had I fucked up so badly?

Remi released his hold on me. I raked my fingers through my hair, pulling too hard at the tangles.

Shane still screamed obscenities as he stumbled out of the parking lot lights. He must live close because he seemed to be walking in a specific direction.

Ransom waited a bit before following him from a fair distance. "Gonna make sure he gets home and doesn't freeze to death."

"You good?" Remi asked.

I looked up from my shoes and found him assessing me. "No. What the fuck was that? I don't do that shit."

"Then why'd you do it?"

"He fuckin' pushed me. He pissed me off, and then he fucking pushed me, and I... I lost my shit."

Remi sucked in a deep breath. "You should go home. Clear your head."

My face and neck grew hot. It was humiliating to be spoken to like child—even worse because he was right.

"Yeah." I sighed. The hope I'd had that my past could be left behind me died. It would never leave, not in this town. It'd always follow me.

It wouldn't hurt just me.

Turning, I found Dennis standing in the doorway, looking like a good Samaritan, Boy Scout who'd never been in a fistfight in his life.

And yet another way he was better for Hazel than me.

Chapter 20
Hazel

"I just wanted to be sure you're okay." Dennis bent to scratch Banjo behind the ears. The dog's tongue lolled out the side of his mouth.

The sky was gray and overcast, the clouds threatening snow. I should have worn my coat, but I wouldn't be outside long. I wrapped my sweater tighter around my middle.

"Uh, I'm good. Just a little shocked. I hadn't heard about this." I looked at my phone—no messages from Elijah. I assumed he was still coming to the clinic, but we hadn't talked today. He also hadn't said anything about the fight he'd gotten into with Shane Briar last night. Finding out from Dennis felt wrong. I couldn't pinpoint what emotion I was feeling.

Concern mixed with apprehension?

Last night had been full of highs—we made our donation, and it'd been fun. But there was also the low of everyone wondering what Elijah was doing with me, and the prickly feeling of being under scrutiny.

"I bet." He straightened and looked at me. "I worry about you. I've heard some things that make me pretty skeptical about this guy."

"You know how rumors work around here. You can't trust everything you hear."

"That's what I thought too, but then there was that fight last night and…" He shrugged. "It made me wonder if there were truths to what I'd heard."

"I'm okay." I pointed my thumb at the employee entrance to the clinic and changed the subject. I didn't want to discuss the state of my relationship with Dennis. "You're sure you can get the stairs fixed before you leave?"

"For sure. I'll get your office door closing properly too, and when I get back, I'll do some more stuff."

"Thank you."

As I hugged him goodbye, tires from a large, rusty, white truck rounded into the parking lot. He pulled away, keeping his hands on my shoulders. "You know he's the lucky one, right?"

My eyebrows shot up. "Uh… sure. Thanks."

Dennis nodded as if everything was resolved, though I was still reeling.

He drove away as I waved one more time. I shivered against the cold breeze, and speed-walked to the building. A door from the truck opened and closed behind me. Glancing over my shoulder, I half-heartedly smiled at whoever this new person was. But when I saw the black and blue bruise on Elijah's face, I skidded to a halt. In just a few strides, I met him in the middle of the parking lot.

"Your face." My hand hovered above his injury.

A muscle flexed in his jaw. "It'll heal."

"What happened? Shane Briar did this?"

"So you heard." He leaned back on his heel, and a bitterness fit strangely at the corners of his mouth. "Right, Ranger Dipshit."

"Don't call him that. He's not the one who got in a fight last night, so you're not in the best position to call him a dipshit, anyway."

He shoved his hands into the pockets of his jeans.

When it was obvious that he wasn't going to elaborate, I asked, "Is your face the worst of it?"

"My pride is."

"What was this about?"

"Nothing." He ran his hands through his hair and gripped the back of his head. "It really was a stupid thing to do."

We agree on that.

"Do you get into fights often?"

"Jesus." He crossed his arms over his chest. "Is that what you think?"

"No, I don't, but like, I also don't know."

"Hazel, I haven't gotten into a fistfight since I lived in this town."

"Okay." I pressed my fingertips to my lips. Changing the subject, I asked, "Whose truck?"

"Ransom's."

"Is your car okay?"

"It's fine. I thought we could go to the medical surplus store in Grand Rapids, my treat."

"I wished you'd checked with my schedule. I don't have time for that today."

"Oh, okay." He scraped the toe of his shoe on the asphalt. "I thought we had the rest of the day together. But we don't. Okay."

He was clearly frustrated, and I was feeling the same way.

"I thought we were just going to do lunch." My words were clipped.

"All right," he said dryly. "Where do you wanna have lunch?"

"How about my place?"

His posture stiffened and his lips pinched. "Don't want to be seen in public with me?"

"What? No." I wanted to be more offended, but as soon as he pointed it out, it occurred to me that it might be a good idea. Even just the idea of being ashamed of him made me feel like a terrible person. Anywhere we went in town would be a sea of eyes fixed on us. It might be better if we got food in Darling, but I doubted it. Not with his black eye. Everyone and their cousin would be asking him what happened.

"You sure?"

"Of course we can go somewhere to eat." I rubbed two fingers at the sudden pain in my forehead. Trying to deflect from my weak words, I added, "Why didn't you tell me about the fight?"

"I wanted to tell you in person. But Ranger"—his pause felt pointed—"Dennis told you first."

"What is this sudden resentment for Dennis? Has he done something to you?"

"I don't resent him."

"Seems like you might." My temper was beginning to bubble over my guilt.

Elijah sucked the front of his teeth, making a *tsking* sound. "I don't know, Hazel. Why would I resent him?"

"Is this because I bid on him last night? You told me to."

"I didn't *tell* you to."

I rolled my eyes, and the grip I had on my anger slipped. "You wanna tell me what the hell is going on, because you're being very shitty."

"I'm *feeling* very shitty."

"Okay, tell me what's going on." I held my hands palms up, but the cold rushed in and I wrapped my arms around myself again.

"I..." he started, then sighed. His eyes swept over me, then to the sparse parking lot. "Can we talk about this at your place?"

"What are you waiting for?" My irritation was flirting with rage, and I wasn't even trying to hold it back anymore.

Scraping both hands through his hair, he glowered at me. "Is this what you want? To fight in your parking lot, while you're freezing and anyone driving by can see us?"

"What fight are we even having?" My voice was pitched high and thin. "You haven't said anything."

He took a step closer to me. With his voice pitched low, he hissed, "You should break up with me before you start up again with Dennis. Or are we not serious, the way you were *not serious* with him?"

I sucked in a sharp breath between my teeth. "Are you accusing me of *cheating*?"

"Not consciously."

"So, just unconsciously? *You* know my mind better than me?"

He let out a humorless laugh, his tongue tucked into his cheek. "That's not what I'm saying."

"Then what are you saying?"

"If you've realized he's better for you, don't string me along."

"That is the most ridiculous thing I've ever heard."

Dennis was sweet, but there wasn't a reality where I'd pick him over Elijah.

"Is it?" He sneered. "For exes, you spend a lot of time together."

For a few moments, all I could do was stare with my mouth open, before bursting out, "I'm his dog's vet! Banjo has diabetes. We've been monitoring his insulin levels."

I took a calming breath, but it didn't stick. Anger still coursed through my veins. I cocked my hip and thrust my chin. "And how dare you compare my relationship with him with what I have with you."

"Don't make it out like what I see isn't real. I'm not the only one; everyone in town sees it."

"Well, if everyone in town sees it!" I took a step closer to him. "You think people didn't warn me about *you*? 'Be careful, you know his reputation.'"

He glared over my shoulder, but didn't speak.

I gestured to the town hub just a few blocks away. "But I'm not listening to a bunch of busybodies over what you tell me."

I'm just letting their picking tear me into shreds, I left unsaid.

"Maybe you should."

My blood ran cold.

"This place—" his voice broke, cutting him off. When he spoke again, it sounded raspy. "My reputation—"

"I don't care—"

"It'll hurt you."

"I don't care," I said again. But even as I said it, I knew he was right. And I knew I cared at least a little.

"Yes, you do. You hate the way everyone's been talking about you, and it won't stop. If you're with me, it won't stop."

"I can handle it."

"Why would you want to?"

"Because I love you." The words were out of my mouth before I knew they were there. I was exposed in their wake. The only comfort I could take in the silence that followed was that they were true.

Elijah's chest sank as if I'd hit him, as if I'd punched all the air from his lungs. His face twisted in pain. He stumbled back under the force of my words—of my feelings. I waited, my heart pumping too fast, my vision darkening around the edges.

He loved me too, didn't he? We *loved* each other. We just hadn't said it, right?

His green eyes met mine, and I was struck by just how sad they were.

"Is that enough?" he whispered.

My sadness warped into something that froze in my chest, heavy, and brittle. It was something to grasp on to. It was something to fill the aching hole Elijah was digging out of me.

I hugged myself tighter, my teeth chattering.

A fine mixture of dread, regret, and resignation was beginning to squeeze my throat. I had to force out, "Isn't it?"

He stared up at the sky as if it held answers. I could practically hear my heart breaking like cracking ice. Tears stung my eyes and clung to my eyelashes.

A crease formed between his eyebrows. His features were etched with pain, a marble statue trapped in grief.

"I love you, too." He bit his lip and his eyes shone.

"Do you?" My last word came out as a sob.

Muscles in his throat flexed. He shook his head as if he didn't want to say what he needed to say next.

He raked his hands down his face, wincing when he touched his bruise. "There will always be a sermon about how I ruin good people. If you're around me, people will talk shit about the company you keep. There will always be a Mrs. Nelson interrupting our dinner."

We both knew it was true.

"So, you're breaking up with me to protect me? Like I can't make that choice for myself?"

"I'm not."

"That's exactly what you're doing."

"It's going to happen again... if you're with me."

"So we can't be together?" Speaking around the grip on my throat hurt almost as much as the clenching vise around my chest. "That's bullshit. If you loved me, you'd fight with me."

The sorrow-ridden resignation fixed into his features was the worst thing I'd ever seen.

He jerked his head to the side and swallowed. "I don't want to hurt you."

"Don't say that. Not while you're destroying me." I was so cold that even the inferno of my anger couldn't warm me.

"I'm sorry, Hazel." I could barely hear his words over the pounding of my heart.

"You really fucking should be." Streams for tears froze on my cheeks. I turned away from him and his beautiful face, so full of anguish. I wanted to give him comfort. I wanted his comfort. I wanted to be mad enough to turn my love to hate, but there just wasn't enough to offset.

Chapter 21
Hazel

"I was hoping you weren't down here," Nora said at the top of the stairs.

There were cobwebs in my messy bun. My hands were filthy from moving dusty cardboard boxes around the clinic basement. A layer of dirt between me and everything I touched. Clearing out the basement was a job I wanted to get done eventually, but it shouldn't have taken precedence over so many other tasks. I'd started opening boxes a couple of days ago, deciding what should stay and should go—mostly go.

It was a comfort to sink beneath the earth, in the musky smell of stale air. Almost like I hit the pause button on every descent down the stairs.

I didn't want to respond to her comment, instead I gestured to the freshly cleared basement floor. "Look at all of this room."

I couldn't see her face, but I could sense her frown—it floated down to cover surfaces like the dust in the air. "Did you sleep last night?"

"Of course I slept."

It wasn't a lie... I'd slept *some*.

She was quiet for a moment. I opened the flaps of the next box and peered inside. Keeping busy was key. If I stopped moving, I'd be able to feel just how devastated I was.

A stair creaked as Nora took a single step down. "Have you eaten?"

My arms jerked to a halt halfway inside the box.

When was the last time I'd eaten?

"I'll take that as a no," she said. "Come on up."

"No, just throw a protein bar at me."

"I am not bringing food down here. That's disgusting. Come up, and wash your hands."

I expected her demanding words, but I didn't expect them to be carried in a gentle tone. It sucked all my resistance out of me. My joints cracked as I stretched my arms over my head. There were squares of cleanish carpet, outlined in brown dust. It danced in the sunlight, too stubborn to be held back by the grimy windows.

The surgical mask I wore over my mouth and nose clung to my cheeks as I peeled it off and set it down. Turning, I moved toward the exit. My movements were sluggish, my arms and legs heavier than normal.

When I got to the bottom step, Nora announced, "I'll be in the break room when you're cleaned up."

The water flowed brown from my hands and arms. My eyes blinked too slowly, they wanted to stay closed. I startled, catching sight of myself in the mirror. My usual dark circles were partially obscured by streaky dirt—at least there was a clean area around my mouth and nose. I took a few more minutes to wipe my face and neck clean.

The smell of cumin and chili powder would have led me to the break room if Nora hadn't already told me she'd be there. There was a steaming bowl of chili on the table when I entered, along with crackers, and a spoon next to it.

"Sit down." Nora nodded toward the chair.

My stomach growled. "That smells so good."

"It is. Sit down. Eat."

She lowered into the seat opposite me. I lifted the spoon to my lips and took a bite of the hearty soup. It tasted similar to my mom's, except spicier.

Nora chewed on a protein bar and stared out the window. At some point while I was in the basement, it had snowed more. It had been two weeks since Elijah had left, and I wished I could bury the memory as easily as the snow buried the grass and trees. Or if I could clean it out like I was the ancient, useless items in the clinic's basement. But those memories and the terrible feelings were always waiting, never quite plucked from my heart.

I looked up to find Nora considering me with sad brown eyes.

She sighed. "Remi said he'd work your shift today."

I swallowed a spoonful of chili too quickly and it burned my throat on the way down. "Why?"

"Because you need to sleep."

"I do not need to sleep. I need to work."

She shook her head.

Rolling my eyes, I leaned back in my chair. "If he's going to do my shift, I'm just going to keep cleaning."

"No, you're gonna go home and go to bed. I'm gonna drive you there."

She was using her "arguing is useless" tone, the one that usually made people buckle under its force. Not me, not now.

I folded my arms on the table and fixed an unwavering glare in her direction. "I don't want to go home. I don't want to sleep. I want to get work done."

Concern pressed into the lines of her forehead and in the depths of her eyes. She opened her mouth and closed it as if reconsidering her words. Then she nodded. "This whole using work as self-abuse has to end. I can't keep watching it."

"I'm not abusing myself."

"I don't know what to do," she continued. "Hazel, you're not okay."

I barked a laugh.

She appeared even more unsettled, which was fair—my laugh *was* a little hysterical.

"I know I'm not okay," I said. "You think that's not obvious to me? I am the furthest from *okay*."

"I don't know what to do for you."

"Leave me alone. Don't *do* anything. Just let me be."

Her leg bounced under the table. She pressed her tongue into her cheek and narrowed her eyes at me. Leaving things be was not the Nora way. "Fine. Do whatever you want today. Remi will be here in a little bit."

"Thank you."

The sun had set hours ago, which meant it was probably late evening. I really didn't care. My time was measured by the number of boxes I cleared away. When heavy steps began descending the stairs, I took a fortifying breath. It didn't sound like Nora, but I couldn't imagine who else it could be.

"Huh," Remi grunted behind me. "It is not clean down here."

I blinked and turned around, mildly surprised it was him. "Yeah."

"So, what are we going to use this space for?"

"I'm not sure. Maybe a physical therapy clinic, eventually."

"Maybe it could be outfitted for a groomer." He pulled a mask over his nose and mouth. "What's your system?"

"My system?"

"Yeah. I'm gonna help you out. Get you above ground sooner."

"No, you don't have to do that."

He pinched the bridge of his nose—I got the feeling he was irritated with me, but that one gesture was the only indication. "I'm going to need you to stop saying that. Every time someone offers you help, you tell them they don't have to. They know they don't have to. Stop fighting help so much."

"*Okay.*" The instinct to argue with him was strong, but I turned toward the mess. "There's really no system. I'm opening a box, deciding if anything is salvageable, can be sold to an antique shop, or donated. Most everything is just getting thrown away."

He stepped up to a stack and pulled the top one down before setting it on the floor. With his height, he did it with a lot more ease, and less danger of being crushed, than I did. "You wanna talk?"

I sighed. "Did Nora send you down here?"

"No, but she's worried about you. We all are."

"I'm fine."

"Yeah, sure."

I leaned over and pulled an unopened bag of towels, but set them in the small pile of "useful things."

"Thank you for working for me today."

"No problem. Brooks said he'll work for you tomorrow, but only if you stay home and sleep."

Rolling my eyes, I swallowed back my irritation. "So, his help comes with stipulations?"

"Can you blame him? If you were watching him work at this level, wouldn't you try to stop him?"

"You can all stop hovering."

He paused, halfway standing, and turned his head to glare at me. "That's hilarious coming from you."

Glaring back, I crossed my arms over my chest. But my annoyance softened slightly at the memory—back when I'd made it a point to call and text at least once a day after his divorce. "That was different. Alicia was your wife, and you were... wrecked when she left."

His Adam's apple bobbed on a swallow. "And you don't think you're wrecked currently?"

Tears that were never far away stung my eyes. "The relationship only lasted a couple of weeks... It's not like it defined my life."

"Is that all it was?"

My throat hurt from holding back my feelings and my jaw clenched. My walls built of muscle and bone were the only barrier between me and the flood of emotions.

Elijah had fit into my life so easily, even if my workflow had suffered. He'd found pockets in my days to see me—lunch here, breakfast there, and every night together. We'd ended things just over two weeks ago, and I still couldn't sleep in my bed. I ached for him, for his body pressed to mine, his arms around me, him inside me.

No matter how often I told myself I missed him disproportionately to the amount of time we'd spent together, I still couldn't make missing him go away.

I couldn't fill the need having him had invoked in my life.

Remi tilted his head, and his features softened with sympathy.

I squeezed my eyes shut, tears leaking down my cheeks. "I'm okay."

He was kind enough not to argue with me.

"I don't want to be a burden," I forced a whisper after a few seconds of silence.

"You're not." He was using the same tone he used to soothe scared animals, and I appreciated it.

I needed to take a steadying breath between each word, but I managed to say, "I. Miss. Him."

It might not have been the boldest declaration of my loss, but it was more than I'd allowed myself since Elijah had left. I wiped the tears from my cheeks and the back of my hand came back streaked with a fine layer of mud. Remi nodded in understanding, the kind of knowing that didn't have to be imagined, the kind that remembered.

"How did you get past it?" I asked.

The haunted look in his eyes told me he hadn't. His pain was still there, present.

Then it was gone. Somewhere under the surface—somewhere close, but hidden.

He lifted a sandy-brown eyebrow. "At first, I did the same thing you're doing. My distractions were a little less... productive." His mouth pulled to one side. "That's not true... I learned a lot."

"What were your distractions?" We'd stayed in touch while he was going through his divorce, but he never confided much in me. At the time, I assumed, hoped, that he was talking to his friend, Owen, from vet school. I probably should have pushed Remi to talk more the way he was for me.

He winced. "Fucking."

My jaw dropped, and I coughed a laugh.

He shrugged. "My body count is... vast. I had quite the ho-phase."

"I mean, I know that. But I didn't realize it was a coping mechanism at the time."

"Yeah. I didn't realize then, either. Therapy helped me identify what I was doing. Someone else touching me made me feel present, but without it, I... was empty."

His choice of word struck the cavernous hollow where my heart was supposed to be. It poked through the paper-thin excuses I'd configured. As if I was a house built of cards, and that word was a puff of air, I crumbled.

My spine curled, and I hugged my middle. Remi moved closer, putting himself within reach, but he didn't touch me until I clung to him. His big arms held me in a hug.

Slowly, he rocked back and forth, murmuring, "I know. I know."

It took a few moments before I caught my breath enough to whisper, "It shouldn't hurt this bad."

"Why not?"

"It was just a couple of weeks…"

He made a tsking sound. "You know it was more than that. It was a future you wanted, and a man you loved."

"I feel dumb."

"Don't judge yourself for caring. It's okay to be sad."

I couldn't respond. All I had energy for was to cling to Remi's middle and cry muddy tears into his blue scrub shirt.

Chapter 22
Hazel

I hadn't been able to bring myself to open the clinic's social media accounts since the auction. Hiding underground—literally—had been more appealing. But after a day of sleeping, per Brooks' stipulation, I felt a little better. My thoughts were clearer. My emotions were still what they were. Today was as good as any to peek through my fingers at the alerts on our profiles.

My cheeks puffed out on an exhale as I considered where to start.

After a brief deliberation, I went to the community page. If it was a garbage fire, I could always go back to the basement. I sat up straighter as I read comment after comment.

Raise of hands, who wishes there was a bachelor auction every weekend? Sterling posted almost three weeks ago, with an emoji guy holding his hand up.

Who knew Hazel could throw a party?! Also, who knew Brooks was hot?! I lost my GD mind! Lindsey Goodman commented underneath. I hadn't actually planned any of it, but it still gave me a little thrill to see my name and party in the same sentence.

OMG! Tell me the bachelor auction will be yearly! I haven't had that much fun in sooooo long! I needed it! Chelsea Thelen commented beneath.

Leaning back in my chair, I let that idea sink in. If there was interest in it being a regular event, then there wasn't any reason for it not to be.

We'd survived the negative attention once, and it more than paid for the donation. It would lift some pressure off me. The relief just the idea gave me was enough to type out. *Start the countdown to next year! The bachelor auction lives! Details to come.*

A "thumbs up" popped under the comment right away.

There was negative attention too, but the excitement and support greatly outweighed the naysayers. Or maybe I was just turning my eyes to the good. Maybe I didn't have to be perfect, to never give them anything bad to say, to always be what they expected me to be. If the busybodies were a part of the town and its energy, then so were my tribe—the people trying to bring kindness to their neighbors; we were here, too.

I was feeling pretty good—breathing more easily—when I caught Ginny's comment, *Bless that Elijah March. My computer hasn't worked this well since I bought it! He even got all those porn pop-ups to stop! To each their own, but some of those were concerning. Informative, but concerning.*

My initial impulse was to text him, ask him what dark corners he'd uncovered, but that wasn't something I could do anymore. He might be nice and respond, but I wasn't ready.

Elijah March. *The* Elijah March. The boy who broke my heart every day of our youth by not noticing my existence. The man whose heart was too broken not to break mine.

He was responsible for his own actions, but I still dished a heaping load of it onto Doc March.

"That bastard," I mumbled to my computer screen.

My social media pennies had been spent, and I braced myself to switch to our banking website. It took one glance for me to freeze in my office chair. The computer screen wouldn't change, no matter how many times I blinked. Unplugging my laptop, I left it open as I carried it from my office in the back of the clinic to the front.

Hopefully, everyone wasn't regretting helping me out.

And hopefully, Nora would understand the balance in the bank account.

Brooks and Remi were still working their last appointments of the day. From the sounds as I walked past Remi's examination room, Mrs. Peters' giant fluffy cat was not happy.

Nora was at the front desk, doing end-of-day paperwork. She glanced over her shoulder as I entered and jerked like she was going to go back to her task, but stopped. "You look not okay."

I set my computer down gently, as if it might contain a bomb. Straightening, I opened my mouth, but words didn't just fall out.

She assessed my face and body language. "You're not going to go back into the basement, are you?"

"What? No." I shook my head, trying to stave away the emotions that had put me in the basement to begin with. There were other fish to fry at the moment. "There's money in the account."

"That's where we usually keep our money."

"Like more than there should be."

Her mouth formed a silent *Oh*. She nodded. "That's the community fund paying for Echo's care."

I leaned back, my eyebrows drawn together. "What?"

"The community fund." She took in my confusion as if searching for understanding.

"I don't know what that is."

She drummed her nails on the countertop. I could practically see gears turning in her mind as she pieced together the information. "Elijah didn't tell you?"

I'd gone most of the day without the threat of tears, but just the mention of his name had me blinking once or twice. Anger weaved into my voice when I asked, "What does he have to do with this?"

"He set it up as a surprise for you; I didn't realize he never told you." Her nails clicked on the laminated surface. When she continued, she sounded almost clinical, as if she'd surgically removed all her opinions. "He coordinated with Mrs. Simons at the library and Deb Creger at city hall for an account to benefit households that can't afford veterinary care."

Everything began shifting around me in a weird swirling motion. The floor rushed up, the walls squeezed closer, and the ceiling dropped.

"Sit down." Nora pushed my shoulders, and I crumpled into a chair.

My head swam in a sickening, lightheaded way. I couldn't identify what was happening with my senses. Was I going to be sick or pass out?

"Breathe," Nora's voice cut through the murkiness.

I sucked in a breath as if I'd been underwater for too long.

"Good. Keep doing that," she said in a stern voice.

My stomach was somewhere near my feet. I felt like I had shrunk to a third of my usual size, too small.

Was he really gone?

I didn't want him to be gone. Why did it have to hurt so badly?

I propped my feet up on the seat and hugged my knees, trying to comfort myself through the pain.

"Hey." Nora sighed.

Her face came into focus.

"Your face is getting color again. I thought you were gonna pass out for a second." She leaned back against the shelves.

"I think I was." I still felt ill and queasy. My chest was still an echo chamber of agony, but I didn't think I'd lose consciousness.

Mrs. Peters walked by, holding her cat carrier. Nora waved goodbye to her as I stared into space, wondering how everything had gone so royally wrong.

A few minutes later, Remi entered the office, covered in white cat hair. He halted at the sight of me. To Nora he asked, "Not the basement?"

"No, I don't think so. She just found out about the community fund," she said.

His chest rose and fell. "Fuck."

"Yeah."

He lowered into the chair across from mine. "You didn't know?"

I shook my head.

"What are you thinking?"

I shook my head, having a hard time focusing on him. "I don't know."

"Have a good night." Brooks led his patient and their owner to the lobby. He turned, and he took in the tableau. His eyes moved from Remi, to me, then to Nora. "Do I need to padlock the basement?"

"No," I whined. "Elijah was just a really great guy, and I miss him, and I feel fucking *terrible*." I hid my face behind my knees. "Please tell me that client is gone."

"He is," Remi assured me.

Nora flicked her wrist. "It was Ol' Terrance Miller, anyway. I don't know if he can complete a sentence without saying, 'fuck.'"

"Small miracles." I set my feet back on the ground.

"What are you thinking?" Remi repeated.

"I don't know."

Brooks' mouth was pulled to one side in distaste.

"What am I supposed to do?" I asked no one in particular.

"What do you have control over?" Tilting his head, Remi watched me and waited.

I shrugged. "I don't think knowing this changes anything. He broke up with me."

My last word was swallowed by a sob. I hid behind my hands and wished they weren't all there to witness my breakdown. With one giant hand, Remi rubbed my shoulders. Nora handed me a box of tissues. I forced my lungs to take in slow breaths to calm my body. After a few moments, I had strung together enough composure to interlace my hands in my lap. "Sorry."

"You're good," Nora mumbled.

Brooks cupped the bill of his baseball cap in both hands—his shoulders lifted toward his ears.

I picked at my fingernails, wondering if I could just leave. Everyone was uncomfortable because of me. I should probably go.

To my surprise, it was Brooks who spoke next. "Would it make you feel better to do something?"

I lifted one shoulder and nodded half-heartedly.

"He did this nice thing for you. If you did something nice for him, it might make it feel more even."

"Wow, I thought you were going to suggest getting drunk or something." Nora voiced my thoughts as well.

Remi's mouth lifted in a lopsided smile. "I did, too."

Brooks' arms dropped to his sides. "Still an option."

Chapter 23
Elijah

"**B**rah," Sebastian's voice was equal parts shock and disgust.

"I know. It's not good." I didn't bother taking in the condition of my living room. I knew without looking that two weeks' worth of dirty laundry, dishes, and takeout containers were still there. I was the only person who lived here, and if I didn't care to clean it up, it wasn't going to happen.

And I didn't give a damn about a whole lot at the moment.

"All right." He spun in a circle. If I knew him, he was looking for his nearest exit.

"What's up, man?"

"Ah." He grimaced and visibly shuddered. "You all right?"

I let out humorless laugh and gestured at the space around me. "No, I'm not great."

There was uncharacteristic concern on his usually happy-go-lucky face. He pressed his lips together and nodded. "Come out. My brothers and I are going to the Outpost to watch the game."

That sounded even less appealing than staying in my messy house. "No."

"You cannot stay here."

"I can."

"Bro, it sucks. You feel like shit. Your heart got all torn to fuck."

I waited for him to make a point as he let the pause become silence.

"And?" I prompted.

He shrugged. "That's it. It sucks."

I snorted, my smile feeling strange. "Wise."

He laughed and gripped my shoulder. "I know. Come on, go get dressed. Come out with me and my brothers. I've already told them to not give you any shit if you talk about her all night."

"They're not gonna listen to that."

"Nah, but at least I told them."

With a sigh, I shook my head. "I really don't want to go out."

"Come anyway."

It was on the tip of my tongue to turn him down. If I stayed, I'd just end up feeling like shit at home. If I joined them, I'd still feel like shit, but at least I wouldn't feel like shit alone. And if he already warned them that I'd be talking about Hazel, then I wouldn't have to feel bad about bringing her up all the time.

As if conjured by an internal timer, I heard her in my mind, *You're destroying me.* My pain was my fault, but worse her pain was my fault, too.

My thumb had hovered over her contact in my phone so many times, but I couldn't bring myself to call her. I wanted to apologize; I wanted to beg her to forgive me, but why would she? After I broke up with her like that, while she asked me not to, should she forgive me?

Swallowing back the memory, I said, "Fine. It's not like I have anything better to do, anyway."

The corners of his mouth pulled down. "That's the enthusiasm I'm looking for."

"Give me a few, I'll get dressed."

Almost a half hour later, I stepped onto the top stair, dressed to go out with my beard trimmed. I had considered shaving it off, but I'd paused with the razor inches from my cheek. I wasn't ready to look different from the version of me that Hazel had loved.

I followed the sound of Seb's voice toward my kitchen. "Sterling, what's happenin', man."

They'd hung out a few times when I'd had different events—birthdays, graduation parties—so I knew they knew each other. Them talking on the phone was still abnormal, but not too weird. Since I could only hear Sebastian's side of the conversation his, "No shit?" put me on guard.

Was Hazel okay? Was my mom?

Patting my pockets, I looked for my phone. I walked faster, finding him with my phone in his hand and his held to his ear by his shoulder. He deftly guarded against my attempt to get my device back as his thumb scrolled *my* Facebook.

"Really?" he said into the speaker, completely ignoring me as I tried again for my phone.

He defended with his back, extending his arm all the way out as he searched. Taking a different tactic, I snatched the phone from his ear. He cursed.

"Sterling, what the hell's goin' on?" I held the phone to my ear. "Is Haz—everybody okay?"

Judging by Sterling's pause and the downturn of Seb's mouth, my stutter did not go unnoticed.

"Yeah, *everybody* is fine," Sterling answered. "I've been trying to get a hold of you. Have you checked the community page?"

I knew he had been, but I'd avoided his calls and texts ever since I overheard him and Ben talk shit about my relationship behind my back.

"No, why?"

"Huh." Seb stopped scrolling. With his eyebrows drawn together, he finally handed me *my* phone.

On the screen, Hazel's grin was huge and proud in her profile photo. She held her arms out, Vana White style, with the clinic in the background. I couldn't help but smile back, even as it twisted my guts into knots. Below her name was a post,

It's been a couple of weeks since the auction, and I don't believe I've properly thanked everyone who came out to offer their hard-earned money, or the gentlemen who gave their time and their trade. I have a special thank you for everyone who coordinated the event, and of course, Benji for hosting.

Our town coming together to support our animals in need means the world to me. It is the subject I am most passionate about.

Thank you.

But there is one person I know I didn't thank. He not only offered his support and time, but he saw a need in our community and coordinated a way to fix it. And because he didn't do it for attention or admiration, very few people know, and I just recently found out.

Because of Elijah March, we now have a fund for households in financial need to get veterinarian help. He sought out the help of Mrs. Simons and Mrs. Creger, and the three of them arranged a collection that will benefit our entire community.

Thank you.

Sterling's voice became background noise as I read and reread Hazel's post. She had to have known it would cause the divided comments—some attacked her personally or promised to take their business elsewhere. The word "socialism" was repeated. Of course, other's came to her defense.

When someone accused her of misusing the business my dad sold her, she openly remarked that he had changed the terms of the deal right before contracts were signed, leaving her in a lurch to provide the donation that the humane society depended on. That she and her staff, along with members of the community, had found a way to make that donation. That she did not apologize, and she would hold the auction again for as long as there was interest.

The long thread of comments asking for another auction next year took a while to scroll through.

But when Tara Nelson made a disparaging comment about me, Hazel argued, *You can make whatever claims you want; I can't change your mind or stop you. But I hope everyone reflects on how Elijah treated them when he was here. Let his actions speak louder than the people who want to do him harm.*

It was exactly the kind of attention she shied away from, but she did it anyway. And more so, she bore it with grace and courage.

For me.

"Eli?" Sterling's voice cut through my thoughts.

"Yeah. I gotta go." I looked up from my phone to find Seb considering me.

He reached his hand out, and I handed him his phone.

After he hung up with Sterling, I said, "I gotta go."

His eyebrows shot up. "Tonight?"

"Yeah."

Blinking, he jerked his head to the side. "Really?"

I looked out the window and saw giant white snowflakes illuminated by the streetlights. My shoulders fell, and I nodded slowly. "Yup."

"Fuck." He groaned. "Let's stop by my place so I can grab my real winter coat and snow boots."

"You're coming?"

"I can't let you drive from Detroit to middle-of-nowhere, Michigan, in this shit by yourself." He pointed at the snow.

"If the roads go sideways, it'll just put you in danger."

"Yeah, but if it gets really sketchy, I'll be able to convince you to pull over."

I opened my mouth to argue, but he cut me off, "Man, I'll just worry about you if I don't come along."

I snorted. "You're a fuckin' sweetheart, man."

His mouth pulled to one side, and he shook his head. "It's fucking annoying."

Chapter 24
Hazel

All I wanted was to be home and in my bed. But with the attention my post had gotten over the past day and a half, I didn't want people to feel like I was hiding. It was probably a ridiculous thing to do, especially since the snow was accumulating quickly outside.

At least the storm had convinced most of the crowd to stay home.

Not me, though. It was leaning toward foolish for me to be out and about with road conditions worsening.

I hadn't been to Benji's since the auction. It might have been the half-filled space, or just my general state of missing Elijah, but I couldn't stop being nostalgic. That was where we swayed—but did not dance—to the music. That booth was where we made out like we were the only two people in the world. That patio was where he told me he wanted to hold my hand and get to know me—to see how we worked together. My nostalgia was turning morose as I just... missed him.

It had felt right to acknowledge his goodness publicly, especially since people so often referred to him as bad news.

It felt right when most everything else felt wrong.

Lifting my drink to my lips, I tried to breathe through the tight squeeze in my chest. Would thinking about him ever stop hurting? It didn't feel like time was doing me any favors.

Nora shot me a concerned look from where she was flirting with a ski tourist at the bar. I waved her off. It had been enough of a struggle to convince her not to hover.

The front door opened and closed. A gust of cold wind swept in. It brushed through the hairs at the nape of my neck. I shivered. I welcomed it. It made me feel like I was present when I'd been feeling absent.

I stared into the middle distance. I planned to finish this hot toddy and then head home. But Nora straightened and looked behind me with her eyes wide, giving me an unsettled apprehension. With my eyebrows drawn together, I followed her gaze.

A man I'd never seen before pushed back the hood of his *huge* bright red coat. From his boots to his head, he looked fortified to scale Mount Everest. He was far too prepared, instantly marking him as an outta towner. His friend was more appropriately clothed.

Pressure crushed my chest, and I sucked in a quick breath.

Elijah licked his lower lip, then bit down on it. His green eyes met mine.

And that *right* feeling fit back into place.

It was as if all the lights had been dimmed, but when he entered the room, they illuminated to their full potential. Shining light into the dark spaces of my heart and putting all the lurking shadows to rest.

I instantly distrusted it. I'd felt this before, and it'd opened me to a hurt too deep. It was terrible to know he was the cause of my pain, and to still want him.

Muscles flexed in his throat as he swallowed.

His friend's attention flicked from me to Elijah, before taking confident strides to the bar.

There were half the number of patrons than usual, but every single one watched us. Their gazes pricked at my skin. I wanted to shrink under the table and hide, but instead, I sat up straighter in the booth.

"Hi." Elijah's voice skimmed over me, pitched low and tentative. Even on just that word, a single syllable that was more breath than language, it lit parts of my brain that had been quiet for the past couple of weeks.

"Hi," I responded, to my surprise. I hadn't realized I was currently verbal.

"Can I join you?"

I chewed on the inside of my cheek, considering all my options for a brief moment before nodding.

He unzipped his coat, it was warm and practical, but hinted at his athletic figure below. I resented him for making winter attire look sexy. I looked like a human-shaped trash bag in my winter coat.

He tossed it into the booth before sitting across from me.

"What are you doing here?" I asked.

I remembered last time when he'd told me, *The woman I like is here, so I'm here.* I remembered the thrill it'd sent through my body. Was he remembering it, too?

"I saw your post." He searched my face, but I couldn't tell if he found what he was looking for there.

"Did you come so I could thank you in person?"

One corner of his lips quirked upward. "No. I came to say sorry."

"About?"

He pulled at the cuffs of his baby blue button-up shirt. After crossing his arms on the table, he tugged at his shirt again. His hand scraped over his beard, but not before I caught his grimace. "I don't know if there's a big enough apology for what I need to apologize for. I had a four-hour drive here to think about what to say, and I still don't know where to start."

I lifted an eyebrow. Externally, I portrayed a woman in control, while internally, I begged him to say all the right things. To ask me to give us another chance. To make me feel safe loving him.

"I've struggled to believe that I'm good for you. Or that someone else wouldn't be better. But then I started seeing signs that I wasn't, and that you knew it."

"What signs?"

He rubbed the back of his neck. "Uh... Dennis being around you so much, helping you—"

"I'm Banjo's vet," I interrupted.

He winced. "I know. I know. But he'd talk like he was still the man you should rely on. Or talking about your work ethic like I don't know how hard you work. That he *knew* you better than I did, knew your needs better than I did. And you... You never contradicted him."

I shook my head, shocked that I could have missed how all that would have made Elijah feel. But then, I wasn't responsible for the feelings he said nothing about, just like he wasn't responsible for the feelings I didn't share.

"I don't think you read all the Dennis stuff correctly. He is... not a deep thinker," I explained. "I don't think he's capable of manipulation."

Elijah raised a skeptical eyebrow.

"Seriously."

"He wants you back."

I threw up my arms. "We. Were. Never. Together."

Elijah looked like he wanted to argue, but stopped himself. "Fine. You know him. I don't. And honestly, this isn't about him."

"No, it's not." I held his gaze. "No one has ever found solutions to my problems the way you did. I mean, that community fund—Elijah, I hope you know what a kindness that is. The *entire* town will benefit from it."

He shifted as if my praise fit uncomfortably around his shoulders. "I wasn't thinking about anyone else."

His words wrapped me up and tied me into knots.

He pushed his hair off his forehead. "Anyway, other people insinuated or outright said you two made more sense."

"Who?" I leaned my head back as the realization dawned. "Shane Briar."

Elijah spread and flexed his fingers. "Him, but before that, I overheard a conversation between Sterling and Ben. And it made my worst insecurities feel real."

"Sterling and Ben?" My mouth hung open in disbelief.

"Yeah... I haven't talked to them about it yet."

"That would feel terrible."

"It did." He kept fidgeting as if he didn't know what to do with himself. It seemed to take a significant amount of willpower to meet my eyes. "But I should have told you... all of that. I shouldn't have decided my paranoia was real, and that I should run away before you could leave me." His voice thickened with emotion, and his eyes shone. "I'm really sorry for that."

"Thank you. You should have talked to me, but it's hard to say things sometimes." I bit my lower lip and felt the tides shift—knowing it was my turn to be honest. "I was also feeling... insecure."

A crease formed between his eyebrows.

"People love you—"

"Not everyone," he pointed out.

I grinned. "No. But even the ones who don't want your attention. I'm always going to be this awkward animal girl to them. I know they wonder what you see in me. And you were right, I don't like their attention."

Staring down at his hands, he said, "They're idiots if they don't see how great you are."

"They are idiots, and I'm sorry that I let their opinions into my head."

My world had shrunk to just Elijah and me. But not knowing what to say, or what all of this could mean for *us*, I rested my chin on my hand, taking in the rest of the bar. Nora lifted a questioning eyebrow, and I shrugged that everything was okayish. His friend in the ridiculous coat watched less directly, lifting a beer to his lips.

"Is that Sebastian?" I asked.

"He insisted on coming." Elijah sounded affectionately annoyed.

"How was the drive?"

"Snowy and long. We went slow."

"Good." The fear that had gripped my throat eased slightly, even if it was technically too late to worry about him. Driving winter roads was a side effect of living in Michigan, but I would have liked if he hadn't taken the risk. "You could have called."

"I..." He sighed, and his shoulders lowered a fraction. Lifting his chin, he looked me straight in the eye. "I don't want to be away from you anymore."

His sincerity took my breath away. Inside the depths of his mossy gaze, I found what I'd been looking for. The promise I'd needed to see in order to trust him again.

"If you need time, I can give you that. But I hope you're willing to... try again." His jaw tightened.

"I want that. I've... I wouldn't let myself hope that we could get back together, but it's all I want."

Little parenthesis pressed around his lips as lines drew from the corners of his eyes. White teeth bit into the flesh of his lower lip. I was pulled in by the magnetism of his smile—one pole finding the other. I was held in his field without being touched. Settling into the power of his draw was as natural as submitting to gravity.

I couldn't have fought back the smile spreading across my face if I'd tried. Happiness flitted and soared inside my ribcage.

It happened in such slow increments that I didn't even realize we were closing the distance between us. Both of us leaning over the table until our mouths finally met. I supported myself on my forearms, standing in a crouch. He had one booted foot on the booth while his palm rested against the sensitive skin of my throat. His thumb stroked from my jaw down my neck and back.

He sucked on my lower lip and I slipped my tongue against the tip of his. Exploring, remembering, reclaiming.

Someone let out a loud whistle, and we pulled apart to find Nora, Sebastian, and Ben clapping.

My face grew hot, but I giggled, sinking down in my seat. Elijah stayed where he was, confident in the attention with an adoring smile directed toward me.

I gasped when he put a knee on the tabletop and then the other. Supported on both knees and a hand, he sank his fingers into the hair at the back of my neck.

"Fuck 'em," he joked. "Come here."

Then his mouth was on mine, hungry and demanding.

I wasn't embarrassed anymore.

Chapter 25
Elijah

"I've missed you," I murmured against Hazel's lips.

She groaned, pawing at the Velcro strip over my coat's zipper. "I missed you. God, Elijah, it was terrible."

The image of her lying awake in her bed, crying and clinging to her pillow the way I had, tore fresh cuts into my heart. "I'm sorry. So sorry."

There were too many layers between us. I needed to feel every inch of her. I needed to bare myself to her in every way.

I needed to soothe all the places I'd harmed.

"I'm sorry, too." Her kisses on my neck were frantic, seeking the few inches of my skin she could reach. Each one imprinted, lingering on my skin and fitting my wounds back together.

I pulled the tab of her zipper down before tearing the Velcro of my coat open, unzipping mine as well. We both struggled to slip out of the garments, laughing and kissing. Her sleeves were inside-out by the time she freed her arms from them. My arm was still trapped in one of my sleeves when she rushed back to my embrace. Undressing would be easier if I could stop kissing her. But every time her mouth left mine, I felt like I was missing something vital to my survival. Her lips were my oxygen.

And I'd been suffocating for weeks.

My fingers sank into the flesh of her ass cheek and my throbbing cock twitched. Two layers of jeans between us was too goddamn much.

I pulled open the closure of my pants with one hand, pushing them and my boxer briefs down.

She wrapped her grip around my hard shaft and stroked once.

My head fell back, my groan nearly a growl.

My hips jerked, fucking into her hand.

She whimpered and shifted, rubbing her thighs together.

I pushed her chin up with my thumb under her jaw. "I love when you do that. Move your hips like you're too horny, and I just know you're so fucking wet."

"I am," she whined.

With my free hand, I unbuttoned her jeans before slipping it inside. My fingers slid down her slit. She was so hot, drenched.

This time I did growl. At some point, I'd pressed her back against her foyer wall. I was sucking and biting too hard on the delicate skin of shoulder, but I couldn't stop.

She sucked on two of my fingers as I finger-fucked her with the other hand. All our hands worked in the same rhythm, her strokes matching mine.

"Your lips are so pretty around my fingers," I ground out.

Spit glistened on my fingers when she released them. She opened her big, brown, lust-soaked eyes. Their heat was enough to incinerate my impulses and leave me at her mercy.

With the lightest push, I stumbled backward a step. She went to her knees. I had barely gained my balance when she swiped the flat of her tongue up my shaft, and I drew in a sharp breath.

She sheathed my head in her mouth and then kept going—taking me deeper, inch after inch. I pulled my hair with both hands, the pain contrasting with the pleasure of her sucking up and down my shaft. It was the only way I could keep from grabbing the back of her head and taking the control from her.

I tilted my head, memorizing the image of her. My jaw hung slack, breathing fast to accommodate the demanding pace of my heart. Fresh tears sprang to her eyes every time she pushed me to the back of her throat.

It was torture to pull myself out of her mouth—her lips swollen and pouting. But I knew a few more minutes of being between them and I'd come down her throat. And that wasn't what I wanted, not what I needed.

"You've proved your point," I gasped. "Your mouth looks pretty around"—I coughed a laugh—"many things."

My balls tightened at her giggle. She pulled her sweater over her head, revealing her tits pressed against her black satin bra. She pulled the straps down, then unclasped it, letting her full tits fall free with a bounce.

I couldn't tell if I went to my knees by choice or because she'd taken my ability to stand away from me.

I cupped her and took one of her nipples into my mouth. Releasing her breast from my lips with a pop, I did the same on her other side.

Her nails dug into my shoulders. "Elijah, I need you so badly. If I don't come soon, I'm gonna die."

We worked together to peel her jeans and panties down her legs. Neither of us even pretended like we could make it to her bed. Instead, she went to her elbows and knees on the carpet. The curly hair on her mound and the skin of her upper thighs shone wetly, and I knew just how good it was going to feel to be inside of her.

I was completely hers. My body, my emotions, my desires open to her.

With the head of my cock at her entrance, I eased my hips to rest against her ass, taking her in one stroke. I stayed there while her muscles tensed and flexed, giving her a moment to get used to me filling her.

I hooked one arm around her waist, and I lowered my chest to her back. I scraped my teeth where her shoulder met her neck and rolled my hips. She met my luxuriating pace. I enjoyed it while I could, but as she neared her orgasm, her body demanded more. She tightened around me, and I knew how to give it to her.

My voice was strained as I asked, "Can you take it hard, baby?"

She arched her back, her pussy squeezing and milking me. "You know I can."

"That's right, you can."

Lifting my torso, I rested one hand between her shoulder blades and took hold of her hip with the other. I pounded into her. Our skin smacked. Sweat beaded on my forehead. Her tits swayed with each thrust. My fingers dug into her flesh so hard there would probably be five bruises left behind.

But then she cried out, her walls spasming around my cock. All my thoughts turned off, and I took even more, everything she would give me.

Both my hands held her hips as I came spilling deep inside her, my head thrown back, every muscle in my body flexed.

It took a moment for me to gain control of my body enough to ease out of her and help her to her feet. I supported most of her weight on our walk down the hall to her bed.

Laying her down, I half noticed the pink carpet burn on her knees before I promptly fell asleep with her in my arms.

Epilogue

Elijah

My mom sat at Hazel's kitchen table with a look on her face I'd never seen before. I didn't think she'd realized I'd seen it. Hazel and I prepared dinner, working around each other in a way that had become comfortable. I'd looked up to ask Mom if she'd heard anything interesting from Euchre Club last night, and caught her expression. Her eyes were a bit brighter than normal and her mouth was tilted upward in something like a smile. Her throat looked like she was swallowing down big emotions as she watched us.

"Hey, Mom, you okay?" I asked.

The corners of her eyes crinkled. "I'm wonderful. Your place is lovely, Hazel."

Hazel's cheeks reddened as she beamed. "Thank you."

"I'm surprised you don't have a pet."

"I want one so badly." She sighed. "I'm just not home enough. I work too much right now."

Mom tilted her head and made eye contact with me. "Hmm… Maybe that'll change soon. Maybe someone else could help you with the pet."

I snorted. "Subtle."

She shrugged, looking very pleased with herself. "You're just cute together."

Hazel didn't look away from the salad she was preparing. Meeting Mom had her feeling anxious the last couple of days, and I knew it meant a lot to her to hear Mom's praise.

"Would you get a dog?" Mom looked out the sliding glass door window. "You have a nice yard."

"I thought maybe, but then I saw Lily Nelson with her new dog," Hazel joked.

Mom barked a laugh. "What was that girl thinking? Adopting that giant puppy."

"She was thinkin' about some alone time with Remi. She bought his vet services at the auction, and then was like, 'Oh no, I don't have a pet.'" I paused, stirring the frying vegetables to gesture with the spatula as I spoke.

"That girl... I remember her from when you were kids. She has grown into the woman version I would have imagined her teenage self to be. Lots of strategy on the back end of a problem she caused."

Hazel nodded. "That's her."

"In her defense," Mom started, "he is a very handsome man, and he seems so nice."

"He is; he's very nice. We've been friends for years now."

"I can't believe he's not taken. He was married once, right?"

"Yeah, his divorce was about five years ago..." Hazel looked up at the ceiling in thought. "Just over five years ago?"

"Does he just like being single?"

I held my hand out to stop the conversation. "Mom, what is this, a fact-seeking mission? Leave Remi alone."

"I'm sorry, you're right. The Euchre Club ladies are turning me into a gossip. I don't *share*, but I like to listen. Hazel, please don't judge me; it is my worst trait." Whispering mostly to herself, she added, "I just like knowing things."

"It's so fun to sit around and dish with your friends," Hazel agreed.

"And some gossip feels so harmless, but some isn't. I probably should not thrive on it. I'm sorry if I was being too nosy about your friend."

"You weren't, but thank you. I know many a mom in the area is wondering what combination of casserole is going to tie him down."

Mom snorted. "Oh goodness, they are."

Dinner was full of easy conversation and stories from my childhood.

The dirty dishes from dinner were sitting in the sink after we cleared the table to play some cards. We'd decided on rummy since we didn't have a fourth player for Euchre.

Mom considered her hand. "I heard Chelsea Thelen's oldest daughter started working at the clinic."

"Yeah, Crystal started just a couple of weeks ago, she's a good kid," Hazel remarked. "I'm glad it works for Chelsea, too."

Hazel still struggled to share responsibilities of the clinic, but she was trying. She was taking coaching from Ben, and little by little, she was striking a healthier balance. It wasn't easy for her, but I made sure she knew how much I appreciated it.

A few minutes before Mom planned to head back in her rental car, I ventured out into the cold to start it.

It was early, but we were calling it a night so I could prepare to drive back to Detroit in the morning. She hugged me as I walked her to her car, the frost on the windshield melting away from the defroster. "Thanks for warming my car up, son."

"You're welcome."

Nodding toward Hazel's front door, Mom said, "I like her."

"I like her, too."

"Will you be up here next weekend?"

I nodded.

"That drive has got to be getting old." She opened her driver's door. "I'd love to cook for you two if it works."

"I'll check with Hazel."

We said goodbye, and I walked back into the house before she'd pulled onto the road—it was a blistery February evening. I found Hazel on the sofa, and I pulled a blanket around the both of us when I snuggled next to her.

"Oh, you're so cold." She scooted tighter against me.

"Yeah." I shivered. "Tonight was good."

"It was. Your mom is fun."

We fell into a comfortable silence, staring out the dark window.

She heaved a heavy sigh. "I don't want you to leave tomorrow."

"I don't want to leave, either."

It was still in the planning stages, but Hazel and I were discussing my moving in with her before spring.

We'd fallen into an easy pattern of driving the distance between us whenever we could. But it was a lot of time in the car, and our phones were dying in the middle of the night because we'd fall asleep talking or listening to each other breathe. We'd talk about anything and everything. Important things, like the growing suspicion around my dad from the community. Or about Sterling and Ben admitting that they'd been talking about Brooks and Olivia after the auction.

Or sometimes we talked idly about things like Remi's new neighbor moving into the other side of his duplex. Olivia and her boyfriend getting engaged—and Hazel's concern for Brooks because of it.

Anything to make it feel like we weren't so far apart.

Hours later, we lay naked in Hazel's bed. She fit perfectly in my arms. Everything felt so right, my body satisfied for the time being, my mind and heart at ease.

Her breathing was growing slow and deep. Her muscles were relaxed, and her head was heavy on my chest.

"I love you," I whispered into the dark room. The feeling was too full for my heart to hold it all in. I needed to say it, even if she was asleep and couldn't hear me.

She gave a little snore in response.

I smiled as I joined her in sleep.

The End

Remi and Alicia Can't Fall Again

Follows *Hazel and Elijah Find Out*

Coming 2025!

Remi has a hot new neighbor. Too bad she's his ex-wife.

Preorder now!

https://www.amazon.com/dp/B0DM2S5P1C

Chapter 1

Alicia

At least eight different cardboard boxes were ripped open—some flaps still stood straight up waving an apology—as water puddled on the linoleum under my feet as I used a dishtowel to dry my hair. When I'd spotted the terry cloth among books and dried goods, I'd thought I'd hit the jackpot. But it turned out to be a single washcloth the size of my hand.

I couldn't recall much of my frenzied packing. I had to of packed towels, though.

"Right?" I spoke to the boxes.

They didn't answer.

I shook my head and changed my voice to an obnoxious mockery. "I'll pack later. I'd rather hang out."

My job brought me to new locations every so often, and I knew what it was to miss Chicago and my friends—mostly my best friend, Sadie. Unlike other travel jobs, I didn't know how long I'd be in Grand Ridge.

So, now I was tits out in a dingy, little kitchen with windows so drafty the sheer curtain fluttered in the blistering breeze.

The sad excuse for a towel was drenched and my hair was still dripping when the front door to the unit connected to mine opened and closed. I slapped the fabric with a wet smack to my chest as if it could provide any modesty and crouched behind the kitchen counters. Heavy boots crunched on the front porch. If my neighbor took a step to the right, they'd see my naked back and probably the top of my ass through the window.

Not exactly the first impression I was hoping to make.

"Is this a new low?" I mumbled under my breath. Goosebumps covered my arms and legs. A shiver passed through my body.

To my immense relief, the footsteps moved in the opposite direction. I summoned all of my courage and lifted my head enough to catch a glimpse of broad shoulders under a brown corduroy coat. The wool lined collar popped to brush the bottom of his stocking cap. There wasn't any reason for me to think it, but I had the sneaking suspicion that he was fine as hell. Not that it mattered—I did not enter the dating pool in these little, middle-of-nowhere towns.

I was here to do a job, and people liking me made it so much easier to do. Stealing the bachelors out of the dating pool would not make me popular, even if it would only be for a short amount of time.

Remaining crouched below counter-height, I shuffled toward the living room. But then a truck engine cranked to life and spurred me to a full dash behind the wall separating the two rooms. With my arms crossed over my breasts, I peaked. Through the long window next to the door, I watched an SUV back down the driveway to the other unit before pulling onto the quiet country highway. The brilliant morning sun reflected off of the windshield blocking the driver from view. Hopefully, it also hid me.

I shivered again, this time it chattered my teeth.

Fuck a towel, I need clothes.

I'd driven myself and my dog, Furgie, up through the night. The town had been asleep and covered in a blanket of white snow as I passed under the single traffic light blinking yellow. Even through the street lights, there were stars dotting the midnight-blue sky. Heading away from town to my new home, the stars brightened and multiplied.

I hadn't seen a night sky like it in years—the Milky Way was a cloudy stripe through the ink.

Parking under the carport on my side of the duplex, I carried my pillow and blanket inside. Furgie trailed behind me on the shoveled walk. The building's interior smelled like stale air and old carpet. Wood paneling lined the bottom half of every wall. In sock covered feet, I climbed the stairs to the single bedroom and bathroom. Then fell face first onto my temporary bed and quickly fell asleep with Furgie curled beside me.

She'd woken me just before seven itching so much the bed shook. When I couldn't fall back asleep, I took her outside before taking a shower with disappointing water pressure.

Probably should have confirmed where my clothes were beforehand, but I didn't.

I left a wet trail on the worn carpet as I rummaged through box after box. For some reason the stupid wash cloth was still clenched in my fist. My body had progressed past goosebumps and a shiver every now and then to shivering constantly. There was a wood-burning stove in the corner opposite the sofa, but even if I did have the necessary fire starting items, I never could get a good fire going. Instead, it mocked me and my frozen state.

"God, I'm like ten minutes away from being hypother—Ah ha!" I exclaimed, pulling a sweatshirt out from among framed photos and a silly old phone shaped like a rainbow and cloud. I slipped the sweatshirt over my head, the soft inside fabric brushed my torso, but ended just above my navel.

"Well, it's something." I set my fists on my naked hips. "At least most of the boxes are open at this point."

On the sofa, Furgie snorted. Her snout wrinkled as she chewed on one of her hind legs. Crouching, I ran a hand down her back. "When I figure out how to leave this place with clothes on, we'll go. We might even be able to walk the wetlands over on Shelby Road and see what we're here to protect."

She continued gnawing.

Technically, my work didn't begin until Monday but I could get a heads start—like visiting local spaces for the vibe of the residence. Maybe I'd figure out the best way to gain footing in the town. It was a fine line to draw between convincing a community that I was here to help and not a busy-body.

Furgie let out a few more snorts, her chewing intensified.

"Girl, you have been so itchy." I scratched my nails along her side and she rolled onto her back. I gasped and pulled my hand back.

Her stomach was lobster colored and splotchy. It clashed with her coppery fur, and was definitely a different color than usual.

"Oh my effing God! Furg, what the hell?"

She flicked her eyes to me, her eyebrows shifting before curling to gnaw on herself again.

"No," I commanded, lifting her head. "You'll make yourself bleed."

The look on her face definitely claimed that would be better than what she was dealing with at the moment.

"I'll figure this out." I looked for my phone and to my immense surprise and relief, I spotted it on the side table.

Googling one handed, I continued searching for pants. My cell service was terrible and the blue line across the top wasn't moving at all. There didn't seem to be any way to increase my reception. It was so easy to take for granted the built in amenities of urban life that rural settings just didn't have.

Pausing my investigation for clothes, I shuffled to a window, hoping that would help.

Apparently, my Wi-Fi needed to be hooked up yesterday.

I left my phone on the sill and went back to my quest for pants. Furgie continued itching, aggressively.

I found sweatpants packed with my cloth shopping bags. I still hadn't found a bra or underwear, and I did not have "bra-less" boobs. But at least returning to my phone next to the condensation dripping window wouldn't be torture anymore.

The Internet still wasn't working. I sent out a text to Sadie, my assistant and best friend, Furgie is all red and itching like a mother fucker. Can you text me the phone number for a vet clinic in the area? I didn't have much hope for the text to send but I was also desperate.

"Okay, let's see if anyone nearby has unsecured Wi-Fi," I said to Furg.

She remained focus on her task to break through her skin either by claw or teeth.

It didn't take long for a list of three networks to appear on my screen. One of them had a really strong signal and didn't require a password, EvrybdyHurts.

My wide eyes scanned the room. "Furguson, who are our neighbors? 'Everybody hurts'? That is alarming. I hope it's a sex dungeon or they're a Dom or something. That is the only scenario I'm comfortable with."

Worrying on my lower lip, I wished I could Google if there was information that the person with the network could learn about me just by connecting to it. On the sofa, Furgie rolled to her other side to scratch with her opposite hind leg.

I sighed. "I'll sleep with a knife under my pillow."

Less than a minute later, I pressed the speaker of my phone to my ear.

"Grand Ridge Animal Clinic, this is Nora. How can I help you?" A polite but uninterested sounding receptionist answered.

"Hi, I'm hoping to get an appointment for my dog. I think she might be having an allergic reaction. She's itching like crazy and she's all red."

"What's your availability?"

"Any time today."

"Oh, today?" I didn't like Nora's skepticism.

"If at all possible. At this rate, she won't have any skin left by tomorrow."

"Oh, no. Can I put you on hold for a moment? I'll see what I can do."

"I can hold."

Her voice changed, growing further away before cutting to silence, "Hey, Peace and Love, you wanna do a lady a solid?"

I puffed a laugh.

"You still there?" she asked.

"I am."

"One of our vets is willing to stay late for your appointment. If the situation becomes more urgent, come as soon as possible."

"Oh my gosh, thank you."

"No problem, so it's still a couple of hours from now, but I have you scheduled for 4:30." She took my information and Furg's. The sofa that came with the rental creaked when I lowered onto the cushion next to her, gently restraining her from itching.

Hanging up, I brushed a hand down Furgie's side. Her leg kicked like it did when something tickled.

"Well, this is one way to introduce ourselves to the town."

https://www.amazon.com/dp/B0DM2S5P1C

Acknowledgements

Writing is often characterized as a lonely task. The actual pounding out of words takes hours of being alone and wondering if you've lost the thread. But creating and sharing stories has brought a beautiful community into my life. From my critique group, the Smut Coven, to the wonderful readers I've been lucky to meet, these bookish spaces have carved out a corner of the internet that I'll be forever grateful for. Belonging is a wonderful thing. HUGS!

Input makes the story stronger. The developmental edits Sarah with Lopt and Cropt gave were invaluable. Thank you, Sarah! A big thank you to Silvia Curry for her copy edits, and Kimberly with Revision Division for her proofread. I could not do such a good job without you!

Kaaaate! This cover! I'm in love! It's perfect!

When I released my first book, I was proud but shy. Through a happy accident, a few of my cousins found out about my public little secret. Those beautiful and wonderful cousins that I've looked up to my *entire* life were so cute and supportive as they read my book. Andrea, Jackie, Angie, and Danielle, you will always be the coolest women in my life. I'm lucky to have you.

Thanks to Mom for her unwavering belief in me. Every person deserves a mom like you. Thanks for being mine.

Nell, thanks for your willingness to give pet medicine advice (and for not giving an ounce of resistance when I told you I would need your help in writing this series.) You're the bestest bestie!

To my husband, you are my favorite romance hero.

Just Fake Married

JUST FAKE MARRIED

JUST... BOOK 1

MARTY VEE

Chapter 1

Emmeline

I ran through the silvery bursts of my breath as my arms pumped at my sides in pace with my legs. My ponytail swung from side to side. Despite the frozen temperatures, sweat dampened my hairline. The path ran along the river. The ice reached from one bank to the other, but the flowing water hadn't frozen over yet. The city traffic elevated at the top of the embankment.

To my left, Owen's feet landed in perfect stride with mine. His hazel eyes fixed to the middle distance, his face stern and lovely.

"What are you doing for Christmas?" I asked. We were more than halfway through our five-mile jog, and he'd been even quieter than usual.

"Family stuff. You?"

Another runner approached from the opposite direction, and Owen fell back behind me, before joining at my side again.

"Same. Spending Christmas Eve at Mom and Dad's—it's tradition. My brother Malcolm and his husband Tom do, too. So, we celebrate for about forty-eight hours. It's... a lot of family time." The cold air bit my lungs, but we kept an easy pace. "You going back home?"

I caught Owen's nod out of the corner of my eye. "Around Grand Rapids, right?"

He nodded again.

If I wanted a chatty running partner, I should have befriended someone else from the running group where I met him. Owen and I had gotten to know each other over the past eleven months, but this level of silence was a bit much, even for him. I'd told him about my work week and a TV show I had watched, a book I wanted to read, and the holiday shopping I still had to get done. It was all a shortened running version, but that was hardly the point. And all he'd said was hello and *"Family stuff. You?"*

I was due some reciprocal conversation.

"What's your deal?" I slowed my pace slightly. "You need to slow down?"

He glanced at me for the first time in about a mile before he focused back on the trail ahead. "No. Why?"

I meant to elbow him, but we weren't close enough. Instead, I passed through the air between us. "You've hardly spoken."

"Thinking."

"About...?"

His sculpted chest rose with an inhale.

We were almost the same height, though he was possibly an inch taller than me. In our many jogs together, I'd collected knowledge about his lean frame. He was attractive, if compactly built men were my type. I tended to go for tall and lean, but over the past few months, Owen had tipped the needle in his direction.

Owen was becoming my type.

Not tall or lean, not compactly built.

Just Owen.

I hadn't even realized my crush on him had gradually developed until I noticed how often I caught myself thinking about him and smiling—or how much I wondered what he looked like under his clothes. Unlike other men I knew, Owen always wore a shirt while working out, even on the hottest days—even if it clung to him like a second skin carving along the ridges of his chest, stomach, and arms.

Of course, currently, he wore layers under a slim-cut coat, unzipped to his waist to ward off the bitter cold.

"I have a donor's New Year's Eve party. I didn't go last year, and he mentioned it to my boss." A crease formed between Owen's eyebrows. Long black eyelashes lowered over his hazel eyes.

Even through Owen's the strong-silent-type, it was obvious he was passionate about the dog rescue he worked with. As a veterinarian, he could probably make more money elsewhere and he wouldn't have to deal with donors, but he loved the dogs.

I wove around a frozen puddle. "Do you have to go?"

"Kinda."

"Is it really that big of a deal? It's just an appearance, right?"

"I hate these things. The donor is a volunteer as well, and..." A muscle flexed in his jaw. "He tried to set me up with his daughter."

"Oh no."

I didn't think Owen had gone on a single date in the time I'd known him. He wasn't really open about it—what with him being such a chatty guy and all. He'd mentioned an ex-girlfriend from vet school that had gotten serious, but nothing else. I spotted a hickey on his neck once, and when I picked on him about it, he just shrugged and replied, "Hookup." It was hard to picture him having casual sex, but it wasn't unthinkable—a puzzle piece I was sure belonged if I could just turn it the right way.

If I just examined it...

And I did.

From. Every. Angle.

Even knowing that, no matter how it fit, casual sex wasn't a good fit for me.

"Yeah, he was persistent," he said.

"He tried more than once?"

Owen snorted. "I don't have a relationship on the radar, but some loud, pushy guy's mystery daughter doesn't appeal to me."

"Can't imagine why not."

"Shocking, I know."

"So, you show up and say you have somewhere else to go."

He nodded, and we ran in silence for a few strides. He looked straight ahead while I stared at him until he noticed. The wind shifted, sending his wintergreen scent my way.

When he raised an eyebrow at me, I suggested, "Wanna do New Year's Eve together? We could be each other's plus-ones."

He focused forward again. "You have a party you have to go to?"

"Work always throws one. I don't have to go, but I probably should. And there's all that mess with Sam... I really don't want to go alone."

Sam and his stupid, good-looking face his with blue eyes and sandy brown hair. He *was* tall and leanly built. We shared an office, and that had been enough for our coworkers to make clumsy insinuations that we should date—no one had less finesse than fifty-year-old men. I would have probably agreed to a date with Sam, but he was obviously not interested.

Did that stop the old men from continuing to make comments about how good we'd look together?

No.

It was very uncomfortable.

Sam *was* my type, but when I caught myself thinking about men, it was Owen who was on my mind more than anyone else.

But when I'd hinted that he and I should go out, he said he had to take care of his dog. It was disappointing, but sometimes interest isn't reciprocated. He was a great running buddy and he made me laugh, and that was enough.

Considering my string of failed past relationships, it was probably better to remain just friends. With my track record, he was bound to have a red-flag then I'd cut ties, and he wouldn't be in my life at all.

"Things still awkward there?" he asked.

I bobbed my head, considering how to answer. "I mean... I didn't like, *throw* myself at him, but I made it clear that I would like to have dinner with him, and he's definitely not interested. And the other guys at work haven't gotten any more subtle in suggesting that we date."

Falling into step behind me again, Owen waited until another jogger passed us. "You don't want me there. I'm shit at these things."

"I wouldn't have asked if I didn't want you there."

"Em, I suck at small talk. I don't dance unless I get way too drunk—"

"Hashtag, goals."

"I'm awkward at parties."

"You're awkward, anyway."

He smirked.

"Come on, man. I need some arm candy."

He coughed out a laugh. "I can go with you, but you don't have to come to this other thing with me."

"What?" My eyebrows shot up. "You're saying that you'll go to my party, but I'm not expected—no, not *invited*—to your party?"

"It's not like you're not invited, but you don't have to go with me."

"Um, weird, but okay."

We were almost halfway through our last mile as a comfortable silence settled with only the sounds of our footfalls on the frozen asphalt.

He came out of his shell once I got to know him, but he avoided crowds and people in general. It was out of character that he volunteered to go to my work event. Honestly, it was peculiar that he'd offered without any real pressure on my end at all.

I studied him out of the corner of my eye. His eyes were deep-set under his dark brows. The straight bridge of his nose cut to his perfect mouth. His lips weren't overly full, but they were sharply ridged and defined. There was a soft knot where the joint of his jaw pushed against his skin. He was artistically beautiful. The ratio of his features would probably fit that "ideal" number for symmetry. And even though his face was distracting, I did not lose my train of thought as I watched him.

This time under my stare, he didn't look back. "What?"

"Why?"

"Why what?"

"Why will you go to my party, but I don't have to go to yours?"

"Does there have to be a reason?" He kept his gaze straight ahead. If I needed any more proof that he was hiding something, it was there when his jaw muscle jumped.

"For you to willingly, and with very little convincing, come with me and get nothing for it? This isn't, like, a movie I wanna go see. This is a pretty big social event." I waited for him to finally look at me. "And you *hate* people."

Dimples pressed into his tan cheeks as he smiled tightly. "It's not that big a deal."

"For some people, no. But for you, it's huge."

His eyebrows peaked like an inverted 'V.' "Can I take it back?"

"Oh no, you're committed now. I'm already planning our coordinating outfits. But you also have to spill."

"You know I don't actually have to do either."

"But you're going to."

Heaving a sigh, he puffed out a steamy breath. "You really don't want to know."

"Will I be implicated in a court of law or something?"

"I don't think I've broken any laws."

"Jesus, what'd you do, Owen?"

"I can't believe I'm about to admit this." He looked up at the gray sky as if it might hold the answers for him.

"Whatever you're about to say, there's no way it can live up to the suspense you're building."

He coughed another laugh, and with a challenging glance my way, he said, "My coworkers think I'm married."

The toe of my shoe caught on the path. I couldn't correct my balance, and I went down with my arms flailing. My gloved hands caught most of the impact, but there was a sharp bite of pain as my knee scraped against the asphalt.

"Shit," Owen exclaimed, turning and running back to me. "Are you okay?"

"Yeah, I just tripped." Rolling onto my butt, I shook out my hands. I looked down where the pain was emanating from my propped-up knee. There was a hole in my leggings, and the skin underneath was scraped, but it didn't look or feel very serious.

He lowered to one knee in front of me. "Didn't live up to the suspense, huh?"

He'd proposed to someone? What the hell... he was married?

"Shut up. You're married?" Why did I sound so angry?

"No." He slipped his gloves off.

My brain trudged through time at a slower pace than his. He wasn't married... but his coworkers thought he was. The unexpected anger was replaced with unexpected relief. Mouth open, I blinked at him.

"May I check your knee?"

I waved him off. "It's fine."

"You sure?"

"Yeah."

"I'd still like to che—"

I leaned forward and cupped his face in my hands. I could feel his heat, even through the layers of fabric. His deep-set hazel eyes snapped to mine. Our faces were close enough that the mist of our breaths met in the space between us like a swirling tangle of steam. It was the closest we'd ever been. It probably would have felt intimate with anyone, and it had nothing to do with the fact that Owen's face was only a foot from mine.

Letting go of him, I wrapped my arms around my thighs. "Why do your coworkers think you're married?"

Marty Vee in the Wild

arty Vee is the midwestern gal who is going to banter her steamy contemporary small town into only one bed, time after time. The friends will become lovers, and so will the enemies.

She lives in the Mitten State with her introverted husband, two feral children, the fluffiest house cat, and her tender-hearted rescue dog.

She loves singing (constantly) and meandering hikes through the woods.

Check Out More of My Books At

https://martyvee.com/books-2/

Vee is for Romance Readers Group

https://www.facebook.com/groups/1161878791021065

The Tiktok

https://www.tiktok.com/@martyveeauthur

Instagram

https://www.instagram.com/martyveeauthor/

Romance Writer's Therapy Podcast

https://romancewriterstherapy.buzzsprout.com/